Margaret Atwood

"Unparalleled among contemporary women novelists at showing the knottiness of human relationships."
—Marilyn R. Abbey,
Chicago Sun-Times

DANCING GIRLS

"The best work she has yet produced . . . [They] illumine areas of the human condition few writers have witnessed with such intelligence and sympathy."

—Robert Taylor,
Boston Globe

"The experience of reading these stories is exhilarating; they remain in your mind."

—Alice Adams

"Margaret Atwood renders visual, aural and tactile events in such crisp, surprising language that her images crackle off the page; readers experience her work viscerally."

—*Washington Post*

"Deft, sardonic: quintessential Atwood."

—*Toronto Globe and Mail*

Bantam Windstone Books
Ask your bookseller for the books you have missed

THE BELL JAR by Sylvia Plath
BODILY HARM by Margaret Atwood
CANCER WARD by Alexander I. Solzhenitsyn
THE CONFESSIONS OF NAT TURNER by William Styron
THE CRYING OF LOT 49 by Thomas Pynchon
DANCING GIRLS AND OTHER STORIES by Margaret Atwood
DELTA OF VENUS Erotica by Anais Nin
THE DIVINERS by Margaret Laurence
THE EDITORS' CHOICE: NEW AMERICAN STORIES,
    George E. Murphy, Jr.—Editor
THE END OF THE ROAD by John Barth
THE FIRST CIRCLE by Alexander I. Solzhenitsyn
FISHER'S HORNPIPE by Todd McEwen
THE FLOATING OPERA by John Barth
THE GOLDEN NOTEBOOK by Doris Lessing
GOODBYE, COLUMBUS by Philip Roth
GRAVITY'S RAINBOW by Thomas Pynchon
THE HEADMASTER'S PAPERS by Richard A. Hawley
HOUSEKEEPING by Marilynne Robinson
HUNGER OF MEMORY by Richard Rodriguez
THE IVORY SWING by Janette Turner Hospital
JOHNNY GOT HIS GUN by Dalton Trumbo
THE KILLING GROUND by Mary Lee Settle
LITTLE BIRDS by Anais Nin
MAGNETIC FIELD(S) by Ron Loewinsohn
A MEASURE OF TIME by Rosa Guy
ONE DAY IN THE LIFE OF IVAN DENISOVICH
    by Alexander I. Solzhenitsyn
PITCH DARK by Renata Adler
THE RIVER WHY by David James Duncan
SET THIS HOUSE ON FIRE by William Styron
SLOW LEARNER by Thomas Pynchon
THE SNOW LEOPARD by Peter Matthiessen
SOMETIMES A GREAT NOTION by Ken Kessey
A SPY IN THE HOUSE OF LOVE by Anais Nin
STATE OF GRACE by Joseph Pintauro
THE STONE ANGEL by Margaret Laurence
THE TIGER IN THE TIGER PIT by Janette Turner Hospital
AN UNKNOWN WOMAN by Alice Koller
V. by Thomas Pynchon

DANCING GIRLS

and Other Stories

Margaret Atwood

BANTAM BOOKS

TORONTO · NEW YORK · LONDON · SYDNEY · AUCKLAND

DANCING GIRLS AND OTHER STORIES
A *Bantam Book / published by arrangement with*
Simon & Schuster
PRINTING HISTORY
Simon & Schuster edition published September 1977
Appeared as a serialization in Redbook magazine, 1982
Seal edition / September 1978
Bantam Trade edition / June 1985

Windstone and accompanying logo of a stylized W are
trademarks of Bantam Books, Inc.

ISBN 0-553-34115-4

PRINTED IN THE UNITED STATES OF AMERICA
O   0 9 8 7 6 5 4 3 2

Acknowledgments

The Man from Mars	1977	*Ontario Review*
Betty		*Ms. Magazine*
Polarities	1971	*Tamarack Review*
Under Glass	1972	*Harper's*
The Grave of the Famous Poet	1973	*Oberon Press*
Hair Jewellery	1976	*Ms. Magazine*
When It Happens	1975	*Chatelaine*
A Travel Piece	1975	*Saturday Night*
The Resplendent Quetzal	1977	*The Malahat Review*
Lives of the Poets	1977	*Saturday Night*
The Sin Eater		*Canadian Broadcasting Corporation*
Giving Birth		*Chatelaine*

Biography of Margaret Atwood

MARGARET ATWOOD is recognized as one of North America's most talented and important writers. She was born on November 18, 1939, in Ottawa, Ontario, Canada. She received her B.A. from the University of Toronto in 1961 and an A.M. degree from Radcliffe College in 1962. She did graduate work at Harvard University and then received her D.Litt. from Trent University in 1973 and an L.L.D. from Queen's University in 1974. She has published nine books of poetry, receiving the Governor General's Award in 1966 for *The Circle Game*. In 1972, she published her respected work of criticism, *Survival: A Thematic Guide to Canadian Literature*. Her six highly acclaimed works of fiction are *Bodily Harm*, *Life Before Man*, *Lady Oracle*, *Surfacing*, *The Edible Woman*, and *Dancing Girls*, a collection of short stories. She frequently writes for *The New York Times*, *Ms*. Magazine, and *The Chicago Sun-Times*. Margaret Atwood has lived and worked in Canada, the United States, England and Italy. She now lives in Toronto, Canada, with novelist Graeme Gibson and their daughter, Jess.

Contents

The Man from Mars   9

Betty   32

Polarities   51

Under Glass   76

The Grave of the Famous Poet   88

Hair Jewellery   101

When It Happens   119

A Travel Piece   130

The Resplendent Quetzal   144

Training   160

Lives of the Poets   183

Dancing Girls   196

The Sin Eater   213

Giving Birth   225

The Man from Mars

A long time ago Christine was walking through the park. She was still wearing her tennis dress; she hadn't had time to shower and change, and her hair was held back with an elastic band. Her chunky reddish face, exposed with no softening fringe, looked like a Russian peasant's, but without the elastic band the hair got in her eyes. The afternoon was too hot for April; the indoor courts had been steaming, her skin felt poached.

The sun had brought the old men out from wherever they spent the winter: she had read a story recently about one who lived for three years in a manhole. They sat weedily on the benches or lay on the grass with their heads on squares of used newspaper. As she passed, their wrinkled toadstool faces drifted towards her, drawn by the movement of her body, then floated away again, uninterested.

The squirrels were out, too, foraging; two or three of them moved towards her in darts and pauses, eyes fixed on her expectantly, mouths with the ratlike receding chins open to show the yellowed front teeth. Christine walked faster, she had nothing to give them. People shouldn't feed them, she thought; it makes them anxious and they get mangy.

Halfway across the park she stopped to take off her cardigan. As she bent over to pick up her tennis racquet again someone touched her on her freshly bared arm. Christine seldom screamed; she straightened up suddenly, gripping the handle of her racquet. It was not one of the old men, however· it was a dark-haired boy of twelve or so.

"Excuse me," he said, "I search for Economics Building. Is it there?" He motioned towards the west.

Christine looked at him more closely. She had been mistaken: he was not young, just short. He came a little above her shoulder, but then, she was above the average height; "statuesque," her mother called it when she was straining. He was also what was referred to in their family as "a person from another culture": oriental without a doubt, though perhaps not Chinese. Christine judged he must be a foreign student and gave him her official welcoming smile. In high school she had been president of the United Nations Club; that year her school had been picked to represent the Egyptian delegation at the Mock Assembly. It had been an unpopular assignment— nobody wanted to be the Arabs—but she had seen it through. She had made rather a good speech about the Palestinian refugees.

"Yes," she said, "that's it over there. The one with the flat roof. See it?"

The man had been smiling nervously at her the whole time. He was wearing glasses with transparent plastic rims, through which his eyes bulged up at her as though through a goldfish bowl. He had not followed where she was pointing. Instead he thrust towards her a small pad of green paper and a ball-point pen.

"You make map," he said.

Christine set down her tennis racquet and drew a careful map. "We are here," she said, pronouncing distinctly. "You go this way. The building is here." She indicated the route with a dotted line and an X. The man leaned close to her, watching the progress of the map attentively; he smelled of cooked cauliflower and an unfamiliar brand of hair grease. When she had finished Christine handed the paper and pen back to him with a terminal smile.

"Wait," the man said. He tore the piece of paper with the map off the pad, folded it carefully and put it in his jacket pocket; the jacket sleeves came down over his wrists and had threads at the edges. He began to write something; she noticed with a slight feeling of revulsion that his nails and the ends of his fingers were so badly bitten they seemed almost deformed. Several of his fingers were blue from the leaky ball-point.

"Here is my name," he said, holding the pad out to her.

Christine read an odd assemblage of Gs, Ys and Ns, neatly printed in block letters. "Thank you," she said.

"You now write *your* name," he said, extending the pen.

Christine hesitated. If this had been a person from her own culture she would have thought he was trying to pick her up. But then, people from her own culture never tried to pick her up; she was too big. The only one who had made the attempt was the Moroccan waiter at the beer parlour where they sometimes went after meetings, and he had been direct. He had just intercepted her on the way to the Ladies' Room and asked and she said no; that had been that. This man was not a waiter though, but a student; she didn't want to offend him. In his culture, whatever it was, this exchange of names on pieces of paper was probably a formal politeness, like saying thank you. She took the pen from him.

"That is a very pleasant name," he said. He folded the paper and placed it in his jacket pocket with the map.

Christine felt she had done her duty. "Well, goodbye," she said. "It was nice to have met you." She bent for her tennis racquet but he had already stooped and retrieved it and was holding it with both hands in front of him, like a captured banner.

"I carry this for you."

"Oh no, please. Don't bother, I am in a hurry," she said, articulating clearly. Deprived of her tennis racquet she felt weaponless. He started to saunter along the path; he was not nervous at all now, he seemed completely at ease.

"*Vous parlez français?*" he asked conversationally.

"*Oui, un petit peu*," she said. "Not very well." How am I

going to get my racquet away from him without being rude? she was wondering.

"*Mais vous avez un bel accent.*" His eyes goggled at her through the glasses: was he being flirtatious? She was well aware that her accent was wretched.

"Look," she said, for the first time letting her impatience show, "I really have to go. Give me my racquet, please."

He quickened his pace but gave no sign of returning the racquet. "Where you are going?"

"Home," she said. "My house."

"I go with you now," he said hopefully.

"No," she said: she would have to be firm with him. She made a lunge and got a grip on her racquet; after a brief tug of war it came free.

"Goodbye," she said, turning away from his puzzled face and setting off at what she hoped was a discouraging jog-trot It was like walking away from a growling dog: you shouldn't let on you were frightened. Why should she be frightened anyway? He was only half her size and she had the tennis racquet, there was nothing he could do to her.

Although she did not look back she could tell he was still following. Let there be a streetcar, she thought, and there was one, but it was far down the line, stuck behind a red light. He appeared at her side, breathing audibly, a moment after she reached the stop. She gazed ahead, rigid.

"You are my friend," he said tentatively.

Christine relented: he hadn't been trying to pick her up after all, he was a stranger, he just wanted to meet some of the local people; in his place she would have wanted the same thing.

"Yes," she said, doling him out a smile.

"That is good," he said. "My country is very far."

Christine couldn't think of an apt reply. "That's interesting," she said. "*Très interessant.*" The streetcar was coming at last; she opened her purse and got out a ticket.

"I go with you now," he said. His hand clamped on her arm above the elbow.

"You . . . stay . . . *here,*" Christine said, resisting the impulse to shout but pausing between each word as though for a deaf person. She detached his hand—his hold was quite feeble and could not compete with her tennis biceps—and leapt off the curb and up the streetcar steps, hearing with relief the doors grind shut behind her. Inside the car and a block away she permitted herself a glance out a side window. He was standing where she had left him; he seemed to be writing something on his little pad of paper.

When she reached home she had only time for a snack, and even then she was almost late for the Debating Society. The topic was, "Resolved: That War Is Obsolete." Her team took the affirmative and won.

Christine came out of her last examination feeling depressed. It was not the exam that depressed her but the fact that it was the last one: it meant the end of the school year. She dropped into the coffee shop as usual, then went home early because there didn't seem to be anything else to do.

"Is that you, dear?" her mother called from the living room. She must have heard the front door close. Christine went in and flopped on the sofa, disturbing the neat pattern of cushions.

"How was your exam, dear?" her mother asked.

"Fine," said Christine flatly. It had been fine; she had passed. She was not a brilliant student, she knew that, but she was conscientious. Her professors always wrote things like "A serious attempt" and "Well thought out but perhaps lacking in élan" on her term papers; they gave her Bs, the occasional B+. She was taking Political Science and Economics, and hoped for a job with the Government after she graduated; with her father's connections she had a good chance.

"That's nice."

Christine felt, resentfully, that her mother had only a hazy idea of what an exam was. She was arranging gladioli in a vase; she had rubber gloves on to protect her hands as she always did when engaged in what she called "housework." As far as Christine could tell her housework consisted of arranging flowers in vases: daffodils and tulips and hyacinths through gladioli, irises and roses, all the way to asters and mums. Sometimes she cooked, elegantly and with chafing-dishes, but she thought of it as a hobby. The girl did everything else. Christine thought it faintly sinful to have a girl. The only ones available now were either foreign or pregnant; their expressions usually suggested they were being taken advantage of somehow. But her mother asked what they would do otherwise; they'd either have to go into a Home or stay in their own countries, and Christine had to agree this was probably true. It was hard, anyway, to argue with her mother. She was so delicate, so preserved-looking, a harsh breath would scratch the finish.

"An interesting young man phoned today," her mother said. She had finished the gladioli and was taking off her rubber gloves. "He asked to speak with you and when I said you weren't in we had quite a little chat. You didn't tell me about him, dear." She put on the glasses which she wore on a decorative chain around her neck, a signal that she was in her modern, intelligent mood rather than her old-fashioned whimsical one.

"Did he leave his name?" Christine asked. She knew a lot of young men but they didn't often call her; they conducted their business with her in the coffee shop or after meetings.

"He's a person from another culture. He said he would call back later."

Christine had to think a moment. She was vaguely acquainted with several people from other cultures, Britain mostly; they belonged to the Debating Society.

"He's studying Philosophy in Montreal," her mother prompted. "He sounded French."

Christine began to remember the man in the park. "I don't think he's French, exactly," she said.

Her mother had taken off her glasses again and was poking absentmindedly at a bent gladiolus. "Well, he sounded French." She meditated, flowery sceptre in hand. "I think it would be nice if you had him to tea."

Christine's mother did her best. She had two other daughters, both of whom took after her. They were beautiful; one was well married already and the other would clearly have no trouble. Her friends consoled her about Christine by saying, "She's not fat, she's just big-bones, it's the father's side," and "Christine is so healthy." Her other daughters had never gotten involved in activities when they were at school, but since Christine could not possibly ever be beautiful even if she took off weight, it was just as well she was so athletic and political, it was a good thing she had interests. Christine's mother tried to encourage her interests whenever possible. Christine could tell when she was making an extra effort, there was a reproachful edge to her voice.

She knew her mother expected enthusiasm but she could not supply it. "I don't know, I'll have to see," she said dubiously.

"You look tired, darling," said her mother. "Perhaps you'd like a glass of milk."

Christine was in the bathtub when the phone rang. She was not prone to fantasy but when she was in the bathtub she often pretended she was a dolphin, a game left over from one of the girls who used to bathe her when she was small. Her mother was being bell-voiced and gracious in the hall; then there was a tap at the door.

"It's that nice young French student, Christine," her mother said.

"Tell him I'm in the bathtub," Christine said, louder than necessary. "He isn't French."

She could hear her mother frowning. "That wouldn't be very polite, Christine. I don't think he'd understand."

"Oh, all right," Christine said. She heaved herself out of the bathtub, swathed her pink bulk in a towel and splattered to the phone.

"Hello," she said gruffly. At a distance he was not pathetic, he was a nuisance. She could not imagine how he had tracked her down: most likely he went through the phone book, calling all the numbers with her last name until he hit on the right one.

"It is your friend."

"I know," she said. "How are you?"

"I am very fine." There was a long pause, during which Christine had a vicious urge to say, "Well goodbye then," and hang up; but she was aware of her mother poised figurine-like in her bedroom doorway. Then he said, "I hope you also are very fine."

"Yes," said Christine. She wasn't going to participate.

"I come to tea," he said.

This took Christine by surprise. "You do?"

"Your pleasant mother ask me. I come Thursday, four o'clock."

"Oh," Christine said, ungraciously.

"See you then," he said, with the conscious pride of one who has mastered a difficult idiom.

Christine set down the phone and went along the hall. Her mother was in her study, sitting innocently at her writing desk.

"Did you ask him to tea on Thursday?"

"Not exactly, dear," her mother said. "I did mention he might come round to tea *some*time, though."

"Well, he's coming Thursday. Four o'clock."

"What's wrong with that?" her mother said serenely. "I think it's a very nice gesture for us to make. I do think you might try to be a little more co-operative." She was pleased with herself.

"Since you invited him," said Christine, "you can bloody well stick around and help me entertain him. I don't want to be left making nice gestures all by myself."

"Christine, *dear*," her mother said, above being shocked. "You ought to put on your dressing gown, you'll catch a chill."

After sulking for an hour Christine tried to think of the tea as a cross between an examination and an executive meeting: not enjoyable, certainly, but to be got through as tactfully as possible. And it *was* a nice gesture. When the cakes her mother had ordered arrived from The Patisserie on Thursday morning she began to feel slightly festive; she even resolved to put on a dress, a good one, instead of a skirt and blouse. After all, she had nothing against him, except the memory of the way he had grabbed her tennis racquet and then her arm. She suppressed a quick impossible vision of herself pursued around the living room, fending him off with thrown sofa cushions and vases of gladioli; nevertheless she told the girl they would have tea in the garden. It would be a treat for him, and there was more space outdoors.

She had suspected her mother would dodge the tea, would contrive to be going out just as he was arriving: that way she could size him up and then leave them alone together. She had done things like that to Christine before; the excuse this time was the Symphony Committee. Sure enough, her mother carefully mislaid her gloves and located them with a faked murmur of joy when the doorbell rang. Christine relished for weeks afterwards the image of her mother's dropped jaw and flawless recovery when he was introduced: he wasn't quite the foreign potentate her optimistic, veil-fragile mind had concocted.

He was prepared for celebration. He had slicked on so much hair cream that his head seemed to be covered with a tight black patent-leather cap, and he had cut the threads off his jacket sleeves. His orange tie was overpoweringly splendid. Christine noticed, however, as he shook her mother's suddenly braced white glove that the ball-point ink on his fingers was indelible. His face had broken out, possibly in anticipation of the delights in store for him; he had a tiny camera slung over his shoulder and was smoking an exotic-smelling cigarette.

Christine led him through the cool flowery softly padded living room and out by the French doors into the garden. "You sit here," she said. "I will have the girl bring tea."

This girl was from the West Indies: Christine's parents had been enraptured with her when they were down at Christmas and had brought her back with them. Since that time she had become pregnant, but Christine's mother had not dismissed her. She said she was slightly disappointed but what could you expect, and she didn't see any real difference between a girl who was pregnant before you hired her and one who got that way afterwards. She prided herself on her tolerance; also there was a scarcity of girls. Strangely enough, the girl became progressively less easy to get along with. Either she did not share Christine's mother's view of her own generosity, or she felt she had gotten away with something and was therefore free to indulge in contempt. At first Christine had tried to treat her as an equal. "Don't call me 'Miss Christine,'" she had said with an imitation of light, comradely laughter. "What you want me to call you then?" the girl had said, scowling. They had begun to have brief, surly arguments in the kitchen, which Christine decided were like the arguments between one servant and another: her mother's attitude towards each of them was similar, they were not altogether satisfactory but they would have to do.

The cakes, glossy with icing, were set out on a plate and the teapot was standing ready; on the counter the electric kettle boiled. Christine headed for it, but the girl, till then sitting with her elbows on the kitchen table and watching her expressionlessly, made a dash and intercepted her. Christine waited until she had poured the water into the pot. Then, "I'll carry it out, Elvira," she said. She had just decided she didn't want the girl to see her visitor's orange tie; already, she knew, her position in the girl's eyes had suffered because no one had yet attempted to get *her* pregnant.

"What you think they pay me for, Miss Christine?" the girl said insolently. She swung towards the garden with the tray; Christine trailed her, feeling lumpish and awkward. The girl was at least as big as she was but in a different way.

"Thank you, Elvira," Christine said when the tray was in place. The girl departed without a word, casting a disdainful backward glance at the frayed jacket sleeves, the stained fingers. Christine was now determined to be especially kind to him.

"You are very rich," he said.

"No," Christine protested, shaking her head, "we're not." She had never thought of her family as rich; it was one of her father's sayings that nobody made any money with the Government.

"Yes," he repeated, "you are very rich." He sat back in his lawn chair, gazing about him as though dazed.

Christine set his cup of tea in front of him. She wasn't in the habit of paying much attention to the house or the garden; they were nothing special, far from being the largest on the street; other people took care of them. But now she looked where he was looking, seeing it all as though from a different height: the long expanses, the border flowers blazing in the early-summer sunlight, the flagged patio and walks, the high walls and the silence.

He came back to her face, sighing a little. "My English is not good," he said, "but I improve."

"You do," Christine said, nodding encouragement.

He took sips of his tea, quickly and tenderly, as though afraid of injuring the cup. "I like to stay here."

Christine passed him the cakes. He took only one, making a slight face as he ate it; but he had several more cups of tea while she finished the cakes. She managed to find out from him that he had come over on a church fellowship—she could not decode the denomination—and was studying Philosophy or Theology, or possibly both. She was feeling well-disposed towards him: he had behaved himself, he had caused her no inconvenience.

The teapot was at last empty. He sat up straight in his chair, as though alerted by a soundless gong. "You look this way, please," he said. Christine saw that he had placed his miniature camera on the stone sundial her mother had shipped back from England two years before. He wanted to take her picture. She was flattered, and settled herself to pose, smiling evenly.

He took off his glasses and laid them beside his plate. For a moment she saw his myopic, unprotected eyes turned towards her, with something tremulous and confiding in them she wanted to close herself off from knowing about. Then he went over and did something to the camera, his back to her. The next instant he was crouched beside her, his arm around her waist as far as it could reach, his other hand covering her own hands which she had folded in her lap, his cheek jammed up against hers. She was too startled to move. The camera clicked.

He stood up at once and replaced his glasses, which glittered now with a sad triumph. "Thank you, miss," he said to her. "I go now." He slung the camera back over his shoulder, keeping his hand on it as though to hold the lid on and prevent escape. "I send to my family; they will like."

He was out the gate and gone before Christine had recovered; then she laughed. She had been afraid he would attack her, she could admit it now, and he had; but not in the usual way. He had raped, *rapeo, rapere, rapui, to seize and carry off*, not herself but her celluloid image, and incidently that of the silver tea service, which glinted mockingly at her as the girl bore it away, carrying it regally, the insignia, the official jewels.

Christine spent the summer as she had for the past three years: she was the sailing instructress at an expensive all-girls camp near Algonquin Park. She had been a camper there, everything was familiar to her; she sailed almost better than she played tennis.

The second week she got a letter from him, postmarked Montreal and forwarded from her home address. It was printed in block letters on a piece of the green paper, two or three sentences. It began, "I hope you are well," then described the weather in monosyllables and ended, "I am fine." It was signed, "Your friend." Each week she got another of these letters, more or less identical. In one of them a colour print was enclosed: himself, slightly cross-eyed and grinning hilariously, even more spindly than she remembered him against her billowing draperies, flowers exploding around them like firecrackers, one of his hands an equivocal blur in her lap, the other out of sight; on her own face, astonishment and outrage, as though he was sticking her in the behind with his hidden thumb.

She answered the first letter, but after that the seniors were in training for the races. At the end of the summer, packing to go home, she threw all the letters away.

When she had been back for several weeks she received another of the green letters. This time there was a return address printed at the top which Christine noted with foreboding was in her own city. Every day she waited for the phone to ring; she was so certain his first attempt at contact would be a disembodied voice that when he came upon her abruptly in mid-campus she was unprepared.

"How are you?"

His smile was the same, but everything else about him had deteriorated. He was, if possible, thinner; his jacket sleeves had sprouted a lush new crop of threads, as though to conceal hands now so badly bitten they appeared to have been gnawed by rodents. His hair fell over his eyes, uncut, ungreased; his eyes in the hollowed face, a delicate triangle of skin stretched on bone, jumped behind his glasses like hooded fish. He had the end of a cigarette in the corner of his mouth, and as they walked he lit a new one from it.

"I'm fine," Christine said. She was thinking, I'm not going to get involved again, enough is enough, I've done my bit for internationalism. "How are you?"

"I live here now," he said. "Maybe I study Economics."

"That's nice." He didn't sound as though he was enrolled anywhere.

"I come to see you."

Christine didn't know whether he meant he had left Montreal in order to be near her or just wanted to visit her at her house as he had done in the spring; either way she refused to be implicated. They were outside the Political Science Building. "I have a class here," she said. "Goodbye." She was being callous, she realized that, but a quick chop was more merciful in the long run, that was what her beautiful sisters used to say.

Afterwards she decided it had been stupid of her to let him find out where her class was. Though a timetable was posted in each of the colleges: all he had to do was look her up and record her every probable movement in block letters on his green notepad. After that day he never left her alone.

Initially he waited outside the lecture rooms for her to come out. She said hello to him curtly at first and kept on going, but this didn't work; he followed her at a distance, smiling his changeless smile. Then she stopped speaking altogether and pretended to ignore him, but it made no difference, he followed her anyway. The fact that she was in some way afraid of him—or was it just embarrassment?—seemed only to encourage him. Her friends started to notice, asking her who he was and why he was tagging along behind her; she could hardly answer because she hardly knew.

As the weekdays passed and he showed no signs of letting up, she began to jog-trot between classes, finally to run. He was tireless, and had an amazing wind for one who smoked so heavily: he would speed along behind her, keeping the distance between them the same, as though he were a pull-toy attached to her by a string. She was aware of the ridiculous spectacle they must make, galloping across campus, something out of a cartoon short, a lumbering elephant stampeded by a smiling, emaciated mouse, both of them locked in the classic pattern of comic pursuit and flight; but she found that to race made her less nervous than to walk sedately, the skin on the back of her neck crawling with the feel of his eyes on it. At least she could use her muscles. She worked out routines, escapes: she would dash in the front door of the Ladies' Room in the coffee shop and out the back door, and he would lose the trail, until he discovered the other entrance. She would try to shake him by detours through baffling archways and corridors, but he seemed as familiar with the architectural mazes as she was herself. As a last refuge she could head for the women's dormitory and watch from safety as he was skidded to a halt by the receptionist's austere voice: men were not allowed past the entrance.

Lunch became difficult. She would be sitting, usually with other members of the Debating Society, just digging nicely into a sandwich, when he would appear suddenly as though he'd come up through an unseen manhole. She then had the choice of barging out through the crowded cafeteria, sandwich half-eaten, or finishing her lunch with him standing behind her chair, everyone at the table acutely aware of him, the conversation stilting and dwindling. Her friends learned to spot him from a distance; they posted lookouts. "Here he comes," they would whisper, helping her collect her belongings for the sprint they knew would follow.

Several times she got tired of running and turned to confront him. "What do you want?" she would ask, glowering belligerently down at him, almost clenching her fists; she felt like shaking him, hitting him.

"I wish to talk with you."

"Well, here I am," she would say. "What do you want to talk about?"

But he would say nothing; he would stand in front of her, shifting his feet, smiling perhaps apologetically (though she could never pinpoint the exact tone of that smile, chewed lips stretched apart over the nicotine-yellowed teeth, rising at the corners, flesh held stiffly in place for an invisible photographer), his eyes jerking from one part of her face to another as though he saw her in fragments.

Annoying and tedious though it was, his pursuit of her had an odd result: mysterious in itself, it rendered her equally mysterious. No one had ever found Christine mysterious before. To her parents she was a beefy heavyweight, a plodder, lacking in flair, ordinary as bread. To her sisters she was the plain one, treated with an indulgence they did not give to each other: they did not fear her as a rival. To her male friends she was the one who could be relied on. She was helpful and a hard worker, always good for a game of tennis with the athletes among them. They invited her along to drink beer with them so they could get into the cleaner, more desirable Ladies and Escorts side of the beer parlour, taking it for granted she would buy her share of the rounds. In moments of stress they confided to her their problems with women. There was nothing devious about her and nothing interesting.

Christine had always agreed with these estimates of herself. In childhood she had identified with the false bride or the ugly sister; whenever a story had begun, "Once there was a maiden as beautiful as she was good," she had known it wasn't her. That was just how it was, but it wasn't so bad. Her parents never expected her to be a brilliant social success and weren't overly disappointed when she wasn't. She was spared the manoeuvring and anxiety she witnessed among others her age, and she even had a kind of special position among men: she was an exception, she fitted none of the categories they commonly used when talking about girls; she wasn't a cock-teaser, a cold fish, an easy lay or a snarky bitch; she was an honorary person. She had grown to share their contempt for most women.

Now, however, there was something about her that could not be explained. A man was chasing her, a peculiar sort of man, granted, but still a man, and he was without doubt attracted to her, he couldn't leave her alone. Other men examined her more closely than they ever had, appraising her, trying to find out what it was those twitching bespectacled eyes saw in her. They started to ask her out, though they returned from these excursions with their curiosity unsatisfied, the secret of her charm still intact. Her opaque dumpling face, her solid bearshaped body became for them parts of a riddle no one could solve. Christine sensed this. In the bathtub she no longer imagined she was a dolphin; instead she imagined she was an elusive water-nixie, or sometimes, in moments of audacity, Marilyn Monroe. The daily chase was becoming a habit; she even looked forward to it. In addition to its other benefits she was losing weight.

All these weeks he had never phoned her or turned up at the house. He must have decided however that his tactics were not having the desired result, or perhaps he sensed she was becoming bored. The phone began to ring in the early morning or late at night when he could be sure she would be there. Sometimes he would simply breathe (she could recognize, or thought she could, the quality of his breathing), in which case she would hang up. Occasionally he would say again that he wanted to talk to her, but even when she gave him lots of time nothing else would follow. Then he extended his range: she would see him on her streetcar, smiling at her silently from a seat never closer than three away; she could feel him tracking her down her own street, though when she would break her resolve to pay no attention and would glance back he would be invisible or in the act of hiding behind a tree or hedge.

Among crowds of people and in daylight she had not really been afraid of him; she was stronger than he was and he had made no recent attempt to touch her. But the days were growing shorter and colder, it was almost November. Often she was arriving home in twilight or a darkness broken only by the feeble orange streetlamps. She brooded over the possibility of razors, knives, guns; by acquiring a weapon he could quickly turn the odds against her. She avoided wearing scarves, remembering the newspaper stories about girls who had been strangled by them. Putting on her nylons in the morning gave her a funny feeling. Her body seemed to have diminished, to have become smaller than his.

Was he deranged, was he a sex maniac? He seemed so harmless, yet it was that kind who often went berserk in the end. She pictured those ragged fingers at her throat, tearing at her clothes, though she could not think of herself as screaming. Parked cars, the shrubberies near her house, the driveways on either side of it, changed as she passed them from unnoticed background to sinister shadowed foreground, every detail distinct and harsh: they were places a man might crouch, leap out from. Yet every time she saw him in the clear light of morning or afternoon (for he still continued his old methods of pursuit), his aging jacket and jittery eyes convinced her that it was she herself who was the tormentor, the persecutor. She was in some sense responsible; from the folds and crevices of the body she had treated for so long as a reliable machine was emanating, against her will, some potent invisible odour, like a dog's in heat or a female moth's, that made him unable to stop following her.

Her mother, who had been too preoccupied with the unavoidable fall entertaining to pay much attention to the number of phone calls Christine was getting or to the hired girl's complaints of a man who hung up without speaking, announced that she was flying down to New York for the weekend; her father decided to go too. Christine panicked: she saw herself in the bathtub with her throat slit, the blood drooling out of her neck and running in a little spiral down the drain (for by this time she believed he could walk through walls, could be everywhere at once). The girl would do nothing to help; she might even stand in the bathroom door with her arms folded, watching. Christine arranged to spend the weekend at her married sister's.

When she arrived back Sunday evening she found the girl close to hysterics. She said that on Saturday she had gone to pull the curtains across the French doors at dusk and had found a strangely contorted face, a man's face, pressed against the glass, staring in at her from the garden. She claimed she had fainted and had almost had her baby a month too early right there on the living-room carpet. Then she had called the police. He was gone by the time they got there but she had recognized him from the afternoon of the tea; she had informed them he was a friend of Christine's.

They called Monday evening to investigate, two of them. They were very polite, they knew who Christine's father was. Her father greeted them heartily; her mother hovered in the background, fidgeting with her porcelain hands, letting them see how frail and worried she was. She didn't like having them in the living room but they were necessary.

Christine had to admit he'd been following her around. She was relieved he'd been discovered, relieved also that she hadn't been the one to tell, though if he'd been a citizen of the country she would have called the police a long time ago. She insisted he was not dangerous, he had never hurt her.

"That kind don't hurt you," one of the policemen said. "They just kill you. You're lucky you aren't dead."

"Nut cases," the other one said.

Her mother volunteered that the thing about people from another culture was that you could never tell whether they were insane or not because their ways were so different. The policemen agreed with her, deferential but also condescending, as though she was a royal halfwit who had to be humoured.

"You know where he lives?" the first policeman asked.

Christine had long ago torn up the letter with his address on it; she shook her head.

"We'll have to pick him up tomorrow then," he said. "Think you can keep him talking outside your class if he's waiting for you?"

After questioning her they held a murmured conversation with her father in the front hall. The girl, clearing away the coffee cups, said if they didn't lock him up she was leaving, she wasn't going to be scared half out of her skin like that again.

Next day when Christine came out of her Modern History lecture he was there, right on schedule. He seemed puzzled when she did not begin to run. She approached him, her heart thumping with treachery and the prospect of freedom. Her body was back to its usual size; she felt herself a giantess, self-controlled, invulnerable.

"How are you?" she asked, smiling brightly.

He looked at her with distrust.

"How have you been?" she ventured again. His own perennial smile faded; he took a step back from her.

"This the one?" said the policeman, popping out from behind a notice board like a Keystone Cop and laying a competent hand on the worn jacket shoulder. The other policeman lounged in the background; force would not be required.

"Don't *do* anything to him," she pleaded as they took him away. They nodded and grinned, respectful, scornful. He seemed to know perfectly well who they were and what they wanted.

The first policeman phoned that evening to make his report. Her father talked with him, jovial and managing. She herself was now out of the picture; she had been protected, her function was over.

"What did they *do* to him?" she asked anxiously as he came back into the living room. She was not sure what went on in police stations.

"They didn't do anything to him," he said, amused by her concern. "They could have booked him for Watching and Besetting, they wanted to know if I'd like to press charges. But it's not worth a court case: he's got a visa that says he's only allowed in the country as long as he studies in Montreal, so I told them to just ship him down there. If he turns up here again they'll deport him. They went around to his rooming house, his rent's two weeks overdue; the landlady said she was on the point of kicking him out. He seems happy enough to be getting his back rent paid and a free train ticket to Montreal." He paused. "They couldn't get anything out of him though."

"*Out* of him?" Christine asked.

"They tried to find out why he was doing it; following you, I mean." Her father's eyes swept her as though it was a riddle to him also. "They said when they asked him about that he just clammed up. Pretended he didn't understand English. He understood well enough, but he wasn't answering."

Christine thought this would be the end, but somehow between his arrest and the departure of the train he managed to elude his escort long enough for one more phone call.

"I see you again," he said. He didn't wait for her to hang up.

Now that he was no longer an embarrassing present reality, he could be talked about, he could become an amusing story. In fact, he was the only amusing story Christine had to tell, and telling it preserved both for herself and for others the aura of her strange allure. Her friends and the men who continued to ask her out speculated about his motives. One suggested he had wanted to marry her so he could remain in the country; another said that oriental men were fond of well-built women: "It's your Rubens quality."

Christine thought about him a lot. She had not been attracted to him, rather the reverse, but as an idea only he was a romantic figure, the one man who had found her irresistible; though she often wondered, inspecting her unchanged pink face and hefty body in her full-length mirror, just what it was about her that had done it. She avoided whenever it was proposed the theory of his insanity: it was only that there was more than one way of being sane.

But a new acquaintance, hearing the story for the first time, had a different explanation. "So he got you, too," he said, laughing. "That has to be the same guy who was hanging around our day camp a year ago this summer. He followed all the girls like that, a short guy, Japanese or something, glasses, smiling all the time."

"Maybe it was another one," Christine said.

"There couldn't be two of them, everything fits. This was a pretty weird guy."

"What . . . *kind* of girls did he follow?" Christine asked.

"Oh, just anyone who happened to be around. But if they paid any attention to him at first, if they were nice to him or anything, he was unshakeable. He was a bit of a pest, but harmless."

Christine ceased to tell her amusing story. She had been one among many, then. She went back to playing tennis, she had been neglecting her game.

A few months later the policeman who had been in charge of the case telephoned her again.

"Like you to know, miss, that fellow you were having the trouble with was sent back to his own country. Deported."

"What for?" Christine asked. "Did he try to come back here?" Maybe she had been special after all, maybe he had dared everything for her.

"Nothing like it," the policeman said. "He was up to the same tricks in Montreal but he really picked the wrong woman this time—a Mother Superior of a convent. They don't stand for things like that in Quebec—had him out of here before he knew what happened. I guess he'll be better off in his own place."

"How old was she?" Christine asked, after a silence.

"Oh, around sixty, I guess."

"Thank you very much for letting me know," Christine said in her best official manner. "It's such a relief." She wondered if the policeman had called to make fun of her.

She was almost crying when she put down the phone. What *had* he wanted from her then? A Mother Superior. Did she really look sixty, did she look like a mother? What did convents mean? Comfort, charity? Refuge? Was it that something had happened to him, some intolerable strain just from being in this country; her tennis dress and exposed legs too much for him, flesh and money seemingly available everywhere but withheld from him wherever he turned, the nun the symbol of some final distortion, the robe and veil reminiscent to his near-sighted eyes of the women of his homeland, the ones he was able to understand? But he was back in his own country, remote from her as another planet; she would never know.

He hadn't forgotten her though. In the spring she got a post-card with a foreign stamp and the familiar block-letter writing. On the front was a picture of a temple. He was fine, he hoped she was fine also, he was her friend. A month later another print of the picture he had taken in the garden arrived, in a sealed manila envelope otherwise empty.

Christine's aura of mystery soon faded; anyway, she herself no longer believed in it. Life became again what she had always expected. She graduated with mediocre grades and went into the Department of Health and Welfare; she did a good job, and was seldom discriminated against for being a woman because nobody thought of her as one. She could afford a pleasant-sized apartment, though she did not put much energy into decorating it. She played less and less tennis; what had been muscle with a light coating of fat turned gradually into fat with a thin substratum of muscle. She began to get headaches.

As the years were used up and the war began to fill the newspapers and magazines, she realized which Eastern country he had actually been from. She had known the name but it hadn't registered at the time, it was such a minor place; she could never keep them separate in her mind.

But though she tried, she couldn't remember the name of the city, and the postcard was long gone—had he been from the North or the South, was he near the battle zone or safely far from it? Obsessively she bought magazines and pored over the available photographs, dead villagers, soldiers on the march, colour blowups of frightened or angry faces, spies being executed; she studied maps, she watched the late-night newscasts, the distant country and terrain becoming almost more familiar to her than her own. Once or twice she thought she could recognize him but it was no use, they all looked like him.

Finally she had to stop looking at the pictures. It bothered her too much, it was bad for her; she was beginning to have nightmares in which he was coming through the French doors of her mother's house in his shabby jacket, carrying a packsack and a rifle and a huge bouquet of richly coloured flowers. He was smiling in the same way but with blood streaked over his face, partly blotting out the features. She gave her television set away and took to reading nineteenth-century novels instead; Trollope and Galsworthy were her favourites. When, despite herself, she would think about him, she would tell herself that he had been crafty and agile-minded enough to survive, more or less, in her country, so surely he would be able to do it in his own, where he knew the language. She could not see him in the army, on either side; he wasn't the type, and to her knowledge he had not believed in any particular ideology. He would be something nondescript, something in the background, like herself; perhaps he had become an interpreter.

Betty

When I was seven we moved again, to a tiny wooden cottage on the Saint Marys River, upstream from Sault Sainte Marie. We were only renting the cottage for the summer, but for the time being it was our house, since we had no other. It was dim and mousy-smelling and very cramped, stuffed with all the things from the place before that were not in storage. My sister and I preferred to spend most of our time outside it.

There was a short beach, behind which the cottages, with their contrasting trim—green against white, maroon against robin's-egg blue, brown against yellow—were lined up like little shoeboxes, each with its matching outhouse at an unsanitary distance behind. But we were forbidden to swim in the water, because of the strong current. There were stories of children who had been swept away, down toward the rapids and the locks and the Algoma Steel fires of the Soo which we could sometimes see from our bedroom window on overcast nights, glowing dull red against the clouds. We were allowed to wade though, no further than the knee, and we would stand in the water, strands of loose weed tangling against our ankles, and wave at the lake freighters as they slid past, so close we could see not only the flags and sea gulls at their sterns but the hands of the sailors and the ovals of their faces as they waved back to us. Then the waves would come, washing over our thighs up to the waists of our bloomered and skirted seersucker bathing suits, and we would scream with delight.

Our mother, who was usually on the shore, reading or talking to someone but not quite watching us, would sometimes mistake the screams for drowning. Or she would say later, "You've been in over your knees," but my sister would explain that it was only the boat waves. My mother would look at me to see if this was the truth. Unlike my sister, I was a clumsy liar.

The freighters were huge, cumbersome, with rust staining the holes for their anchor chains and enormous chimneys from which the smoke spurted in grey burps. When they blew their horns, as they always did when approaching the locks, the windows in our cottage rattled. For us, they were magical. Sometimes things would drop or be thrown from them, and we would watch these floating objects eagerly, running along the beach to be there when they landed, wading out to fish them in. Usually these treasures turned out to be only empty cardboard boxes or punctured oil cans, oozing dark brown grease and good for nothing. Several times we got orange crates, which we used as cupboards or stools in our hideouts.

We liked the cottage partly because we had places to make these hideouts. There had never been room before, since we had always lived in cities. Just before this it was Ottawa, the ground floor of an old three-tiered red-brick apartment building. On the floor above us lived a newly married couple, the wife English and Protestant, the husband French and Catholic. He was in the Air Force, and was away a lot, but when he came back on leave he used to beat up his wife. It was always about eleven o'clock at night. She would flee downstairs to my mother for protection, and they would sit in the kitchen with cups of tea. The wife would cry, though quietly, so as not to wake us—my mother insisted on that, being a believer in twelve hours of sleep for children—display her bruised eye or cheek, and whisper about his drinking. After an hour or so there would be a discreet knock on the door, and the airman, in full uniform, would ask my mother politely if he could have his wife back upstairs where she belonged. It was a religious dispute, he would say. Besides, he'd given her fifteen dollars to spend on food and she had served him fried Kam. After being away a month, a man expected a good roast, pork or beef, didn't my mother agree? "I kept my mouth shut and my eyes open," my mother would say. He never seemed that drunk to her, but with the polite kind you couldn't tell what they would do.

I wasn't supposed to know about any of this. I was considered either too young or too good; but my sister, who was four years older, was given hints, which she passed along to me with whatever she thought fit to add. I saw the wife a number of times, going up or down the stairs outside our door, and once she did have a black eye. I never saw the man, but by the time we left Ottawa I was convinced he was a murderer.

This might have explained my father's warning when my mother told him she had met the young couple who lived in the right-hand cottage. "Don't get too involved," he said. "I don't want her running over here at all hours of the night." He had little patience with my mother's talents as a sympathetic listener, even when she teased him by saying, "But I listen to *you*, dear." She attracted people he called "sponges."

He didn't seem to have anything to worry about. This couple was very different from the other one. Fred and Betty insisted on being called Fred and Betty, right away. My sister and I, who had been drilled to call people Mr. and Mrs., had to call them Fred and Betty also, and we could go over to their house whenever we wanted to. "I don't want you to take that at face value," our mother said. Times were hard but our mother had been properly brought up, and we were going to be, too. Nevertheless, at first we went to Fred and Betty's as often as we could.

Their cottage was exactly the same size as ours, but since there was less furniture in it it seemed bigger. Ours had Ten-Test walls between the rooms, painted lime green, with lighter squares on the paint where other people had once hung pictures. Betty had replaced her walls with real plywood and painted the inside bright yellow, and she'd made yellow-and-

34

white curtains for the kitchen, a print of chickens coming out of eggshells. She'd sewed herself a matching apron from the leftover material. They owned their cottage rather than renting it; as my mother said, you didn't mind doing the work then. Betty called the tiny kitchen a kitchenette. There was a round ironwork table tucked into one corner, with two scrolled ironwork chairs, painted white, one for Betty and one for Fred. Betty called this corner the breakfast nook.

There was more to do at Fred and Betty's than at our house. They had a bird made of hollow coloured glass that perched on the edge of a tumbler of water, teetering back and forth until it would finally dip its head into the water and take a drink. They had a front-door knocker in the shape of a woodpecker: you pulled a string, and the woodpecker pecked at the door. They also had a whistle in the shape of a bird that you could fill with water and blow into and it would warble, "like a canary," Betty said. And they took the Saturday coloured funnies. Our parents didn't, and they didn't like us reading trash, as they called it. But Fred and Betty were so friendly and kind to us, what, as my mother said, could they do?

Beyond all these attractions there was Fred. We both fell in love with Fred. My sister would climb into his lap and announce that he was her boyfriend and she was going to marry him when she grew up. She would then make him read the funnies to her and tease him by trying to take the pipe out of his mouth or by tying his shoelaces together. I felt the same way, but I knew it was no good saying so. My sister had staked her claim: when she said she was going to do a thing she usually did it. And she hated my being what she called a copycat. So I would sit in the breakfast nook on one of the scrolled ironwork chairs while Betty made coffee, watching my sister and Fred on the living-room couch.

There was something about Fred that attracted people. My mother, who was not a flirtatious woman—she went in for wisdom, instead—was livelier when he was around. Even my father liked him, and would sometimes have a beer with him when he got back from the city. They would sit on the porch of Fred's cottage in Betty's yellow wicker chairs, swatting at the sand flies and discussing baseball scores. They seldom mentioned their jobs. I'm not sure what Fred did, but it was in an office. My father was "in wallpaper," my mother said, but I was never very clear about what that meant. It was more exciting when they talked about the war. My father's bad back had kept him out of it, much to his disgust, but Fred had been in the Navy. He never said too much about it, though my father was always prompting him; but we knew from Betty that they were engaged just before Fred left and married right after he came back. Betty had written letters to him every single night and mailed them once a week. She did not say how often Fred had written to her. My father didn't like many people, but he said that Fred wasn't a fool.

Fred didn't seem to make any efforts to be nice to people. I don't think he was even especially handsome. The difficulty is that though I can remember Betty down to the last hair and freckle, I can't remember what Fred looked like. He had dark hair and a pipe, and he used to sing to us if we pestered him enough. "Sioux City Sue," he would sing, "Your hair is red, your eyes are blue, I'd swap my horse and dog for you . . ." Or he would sing "Beautiful Brown Eyes" to my sister, whose eyes were brown as compared with my own watery blue. This hurt my feelings, as the song contained the line, "I'll never love blue eyes again." It seemed so final, a whole lifetime of being unloved by Fred. Once I cried, which was made worse by the fact that I couldn't explain to anyone what was wrong; and I had to undergo the humiliation of Fred's jocular concern and my sister's scorn, and the worse humiliation of being comforted by Betty in the kitchenette. It was a humiliation because it was obvious even to me that Betty didn't grasp things very well. "Don't pay any attention to *him*," she said, having guessed that my tears had something to do with Fred. But that was the one piece of advice I couldn't take.

Fred, like a cat, wouldn't go two steps out of his way for you really, as my mother said later. So it was unfair that everyone was in love with Fred, but no one, despite her kindness, was in love with Betty. It was Betty who always greeted us at the door, asked us in, and talked to us while Fred slouched on the couch reading the paper. She fed us cookies and milk shakes and let us lick out the bowls when she was baking. Betty was such a nice person; everyone said so, but no one would have called Fred exactly that. Fred, for instance, did not laugh much, and he only smiled when he was making rude remarks, mostly to my sister. "Stuffing your face again?" he would say. "Hey, baggy-pants." Whereas Betty never said things like that, and she was always either smiling or laughing.

She laughed a lot when Fred called her Betty Grable, which he did at least once a day. I couldn't see why she laughed. It was supposed to be a compliment, I thought. Betty Grable was a famous movie star; there was a picture of her thumb-tacked to the wall in Fred and Betty's outhouse. Both my sister and I preferred Fred and Betty's outhouse to our own. Theirs had curtains on the window, unlike ours, and it had a little wooden box and a matching wooden scoop for the lye. We only had a cardboard box and an old trowel.

Betty didn't really look like Betty Grable, who was blonde and not as plump as our Betty. Still, they were both beautiful, I thought. I didn't realize until much later that the remark was cruel; for Betty Grable was renowned for her legs, whereas our Betty had legs that started at her waist and continued downwards without a curve or a pause until they reached her feet. At the time they seemed like ordinary legs. Sitting in the kitchenette, I saw a lot of Betty's legs, for she wore halter tops and shorts, with her yellow apron over them. Somehow Betty could never get her legs to tan, despite the hours she spent crocheting in her wicker chair, the top part of her in the shade of the porch but her legs sticking out into the sun.

My father said that Betty had no sense of humour. I couldn't understand this at all. If you told her a joke she would always laugh, even if you got it mixed up, and she told jokes of her own, too. She would print the word "BED," making the E smaller and thicker than the B and the D. "What's this?" she would say. "It's the little dark E in BED." I didn't get this joke the first time she told it and she had to explain it to me. "Little darkie," she said, her slightly protruding teeth shining with good humour. We had never been to the United States, even though we could see it across the river, a strip of green trees that faded west into the blue of Lake Superior, and the only black people I had seen were the characters in the comics. There was L'il 8-Ball, and the Africans in Tarzan, and Lothar in Mandrake the Magician, who wore a lion skin. I couldn't see what any of them had to do with the word "bed."

My father also said that Betty had no sex appeal. This didn't seem to bother my mother in the least. "She's a very nice girl," she would answer complacently, or, "She has very nice colouring." My mother and Betty were soon collaborating on a scheme for making the preserving easier. Most people still had Victory gardens, though the war was over, and the months of July and August were supposed to be spent putting up as many jars of fruit and vegetables as you could. My mother's garden was half-hearted, like most of her housekeeping efforts. It was a small patch beside the outhouse where squash vines rambled over a thicket of overgrown tomato plants and a few uneven lines of dwarfed carrots and beets. My mother's talent, we had heard her say, was for people. Betty and Fred didn't have a garden at all. Fred wouldn't have worked in it, and when I think of Betty now I realize that a garden would have been too uncontained for her. But she had Fred buy dozens of six-quart baskets of strawberries, peaches, beans, tomatoes and Concord grapes, on his trips into the city; and she persuaded my mother to give up on her own garden and join her in her mammoth canning sessions.

My mother's wood stove was unbearably hot for such an operation, and Betty's little electric range was too small; so Betty got "the boys," as she called Fred and my father, to set up the derelict wood stove that until then had been rusting behind Betty's outhouse. They put it in our backyard, and my mother and Betty would sit at our kitchen table, which had been carried outside, peeling, slicing and talking, Betty with her round pincushion cheeks flushed redder than usual by the heat and my mother with an old bandanna wrapped around her head, making her look like a gypsy. Behind them the canning kettles bubbled and steamed, and on one side of the table the growing ranks of Crown jars, inverted on layers of newspapers, cooled and sometimes leaked or cracked. My sister and I hung around the edges, not wanting to be obvious enough to be put to work, but coveting the empty six-quart baskets. We could use them in our hideout, we felt; we were never sure what for, but they fitted neatly into the orange crates.

I learned a lot about Fred during Betty's canning sessions: how he liked his eggs, what size socks he took (Betty was a knitter), how well he was doing at the office, what he refused to eat for dinner. Fred was a picky eater, Betty said joyfully. Betty had almost nothing else to talk about, and even my mother, veteran of many confidences, began to talk less and smoke more than usual when Betty was around. It was easier to listen to disasters than to Betty's inexhaustible and trivial cheer. I began to think that I might not want to be married to Fred after all. He unrolled from Betty's mouth like a long ribbon of soggy newspaper printed from end to end with nothing but the weather. Neither my sister nor I was interested in sock sizes, and Betty's random, unexciting details diminished Fred in our eyes. We began to spend less of our playtime at Fred and Betty's and more in our hideout, which was in a patch of scrubby oak on a vacant lot along the shore. There we played complicated games of Mandrake the Magician and his faithful servant Lothar, with our dolls as easily hypnotized villains. My sister was always Mandrake. When we tired of this, we would put on our bathing suits and go wading along the shore, watching for freighters and throwing acorns into the river to see how quickly they would be carried away by the current.

It was on one of these wading expeditions that we met Nan. She lived ten lots down, in a white cottage with red trim. Unlike many of the other cottages, Nan's had a real dock, built out into the river and anchored around the posts with piles of rocks. She was sitting on this dock when we first saw her, chewing gum and flipping through a stack of airplane cards from Wings cigarettes. Everyone knew that only boys collected these. Her hair and her face were light brown, and she had a sleek plump sheen, like caramel pudding.

"What're you doing with *those?*" were my sister's first words. Nan only smiled.

That same afternoon Nan was allowed into our hideout, and after a cursory game of Mandrake, during which I was demoted to the lowly position of Narda, the two of them sat on our orange crates and exchanged what seemed to me to be languid and pointless comments.

"You ever go to the store?" Nan asked. We never did. Nan smiled some more. She was twelve; my sister was only eleven and three-quarters.

"There's cute boys at the store," Nan said. She was wearing a peasant blouse with a frill and an elastic top that she could slide down over her shoulders if she wanted too. She stuck her airplane cards into her shorts pocket and we went to ask my mother if we could walk to the store. After that, my sister and Nan went there almost every afternoon.

The store was a mile and a half from our cottage, a hot walk along the shore past the fronts of other cottages where fat mothers basked in the sun and other, possibly hostile children paddled in the water; past rowboats hauled up on the sand, along cement breakwaters, through patches of beach grass that cut your ankles if you ran through it and beach peas that were hard and bitter-tasting. In some places we could smell the outhouses. Just before the store, there was an open space with poison ivy, which we had to wade around.

The store had no name. It was just "the store," the only store for the cottagers since it was the only one they could walk to. I was allowed to go with my sister and Nan, or rather, my mother insisted that I go. Although I hadn't said anything to her about it, she could sense my misery. It wasn't so much my sister's desertion that hurt, but her blithe unconsciousness of it. She was quite willing to play with me when Nan wasn't around.

Sometimes, when the sight of my sister and Nan conspiring twenty paces ahead of me made me too unhappy, I would double back and go to Fred and Betty's. There I would sit facing backwards on one of Betty's kitchen chairs, my two hands rigid in the air, holding a skein of sky-blue wool while Betty wound it into balls. Or, under Betty's direction, I crocheted sweaty, uneven little pink and yellow dolls' dresses for the dolls my sister was, suddenly, too old to play with.

On better days I would make it as far as the store. It was not beautiful or even clean, but we were so used to wartime drabness and grime that we didn't notice. It was a two-storey building of unpainted wood which had weathered grey. Parts of it were patched with tar paper, and it had coloured metal signs nailed around the front screen door and windows: Coca-Cola, 7-Up, Salada Tea. Inside, it had the sugary, mournful smell of old general stores, a mixture of the cones for the ice-cream cones, the packages of Oreo cookies, the open boxes of jawbreakers and licorice whips that lined the counter, and that other smell, musky and sharp, part dry-rot and part sweat. The bottles of pop were kept in a metal cooler with a heavy lid, filled with cold water and chunks of ice melted to the smoothness of the sand-scoured pieces of glass we sometimes found on the beach.

The owner of the store and his wife lived on the second floor, but we almost never saw them. The store was run by their two daughters, who took turns behind the counter. They were both dark and they both wore shorts and polka-dot halter tops, but one was friendly and the other one, the thinner, younger one, was not. She would take our pennies and ring them into the cash register without saying a word, staring over our heads out the front window with its dangling raisin-covered fly-papers as if she was completely detached from the activity her hands were performing. She didn't dislike us; she just didn't see us. She wore her hair long and done in a sort of roll at the front, and her lipstick was purplish.

The first time we went to the store we found out why Nan collected airplane cards. There were two boys there, sitting on the grey, splintery front steps, their arms crossed over their knees. I had been told by my sister that the right thing to do with boys was to ignore them; otherwise they would pester you.

But these boys knew Nan, and they spoke to her, not with the usual taunts, but with respect.

"You got anything new?" one of them said.

Nan smiled, brushed back her hair and wiggled her shoulders a little inside her peasant blouse. Then she slid her airplane cards slowly out of her shorts pocket and began riffling through them.

"You got any?" the other boy said to my sister. For once she was humbled. After that, she got my mother to switch brands and built up her own pack. I saw her in front of the mirror about a week later, practising that tantalizing slide, the cards coming out of her pocket like a magician's snake.

When I went to the store I always had to bring back a loaf of wax-papered bread for my mother, and sometimes a package of "Jiffy" Pie Crust, if they had any. My sister never had to: she had already discovered the advantages of being unreliable. As payment, and, I'm sure, as compensation for my unhappiness, my mother gave me a penny a trip, and when I had saved five of these pennies I bought my first Popsicle. Our mother had always refused to buy them for us, although she permitted ice-cream cones. She said there was something in Popsicles that was bad for you, and as I sat on the front steps of the store, licking down to the wooden stick, I kept looking for this thing. I visualized it as a sort of core, like the white fingernail-shaped part in a kernel of corn, but I couldn't find anything.

My sister and Nan were sitting beside me on the front steps. There were no boys at the store that day, so they had nothing else to do. It was even hotter than usual, and airless; there was a shimmer over the river, and the freighters wavered as they passed through it. My Popsicle was melting almost before I could eat it. I had given my sister half of it, which she had taken without the gratitude I had hoped for. She was sharing it with Nan.

Fred came around the corner of the building and headed towards the front door. This was no surprise, as we had seen him at the store several times before.

"Hi, beautiful," he said to my sister. We moved our rumps along the step to let him in the door.

After quite a long time he came out, carrying a loaf of bread. He asked us if we wanted a lift with him in his car: he was just coming back from the city, he said. Of course we said yes. There was nothing unusual about any of this, except that the daughter, the thinner, purple one, stepped outside the door and stood on the steps as we were driving off. She folded her arms across her chest in that slump-shouldered pose of women idling in doorways. She wasn't smiling. I thought she had come out to watch the Canada Steamship Lines freighter that was going past, but then I saw that she was staring at Fred. She looked as if she wanted to kill him.

Fred didn't seem to notice. He sang all the way home. "Katy, oh beautiful Katy," he sang, winking at my sister, whom he sometimes called Katy since her name was Catherine. He had the windows open, and dust from the rutted gravel road poured over us, whitening our eyebrows and turning Fred's hair grey. At every jolt my sister and Nan screamed gleefully, and after a while I forgot my feelings of exclusion and screamed too.

It seemed as if we had lived in the cottage for a long time, though it was only one summer. By August I could hardly remember the apartment in Ottawa and the man who used to beat up his wife. That had happened in a remote life; and, despite the sunshine, the water, the open space, a happier one. Before, our frequent moves and the insecurities of new schools had forced my sister to value me: I was four years younger, but I was loyal and always there. Now those years were a canyon between us, an empty stretch like a beach along which I could see her disappearing ahead of me. I longed to be just like her, but I could no longer tell what she was like.

In the third week of August the leaves started to turn, not all at once, just a single red one here and there, like a warning. That meant it would soon be time for school and another move. We didn't even know where we would be moving to this time, and when Nan asked us what school we went to, we were evasive.

"I've been to eight different schools," my sister said proudly.

Because I was so much younger, I had only been to two. Nan, who had been to the same one all her life, slipped the edge of her peasant blouse over her shoulders and down to her elbows to show us that her breasts were growing. The rings around her nipples had softened and started to puff out; otherwise she was as flat as my sister.

"So what," said my sister, rolling up her jersey. This was a competition I couldn't be part of. It was about change, and, increasingly, change frightened me. I walked back along the beach to Betty's house, where my latest piece of grubby crocheting was waiting for me and where everything was always the same.

I knocked on the screen door and opened it. I meant to say, "Can I come in?" the way we always did, but I didn't say it. Betty was sitting by herself at the iron table of the breakfast nook. She had on her shorts and a striped sailor top, navy blue and white with a little anchor pin, and the apron with the yellow chickens coming out of their eggs. For once she wasn't doing anything, and there was no cup of coffee in front of her. Her face was white and uncomprehending, as if someone had just hit her for no reason.

She saw me, but she didn't smile or ask me in. "What am I going to do?" she said.

I looked around the kitchen. Everything was in its place: the percolator gleamed from the stove, the glass bird was teetering slowly down, there were no broken dishes, no water on the floor. What had happened?

"Are you sick?" I said.

"There's nothing I can do," Betty said.

She looked so strange that I was frightened. I ran out of the kitchen and across the hillocky grass to get to my mother, who always knew what should be done.

"There's something wrong with Betty," I said.

My mother was mixing something in a bowl. She rubbed her hands together to get the dough off, then wiped them on her apron. She didn't look surprised or ask me what it was. "You stay here," she said. She picked up her package of cigarettes and went out the door.

That evening we had to go to bed early because my mother wanted to talk to my father. We listened, of course; it was easy through the Ten-Test walls.

"I saw it coming," my mother said. "A mile away."

"Who is it?" my father said.

"She doesn't know," said my mother. "Some girl from town."

"Betty's a fool," my father said. "She always was." Later, when husbands and wives leaving each other became more common, he often said this, but no matter which one had left it was always the woman he called the fool. His highest compliment to my mother was that she was no fool.

"That may be," said my mother. "But you'd never want to meet a nicer girl. He was her whole life."

My sister and I whispered together. My sister's theory was that Fred had run away from Betty with another woman. I couldn't believe this: I had never heard of such a thing happening. I was so upset I couldn't sleep, and for a long time after that I was anxious whenever my father was away overnight, as he frequently was. What if he never came back?

We didn't see Betty after that. We knew she was in her cottage, because every day my mother carried over samples of her tough and lumpy baking, almost as if someone had died. But we were given strict orders to stay away, and not to go peering in the windows as our mother must have known we longed to do. "She's having a nervous breakdown," our mother said, which for me called up an image of Betty lying disjointed on the floor like a car at the garage.

We didn't even see her on the day we got into my father's second-hand Studebaker, the back seat packed to the window-tops with only a little oblong space for me to crouch in, and drove out to the main highway to begin the six-hundred-mile journey south to Toronto. My father had changed jobs again; he was now in building materials, and he was sure, since the country was having a boom, that this was finally the right change. We spent September and part of October in a motel while my father looked for a house. I had my eighth birthday and my sister turned twelve. Then there was another new school, and I almost forgot about Betty.

But a month after I had turned twelve myself, Betty was suddenly there one night for dinner. We had people for dinner a lot more than we used to, and sometimes the dinners were so important that my sister and I ate first. My sister didn't care, as she had boyfriends by that time. I was still in public school and had to wear lisle stockings instead of the seamed nylons my sister was permitted. Also, I had braces. My sister had had braces at that age too, but she had somehow managed to make them seem rakish and daring, so that I had longed for a mouthful of flashing silver teeth like hers. But she no longer had them, and my own mouth in its shackles felt clumsy and muffled.

"You remember Betty," my mother said.

"Elizabeth," Betty said.

"Oh yes, of course," said my mother.

Betty had changed a lot. Before, she had been a little plump; now she was buxom. Her cheeks were as round and florid as two tomatoes, and I thought she was using too much rouge until I saw that the red was caused by masses of tiny veins under her skin. She was wearing a long black pleated skirt, a white short-sleeved angora sweater with a string of black beads, and open-toed black velvet pumps with high heels. She smelled strongly of Lily of the Valley. She had a job, my mother told my father later, a very good job. She was an executive secretary, and now called herself Miss instead of Mrs.

"She's doing very well," my mother said, "considering what happened. She's pulled herself together."

"I hope you don't start inviting her to dinner all the time," said my father, who still found Betty irritating in spite of her new look. She laughed more than ever now, and crossed her legs frequently.

"I feel I'm the only real friend she has," said my mother. She didn't say Betty was the only real friend she had, though when my father said "your friend" everyone knew who he meant. My mother had a lot of friends, and her talent for wise listening was now a business asset for my father.

"She says she'll never marry again," said my mother.

"She's a fool," my father said.

"If I ever saw anyone cut out for marriage, it was her," said my mother. This remark increased my anxiety about my own future. If all Betty's accomplishments had not been enough for Fred, what hope was there for me? I did not have my sister's natural flair, but I had thought there would be some tricks I could learn, dutifully, painstakingly. We were taking Home Economics at school and the teacher kept saying that the way to a man's heart was through his stomach. I knew this wasn't true—my mother was still a slapdash cook, and when she gave the best dinners she had a woman in to help— but I laboured over my blancmange and Harvard beets as if I believed it.

My mother started inviting Betty to dinner with men who were not married. Betty smiled and laughed and several of the men seemed interested, but nothing came of it.

"After the way she was hurt, I'm not surprised," my mother said. I was now old enough to be told things, and besides, my sister was never around. "I heard it was a secretary at his company he ran off with. They even got married, after the divorce." There was something else about Betty, she told me, although I must never mention it as Betty found it very distressing. Fred's brother, who was a dentist, had killed his wife because he got involved—my mother said "involved" richly, as if it was a kind of dessert—with his dental technician. He had put his wife into the car and run a tube in from the exhaust pipe, and then tried to pretend it was suicide. The police had found out though, and he was in jail.

This made Betty much more interesting in my eyes. It was in Fred's blood, then, this tendency towards involvement. In fact it could just as easily have been Betty herself who had been murdered. I now came to see Betty's laugh as the mask of a stricken and martyred woman. She was not just a wife who had been deserted. Even I could see that this was not a tragic position, it was a ridiculous and humiliating one. She was much more than that: she was a woman who had narrowly escaped death. That Betty herself saw it this way I soon had no doubt. There was something smug and even pious about the way she kept Mother's single men at a polite distance, something faintly nunlike. A lurid aura of sacrificial blood surrounded her. Betty had been there, she had passed through it, she had come out alive, and now she was dedicating herself to, well, to something else.

But it was hard for me to sustain this version of Betty for long. My mother soon ran out of single men and Betty, when she came to dinner, came alone. She talked as incessantly about the details surrounding the other women at her office as she had about Fred. We soon knew how they all took their coffee, which ones lived with their mothers, where they had their hair done, and what their apartments looked like. Betty herself had a darling apartment on Avenue Road, and she had re-done it all herself and even made the slipcovers. Betty was as devoted to her boss as she had once been to Fred. She did all his Christmas shopping, and each year we heard what he had given to his employees, what to his wife and children, and what each item had cost. Betty seemed, in a way, quite happy.

We saw a lot of Betty around Christmas; my mother said she felt sorry for her because she had no family. Betty was in the habit of giving us Christmas presents that made it obvious she thought we were younger than we were. She favoured Parcheesi sets and angora mittens a size too small. I lost interest in her. Even her unending cheerfulness came to seem like a perversion, or a defect almost like idiocy. I was fifteen now and in the throes of adolescent depression. My sister was away at Queen's; sometimes she gave me clothes she no longer wanted. She was not exactly beautiful—both her eyes and her mouth were too large—but everyone called her vivacious. They called me nice. My braces had come off, but it didn't seem to make any difference. What right had Betty to be cheerful? When she came to dinner, I excused myself early and went to my room.

One afternoon, in the spring of Grade Eleven, I came home from school to find my mother sitting at the dining-room table. She was crying, which was so rare that my immediate fear was that something had happened to my father. I didn't think he had left her; that particular anxiety was past. But perhaps he had been killed in a car crash.

"Mum, what is it?" I said.

"Bring me a glass of water," she said. She drank some of it and pushed back her hair. "I'm all right now," she said. "I just had a call from Betty. It was very upsetting; she said horrible things to me."

"Why?" I said. "What did you do?"

"She accused me of . . . horrible things." My mother swabbed at her eyes. "She was screaming. I've never heard Betty scream in my life before. After all that time I spent with her. She said she never wanted to speak to me again. Where would she get such an idea?"

"What idea?" I said. I was just as mystified as my mother was. My mother was a bad cook, but she was a good woman. I could not imagine her doing anything that would make anyone want to scream at her.

My mother held back slightly. "Things about Fred," she said. "She must be crazy. I hadn't seen her for a couple of months, and then suddenly, just like that."

"There must be something wrong with her," my father said at dinner that night. Of course he was right. Betty had an undetected brain tumour, which was discovered when her strange behaviour was noticed at the office. She died in the hospital two months later, but my mother didn't hear about it till afterwards. She was contrite; she felt she should have visited her friend in the hospital, despite the abusive phone call.

"I ought to have known it was something like that," she said. "Personality change, that's one of the clues." In the course of her listening, my mother had picked up a great deal of information about terminal illnesses.

But for me, this explanation wasn't good enough. For years after that, Betty followed me around, waiting for me to finish her off in some way more satisfactory to both of us. When I first heard about her death I felt doomed. This, then, was the punishment for being devoted and obliging, this was what happened to girls such as (I felt) myself. When I opened the high-school yearbook and my own face, in pageboy haircut and tentative, appeasing smile, stared back at me, it was Betty's eyes I superimposed on mine. She had been kind to me when I was a child, and with the callousness of children towards those who are kind but not enchanting, I had preferred Fred. In my future I saw myself being abandoned by a succession of Freds who were running down the beach after a crowd of vivacious girls, all of whom looked remarkably like my sister. As for Betty's final screams of hatred and rage, they were screams of protest against the unfairness of life. That anger, I knew, was my own, the dark side of that terrible and deforming niceness that had marked Betty like the aftermath of some crippling disease.

People change, though, especially after they are dead. As I passed beyond the age of melodrama I came to see that if I did not want to be Betty, I would have to be someone else. Furthermore, I was already quite different from Betty. In a way, she had absolved me from making the demanded choices by having made them so thoroughly herself. People stopped calling me a nice girl and started calling me a clever one, and after a while I enjoyed this. Betty herself, baking oatmeal cookies in the ephemeral sunlight of fifteen years before, slid back into three dimensions. She was an ordinary woman who had died too young of an incurable disease. Was that it, was that all?

From time to time I would like to have Betty back, if only for an hour's conversation. I would like her to forgive me for my rejection of her angora mittens, for my secret betrayals of her, for my adolescent contempt. I would like to show her this story I have told about her and ask her if any of it is true. But I can think of nothing I want to ask her that I could phrase in a way that she would care to understand. She would only laugh in her accepting, uncomprehending way and offer me something, a chocolate brownie, a ball of wool.

Fred, on the other hand, no longer intrigues me. The Freds of this world make themselves explicit by what they do and choose. It is the Bettys who are mysterious.

Polarities

Gentle and just pleasure
It is, being human, to have won from space
This unchill, habitable interior

—MARGARET AVISON,
"New Year's Poem"

He hadn't seen her around for a week, which was unusual: he asked her if she'd been sick.

"No," she said, "working." She always spoke of what she
had been doing with organizational, almost military briskness.
She had a little packsack in which she carried around her books
and notebooks. To Morrison, whose mind shambled from one
thing to another, picking up, fingering, setting down, she was a
small model of the kind of efficiency he ought to be displaying
more of. Perhaps that was why he had never wanted to touch
her: he liked women who were not necessarily more stupid but
lazier than himself. Sloth aroused him: a girl's unwashed dishes
were an invitation to laxity and indulgence.

She marched beside him along the corridor and down the
stairs, her short clipped steps syncopating with his own lank
strides. As they descended, the smell of straw, droppings and
formaldehyde grew stronger: a colony of overflow experimental
mice from the Science Building lived in the cellar. When he
saw that she was leaving the building too and probably going
home, he offered her a lift.

"Only if you're heading that way anyway." Louise didn't accept favours, she had made that clear from the start. When he'd asked her if she wanted to take in a film with him she said, "Only if you let me pay for my own ticket." If she had been taller he might have found this threatening.

It was colder, the weak red sun almost down, the snow purpling and creaky. She jumped up and down beside the car till he got the plug-in engine heater untangled and the door opened, her head coming out of the enormous second-hand fur coat she wore like a gopher's out of its burrow. He had seen a lot of gophers on the drive across, many of them dead; one he had killed himself, an accident, it had dived practically under the car wheels. The car itself hadn't held up either: by the time he'd made it to the outskirts—though later he realized that this was in fact the city—a fender had come off and the ignition was failing. He'd had to junk it, and had decided stoically to do without a car until he found he couldn't.

He swung the car onto the driveway that led from the university. It bumped as though crossing a metal-plated bridge: the tires were angular from the cold, the motor sluggish. He should take the car for long drives more often; it was getting stale. Louise was talking more than she normally did; she was excited about something. Two of her students had been giving her a hassle, but she told them they didn't have to come to class. "It's your heads, not mine." She knew she had won, they would shape up, they would contribute. Morrison was not up on the theories of group dynamics. He liked the old way: you taught the subject and forgot about them as people. It disconcerted him when they slouched into his office and mumbled at him, fidgeting and self-conscious, about their fathers or their love lives. He didn't tell them about his father or his love life and he wished they would observe the same reticence, though they seemed to think they had to do it in order to get extensions on their term papers. At the beginning of the year one of his students had wanted the class to sit in a circle but luckily the rest of them preferred straight lines.

"It's right here," she said; he had been driving past it. He crunched the car to a halt, fender against the rockbank, snowbank. Here they did not take the snow away; they spread sand on it, layer by layer as it fell, confident there would be no thaw.

"It's finished; you can come in and see it," she said, suggesting but really demanding.

"What's finished?" he asked. He hadn't been paying attention.

"I told you. My place, my apartment, that's what I've been working on."

The house was one of the featureless two-storey boxes thrown up by the streetful in the years after the war when there was a housing boom and materials were scarce. It was stuccoed with a greyish gravel Morrison found spiritually depleting. There were a few older houses, but they were quickly being torn down by developers; soon the city would have no visible past at all. Everything else was high-rises, or worse, low barrack-shaped multiple-housing units, cheaply tacked together. Sometimes the rows of flimsy buildings—snow on their roofs, rootless white faces peering suspiciously out through their windows, kids' toys scattered like trash on the walks—reminded him of old photographs he had seen of mining camps. They were the houses of people who did not expect to be living in them for long.

Her apartment was in the basement. As they went around to the back and down the stairs, avoiding on the landing a newspaper spread with the overshoes and boots of the family living upstairs, Morrison remembered vividly and with a recurrence of panic his own search for a place, a roof, a container, his trudges from address to address, his tours of clammy, binlike cellars hastily done up by the owners in vinyl tile and sheets of cheap panelling to take advantage of the student inflow and the housing squeeze. He'd known he would never survive a winter buried like that or closed in one the glass-sided cardboard-carton apartment buildings. Were there no real ones, mellowed, interesting, possible? Finally he had come upon an available second storey; the house was pink gravel instead of grey, the filth was daunting and the landlady querulous, but he had taken it immediately just to be able to open a window and look out. /

He had not known what to expect of Louise's room. He had never visualized her as living anywhere, even though he had collected her and dropped her off outside the house a number of times.

"I finished the bookshelves yesterday," she said, waving at a wall-length structure of varnished boards and cement blocks. "Sit down, I'll make you some cocoa." She went into the kitchen, still with her fur coat on, and Morrison sat down in the leatherette swivel armchair. He swivelled, surveying, comparing it with the kind of interior he thought of himself as inhabiting but never got around to assembling.

She had obviously put a lot of energy into it, but the result was less like a room than like several rooms, pieces of which had been cut out and pasted onto one another. He could not decide what created this effect: it was the same unity in diversity he had found in the motels on the way across, the modernish furniture, the conventional framed northern landscapes on the walls. But her table was ersatz Victorian and the prints Picasso. The bed was concealed behind a partly drawn dyed burlap curtain at the end of the room, but visible on the bedside rug were two light blue fuzzy slippers that startled, almost shocked him: they were so unlike her.

Louise brought the cocoa and sat down opposite him on the floor. They talked as usual about the city: they were both still looking for things to do, a quest based on their shared Eastern assumption that cities ought to be entertaining. It was this rather than mutual attraction which led them to spend as much time together as they did; most of the others were married or had been here too long and had given up.

The films changed slowly; the one theatre, with its outdated popular comedies, they had sneered at. They had gone to the opera together when it had come, though: local chorus and imported stars—*Lucia*, it had been, and really quite well done, considering. At intermission Morrison had glanced around at the silent, chunky audience in the lobby, some of the women still in early-sixties pointed-toe spike heels, and murmured to Louise that it was like tourist brochures from Russia.

One Sunday before the snow came they had gone for an impromptu drive; at her suggestion they had aimed for the zoo twenty miles from the city. After they made it through the oil derricks there had been trees; not the right kind of trees—he had felt, as he had on the way across, that the land was keeping itself apart from him, not letting him in; there had to be more to it than this repetitive, non-committal drabness—but still trees; and the zoo once they reached it was spacious, the animals kept in enclosures large enough for them to run in and even hide in if they wanted to.

Louise had been there before—how, since she had no car, he didn't ask—and showed him around. "They choose animals that can survive the winter," she said. "It's open all year. They don't even know they're in a zoo." She pointed out the artificial mountain made of cement blocks for the mountain goats to climb on. Morrison didn't as a rule like any animal bigger and wilder than a cat, but these kept far enough away to be tolerable. That day she had told him a little about herself, a departure: mostly she talked about her work. She had travelled in Europe, she told him, and had spent a year studying in England.

"What are you doing here?" he had asked.

She shrugged. "They gave me money; nobody else would."

Essentially it was his reason too. It wasn't the draft; he was really overage, though here they kept wanting to think he was a dodger, it made his presence more acceptable to them. The job market had been tight back in the States and also, when he tried later, in what they called here the East. But in all fairness it hadn't been only the money or the dismalness of the situation back home. He had wanted something else, some adventure; he felt he might learn something new. He had thought the city would be near the mountains. But except for the raw gully through which the brownish river curved, it was flat.

"I don't want you to think of it as typical," Louise was saying. "You ought to see Montreal."

"Are *you* typical?" he asked.

She laughed. "None of us are typical, or do we all look alike to you? I'm not typical, I'm all-inclusive."

She let her fur coat fall down from around her shoulders as

she said this, and he wondered again whether he was expected to make a move, to approach her. He ought to approach someone or something; he was beginning to feel isolated inside his clothes and skin. His students were out of the question; besides, they were so thick, so impermeable; the girls, even the more slender ones, made him think of slabs of substance white and congealed, like lard; and the other single women on staff were much older than he was: in them Louise's briskness had degenerated into a pinpointing, impaling quality.

There must be a place where he could meet someone, some nice loosely structured girl with ungroomed, seedy breasts, more thing than idea, slovenly and gratuitous. They existed, he was familiar with them from what he had begun to think of as his previous life, but he had not kept in touch with any of them. They had all been good at first but even the sloppiest had in time come to require something from him he thought he was not yet ready to give: they wanted him to be in love with them, an exertion of the mind too strenuous for him to undertake. His mind, he felt, was needed for other things, though he wasn't quite sure what they were. He was tasting, exploring: goals would come later.

Louise wasn't at all like them; she would never lend him her body for nothing, even temporarily, though she had the fur spread out around her now like a rug and had raised one corduroy-trousered knee, letting him see in profile the taut bulge of her somewhat muscular thigh. She probably went skiing and ice skating. He imagined his long body locked in that athletic, chilly grip, his eyes darkened by fur. Not yet, he thought, raising his half-full cocoa cup between them. I can do without, I don't need it yet.

It was the weekend and Morrison was painting his apartment as he habitually did on weekends; he had been at it off and on since he moved in.

"You'll have to have it painted, of course," he'd said smoothly to the landlady when inspecting it, but he had already shown himself too eager and she'd outfoxed him. "Well, I don't know, there's another boy wants it says he'll paint it himself. . . ." So of course Morrison had to say he would too. This was the third coat.

Morrison's vision of wall-painting had been drawn from the paint ads—spot-free housewives gliding it on, one-handed and smiling—but it wasn't easy. The paint got on the floor, on the furniture, in his hair. Before he could even begin he had to cart out the accumulated discards of several generations of previous tenants: baby clothes, old snapshots, an inner tube, heaps of empty liquor bottles and (intriguingly) a silk parachute. Messiness interested him only in women; he could not live surrounded by it himself.

One wall of the living room had been pink, one green, one orange and one black. He was painting them white. The last tenants, a group of Nigerian students, had left weird magic-looking murals on the walls: a sort of swamp, in black on the orange wall, and an upright shape, in pink on the green wall, was either a very poorly done Christ Child or—could it be?—an erect penis with a halo around it. Morrison painted these two walls first, but it made him uneasy to know the pictures were still there underneath the paint. Sometimes as he rollered his way around the room he wondered what the Nigerians had thought the first time it hit forty below.

The landlady seemed to prefer foreign students, probably because they were afraid to complain: she had been aggrieved when Morrison had demanded a real lock for his door. The cellar was a warren of cubbyholes; he was not sure yet exactly who lived in them. Soon after he had moved in a Korean had appeared at his door, hopefully smiling. He wanted to talk about income tax.

"I'm sorry," Morrison had said, "some other time, okay? I have a lot of work to do." He was nice enough, no doubt, but Morrison didn't want to get involved with someone he didn't know; and he did have work to do. He felt picayune about it later when he discovered the Korean had a wife and child down in his cubbyhole with him; often in the fall they had put fishes out to dry, stringing them on the clotheslines where they twirled in the wind like plastic gas-station decorations.

He was doing the ceiling, craning his neck, with the latex oozing down the handle of the roller onto his arm, when the buzzer went. He almost hoped it was the Korean, he seldom saw anyone on the weekends. But it was Louise.

"Hi," he said, surprised.

"I just thought I'd drop in," she said. "I don't use the phone any more."

"I'm painting," he said, partly as an excuse: he wasn't sure he wanted her in the house. What would she demand from him?

"Can I help?" she asked, as though it was a big treat.

"Actually I was about to stop for the day," he lied. He knew she would be better at it than he was.

He made tea in the kitchen and she sat at the table and watched him.

"I came to talk about Blake," she said. "I have to do a paper." Unlike him she was only a Graduate Assistant, she was taking a course.

"What aspect?" Morrison asked, not interested. Blake wasn't his field. He didn't mind the earlier lyrics but the prophecies bored him and the extravagant letters in which Blake called his friends angels of light and vilified his enemies he found in bad taste.

"We each have to analyze one poem in *Songs of Experience*. I'm supposed to do the Nurse's Song. But they don't know what's going on in that course, he doesn't know what's going on. I've been trying to get through to them but they're all doing the one-up thing, they don't know what's happening. They sit there and pull each other's papers apart, I mean, they don't know what poetry's supposed to be *for*." She wasn't drinking her tea.

"When's it due?" he asked, keeping on neutral ground.

"Next week. But I'm not going to do it, not the way *they* want. I'm giving them one of my own poems. That says it all. I mean, if they have to read one right there in the class they'll get what Blake was trying to do with *cadences*. I'm getting it photocopied." She hesitated, less sure of herself. "Do you think that'll be all right?"

Morrison wondered what he would do if one of his own students tried such a ploy. He hadn't thought of Louise as the poetry-writing type. "Have you checked with Professor about it?"

"I try to talk to him," she said. "I try to *help* him but I can't get *through* to him. If they don't get what I mean though I'll know they're all phonies and I can just walk out." She was twisting her cup on the tabletop, her lips were trembling.

Morrison felt his loyalties were being divided; also he didn't want her to cry, that would involve dangerous comforting pats, even an arm around her shoulder. He tried to shut out an involuntary quick image of himself on top of her in the middle of the kitchen floor, getting white latex all over her fur. *Not today*, his mind commanded, pleaded.

As if in answer the reverberations of an organ boomed from beneath their feet, accompanied by a high quavering voice: "*Rock of a-ges, cleft for me . . . Let me* HIIIDE *myself . . .*" Louise took it as a signal. "I have to go," she said. She got up and went out as abruptly as she had come, thanking him perfunctorily for the tea she hadn't drunk.

The organ was a Hammond, owned by the woman downstairs, a native. When her husband and nubile child were home she shouted at them. The rest of the time she ran the vacuum cleaner or picked out hymn tunes and old favourites on the organ with two fingers, singing to herself. The organ was to Morrison the most annoying. At first he tried to ignore it; then he put on opera records, attempting to drown it out. Finally he recorded it with his tape recorder. When the noise got too aggravating he would aim the speakers down the hot air register and run the tape through as loudly as possible. It gave him a sense of participation, of control.

He did this now, admiring the way the tape clashed with what she was currently playing: "Whispering Hope" with an overlay of "Annie Laurie"; "The Last Rose of Summer" counterpointing "Come to the Church in the Wildwood." He was surprised at how much he was able to hate her: he had only seen her once, looking balefully out at him from between her hideous flowered drapes as he wallowed through the snow on his way to the garage. Her husband was supposed to keep the walk shovelled but didn't.

Louise came back the next day before Morrison was up. He was awake but he could tell by the chill in the room—his breath was visible—and by the faint smell of oil that something had gone wrong with the furnace again. It was less trouble to stay in bed, at least till the sun was well risen, than to get up and try the various ways of keeping warm.

When the buzzer went he pulled a blanket around himself and stumbled to the door.

"I thought of something," Louise said tragically. She was in the door before he could fend her off.

"I'm afraid it's cold in here," he said.

"I had to come over and tell you. I don't use the phone any more. You should have yours taken out."

She stomped the snow from her boots while Morrison retreated into the living room. There was a thick crust of frost on the insides of the windows; he lit the gas fireplace. Louise stalked impatiently around the uncarpeted floor.

"You aren't listening," she said. He looked out obediently at her from his blanket. "What I thought of is this: *The city has no right to be here.* I mean, why is it? No city should be here, this far north; it isn't even on a lake or an important river, even. Why is it here?" She clasped her hands, gazing at him as though everything depended on his answer.

Morrison, standing on one bare foot, reflected that he had often since his arrival asked himself the same question. "It started as a trading post," he said, shivering.

"But it doesn't *look* like one. It doesn't look like anything, it doesn't *have* anything, it could be anywhere. Why is it *here*?" She implored; she even clutched a corner of his blanket.

Morrison shied away. "Look," he said, "do you mind if I get some clothes on?"

"Which room are they in?" she asked suspiciously.

"The bedroom," he said.

"That's all right. That room's all right," she said.

Contrary to his fear she made no attempt to follow him in. When he was dressed he returned to find her sitting on the floor with a piece of paper. "We have to complete the circle," she said. "We need the others."

"What others?" He decided she was overtired, she had been working too hard: she had deep red blotches around her eyes and the rest of her face was pale green.

"I'll draw you a diagram of it," she said. But instead she sat on the floor, jabbing at the paper with the pencil point. "I wanted to work out my own system," she said plaintively, "but they wouldn't let me." A tear slid down her cheek.

"Maybe you need to talk to someone," Morrison said, over-casually.

She raised her head. "But I'm talking to you. Oh," she said, reverting to her office voice, "you mean a shrink. I saw one earlier. He said I was very sane and a genius. He took a reading of my head: he said the patterns in my brain are the same as Julius Caesar's, only his were military and mine are creative." She started jabbing with the pencil again.

"I'll make you a peanut butter sandwich," Morrison said, offering the only thing he himself wanted right then. It did not occur to him until months later when he was remembering it to ask himself how anyone could have known about the patterns in Julius Caesar's brain. At the moment he was wondering whether Louise might not in fact be a genius. He felt helpless because of his own inability to respond; she would think him as obtuse as the others, whoever they were.

At first she did not want him to go into the kitchen: she knew the telephone was in there. But he promised not to use it. When he came out again with a piece of bread on which he had spread with difficulty the gelid peanut butter, she was curled inside her coat in front of the fire, sleeping. He laid the bread gently beside her as if leaving crumbs on a stump for unseen animals. Then he changed his mind, retrieved it, took it on tiptoe into the kitchen and ate it himself. He turned on the oven, opened the oven door, wrapped himself in a blanket from the bedroom and read Marvell.

She slept for nearly three hours; he didn't hear her get up. She appeared in the kitchen doorway, looking much better, though a greyish-green pallor still lingered around her mouth and eyes.

"That was just what I needed," she said in her old brisk voice. "Now I must be off; I have lots of work to do." Morrison took his feet off the stove and saw her to the door.

"Don't fall," he called after her cheerfully as she went down the steep wooden steps, her feet hidden under the rim of her coat. The steps were icy, he didn't keep them cleared properly. His landlady was afraid someone would slip on them and sue her.

At the bottom Louise turned and waved at him. The air was thickening with ice fog, frozen water particles held in suspension; if you ran a horse in it, they'd told him, the ice pierced its lungs and it bled to death. But they hadn't told him that till after he'd trotted to the university in it one morning when the car wouldn't start and complained aloud in the coffee room about the sharp pains in his chest.

He watched her out of sight around the corner of the house. Then he went back to the living room with a sense of recapturing lost territory. Her pencil and the paper she had used, covered with dots and slashing marks, an undeciphered code, were still by the fireplace. He started to crumple the paper up, but instead folded it carefully and put it on the mantelpiece where he kept his unanswered letters. After that he paced the apartment, conscious of his own work awaiting him but feeling as though he had nothing to do.

Half an hour later she was back again; he discovered he had been expecting her. Her face was mournful, all its lines led downwards as though tiny hands were pulling at the jawline skin.

"Oh, you have to come out," she said, pleading. "You have to come out, there's too much fog."

"Why don't you come in?" Morrison said. That would be

easier to handle. Maybe she'd been into something, if that was all it was he could wait it out. He'd been cautious himself; it was a small place and the local pusher was likely to be one of your own students; also he had no desire to reduce his mind to oatmeal mush.

"No," she said, "I can't go through this door any more. It's wrong. You have to come out." Her face became crafty, as though she was planning. "It will do you good to get out for a walk," she said reasonably.

She was right, he didn't get enough exercise. He pulled on his heavy boots and went to find his coat.

As they creaked and slid along the street Louise was pleased with herself, triumphant; she walked slightly ahead of him as if determined to keep the lead. The ice fog surrounded them, deadened their voices, it was crystallizing like a growth of spruce needles on the telephone wires and the branches of the few trees which he could not help thinking of as stunted, though to the natives, he supposed, they must represent the normal size for trees. He took care not to breathe too deeply. A flock of grosbeaks whirred and shrilled up ahead, picking the last few red berries from a mountain ash.

"I'm glad it isn't sunny," Louise said. "The sun was burning out the cells in my brain, but I feel a lot better now."

Morrison glanced at the sky. The sun was up there somewhere, marked by a pale spot in the otherwise evenly spread grey. He checked an impulse to shield his eyes and thereby protect his brain cells: he realized it was an attempt to suppress the undesired knowledge that Louise was disturbed or, out with it, she was crazy.

"Living here isn't so bad," Louise said, skipping girlishly on the hard-packed snow. "You just have to have inner resources. I'm glad I have them; I think I have more than you, Morrison, I have more than most people. That's what I said to myself when I moved here."

"Where are we going?" Morrison asked when they had accomplished several blocks. She had taken him west, along a street he was not familiar with, or was it the fog?

"To find the others, of course," she said, glancing back at

him contemptuously. "We have to complete the circle."

Morrison followed without protest; he was relieved there would soon be others.

She stopped in front of a medium-tall high-rise. "They're inside," she said. Morrison went towards the front door, but she tugged at his arm.

"You can't go in that door," she said. "It's facing the wrong way. It's the wrong door."

"What's the matter with it?" Morrison asked. It might be the wrong door (and the longer he looked at it, plate glass and shining evilly, the more he saw what she meant), but it was the only one.

"It faces east," she said. "Don't you know? The city is polarized north and south; the river splits it in two; the poles are the gas plant and the power plant. Haven't you ever noticed the bridge joins them together? That's how the current gets across. We have to keep the poles in our brains lined up with the poles of the city, that's what Blake's poetry is all about. You can't break the current."

"Then how do we get in?" he said. She sat down in the snow; he was afraid again she was going to cry.

"Listen," he said hastily, "I'll go in the door sideways and bring them out; that way I won't break the current. You won't have to go through the door at all. Who are they?" he asked as an afterthought.

When he recognized the name he was elated: she wasn't insane after all, the people were real, she had a purpose and a plan. This was probably just an elaborate way of arranging to see her friends.

They were the Jamiesons. Dave was one of those with whom Morrison had exchanged pleasantries in the hallways but nothing further. His wife had a recent baby. Morrison found them in their Saturday shirts and jeans; he tried to explain what he wanted, which was difficult because he wasn't sure. Finally he said he needed help. Only Dave could come, the wife had to stay behind with the baby.

"I hardly know Louise, you know," Dave volunteered in the elevator.

"Neither do I," said Morrison.

Louise was waiting behind a short fir tree on the front lawn. She came out when she saw them. "Where's the baby?" she said. "We need the baby to complete the circle. We *need* the baby. Don't you know the country will split apart without it?" She stamped her foot at them angrily.

"We can come back for it," Morrison said, which pacified her. She said there were only two others they had to collect; she explained that they needed people from both sides of the river. Dave Jamieson suggested they take his car, but Louise was now off cars: they were as bad as telephones, they had no fixed directions. She wanted to walk. At last they persuaded her onto the bus, pointing out that it ran north and south. She had to make certain first that it went over the right bridge, the one near the gas plant.

The other couple Louise had named lived in an apartment over-looking the river. She seemed to have picked them not because they were special friends but because from their living room, which she had been in once, both the gas plant and the power plant were visible. The apartment door faced south; Louise entered the building with no hesitation.

Morrison was not overjoyed with Louise's choice. This couple was foremost among the local anti-Americans: he had to endure Paul's bitter sallies almost daily in the coffee room, while Leota at staff parties had a way of running on in his presence about the wicked Americans and then turning to him and saying, mouth but not eyes gushing, "Oh, but I forgot—*you're* an American." He had found the best defence was to agree. "You Yanks are coming up and taking all our jobs," Paul would say, and Morrison would nod affably. "That's right, you shouldn't let it happen. I wonder why you hired me?" Leota would start in about how the Americans were buying up all the industry, and Morrison would say, "Yes, it's a shame. Why are you selling it to us?" He saw their point, of course, but he wasn't Procter & Gamble. What did they want him to do? What were they doing themselves, come to think of it? But Paul had once broken down after too many beers in the Faculty Club and confided that Leota had been thin when he married her but now she was fat. Morrison held the memory of that confession as a kind of hostage.

He had to admit though that on this occasion Paul was much more efficient than he himself was capable of being. Paul saw at once what it had taken Morrison hours, perhaps weeks, to see: that something was wrong with Louise. Leota decoyed her into the kitchen with a glass of milk while Paul conspired single-handedly in the living room.

"She's crazy as a coot. We've got to get her to the loony bin. We'll pretend to go along with her, this circle business, and when we get her downstairs we'll grab her and stuff her into my car. How long has this been going on?"

Morrison didn't like the sound of the words "grab" and "stuff." "She won't go in cars," he said.

"Hell," said Paul, "I'm not walking in this bloody weather. Besides, it's miles. We'll use force if necessary." He thrust a quick beer at each of them, and when he judged they ought to have finished they all went into the kitchen and Paul carefully told Louise that it was time to go.

"Where?" Louise asked. She scanned their faces: she could tell they were up to something. Morrison felt guilt seeping into his eyes and turned his head away.

"To get the baby," Paul said. "Then we can form the circle."

Louise looked at him strangely. "What baby? What circle?" she said testing him.

"*You* know," Paul said persuasively. After a moment she put down her glass of milk, still almost full, and said she was ready.

At the car she balked. "Not in there," she said, planting her feet. "I'm not going in there." When Paul gripped her arm and said, soothingly and menacingly, "Now be a good girl," she broke away from him and ran down the street, stumbling and sliding. Morrison didn't have the heart to run after her; already he felt like a traitor. He watched stupidly while Dave and Paul chased after her, catching her at last and half-carrying her back; they held her wriggling and kicking inside her fur coat as though it was a sack. Their breath came out in white spurts.

"Open the back door, Morrison," Paul said, sergeant-like, giving him a scornful glance as though he was good for nothing else. Morrison obeyed and Louise was thrust in, Dave holding her more or less by the scruff of the neck and Paul picking up her feet. She did not resist as much as Morrison expected. He got in on one side of her; Dave was on the other. Leota, who had waddled down belatedly, had reached the front seat; once they were in motion she turned around and made false, cheering-up noises at Louise.

"Where are they taking me?" Louise whispered to Morrison. "It's to the hospital, isn't it?" She was almost hopeful, perhaps she had been depending on them to do this. She snuggled close to Morrison, rubbing her thigh against his; he tried not to move away.

As they reached the outskirts she whispered to him again. "This is silly, Morrison. They're being silly, aren't they? When we get to the next stoplight, open the door on your side and we'll jump out and run away. We'll go to my place."

Morrison smiled wanly at her, but he was almost inclined to try it. Although he knew he couldn't do anything to help her and did not want the responsibility anyway, he also didn't want his mind burdened with whatever was going to happen to her next. He felt like someone appointed to a firing squad: it was not his choice, it was his duty, no one could blame him.

There was less ice fog now. The day was turning greyer, bluer: they were moving east, away from the sun. The mental clinic was outside the city, reached by a curving, expressionless driveway. The buildings were the same assemblage of disparate once-recent styles as those at the university: the same jarring fragmentation of space, the same dismal failure at modishness. Government institutions, Morrison thought; they were probably done by the same architect.

Louise was calm as they went to the reception entrance. Inside was a glass-fronted cubicle, decorated with rudimentary Christmas bells cut from red and green construction paper. Louise stood quietly, listening with an amused, tolerant smile, while Paul talked with the receptionist; but when a young intern appeared she said, "I must apologize for my friends; they've been drinking and they're trying to play a practical joke on me."

The intern frowned enquiringly. Paul blustered, relating Louise's theories of the circle and the poles. She denied everything and told the intern he should call the police; a joke was a joke but this was a misuse of public property.

Paul appealed to Morrison: he was her closest friend. "Well," Morrison hedged, "she *was* acting a little strange, but maybe not enough to . . ." His eyes trailed off to the imitation-modern interior, the corridors leading off into god knew where. Along one of the corridors a listless figure shuffled.

Louise was carrying it off so well, she was so cool, she had the intern almost convinced; but when she saw she was winning she lost her grip. Giving Paul a playful shove on the chest, she said, "We don't need *your* kind here. *You* won't get into the circle." She turned to the intern and said gravely, "Now I have to go. My work is very important, you know. I'm preventing the civil war."

After she had been registered, her few valuables taken from her and locked in the safe ("So they won't be stolen by the patients," the receptionist said), her house keys delivered to Morrison at her request, she disappeared down one of the corridors between two interns. She was not crying. She didn't say goodbye to any of them, though she gave Morrison a dignified, freezing nod. "I expect you to bring my notebook to me," she said with a pronounced English accent. "The black one, I need it. You'll find it on my desk. And I'll need some underwear. Leota can bring that."

Morrison, shamed and remorseful, promised he would visit.

When they got back to the city they dropped Dave Jamieson off at his place; then the three of them had pizza and Cokes together. Paul and Leota were friendlier than usual: they wanted to find out more. They leaned across the table, questioning, avid, prying; they were enjoying it. This, he realized, was for them the kind of entertainment the city could best afford.

Afterwards they all went to Louise's cellar to gather up for her those shreds of her life she had asked them to allow her. Leota found the underwear (surprisingly frilly, most of it purple and black) after an indecently long search through Louise's bureau drawers; he and Paul tried to decide which of the black notebooks on her desk she would want. There were eight or nine of them; Paul opened a few and read excerpts at random, though Morrison protested weakly. References to the poles and the circle dated back several months; before he had known her, Morrison thought.

In her notebooks Louise had been working out her private system, in aphorisms and short poems which were thoroughly sane in themselves but which taken together were not; though, Morrison reflected, the only difference is that she's taken as real what the rest of us pretend is only metaphorical. Between the aphorisms were little sketches like wiring diagrams, quotations from the English poets and long detailed analyses of her acquaintances at the university.

"Here's you, Morrison," Paul said with a relishing chuckle. "'Morrison is not a complete person. He needs to be completed, he refuses to admit his body is part of his mind. He can be in the circle possibly, but only if he will surrender his role as a fragment and show himself willing to merge with the greater whole.' Boy, she must've been nutty for months."

They were violating her, entering her privacy against her will. "Put that away," Morrison said, more sharply than he ordinarily dared speak to Paul. "We'll take the half-empty notebook, that must be the one she meant."

There were a dozen or so library books scattered around the room, some overdue: geology and history for the most part, and one volume of Blake. Leota volunteered to take them back.

As he was about to slip the catch on the inside lock Morrison glanced once more around the room. He could see now where it got its air of pastiche: the bookcase was a copy of the one in Paul's living room, the prints and the table were almost identical with those at the Jamiesons'. Other details stirred dim images of objects half-noted in the various houses, at the various but nearly identical get-acquainted parties. Poor Louise

69

had been trying to construct herself out of the other people she had met. Only from himself had she taken nothing; thinking of his chill interior, embryonic and blighted, he realized it had nothing for her to take.

He kept his promise and went to see her. His first visit was made with Paul and Leota, but he sensed their resentment: they seemed to think their countrywoman should be permitted to go mad without witness or participation by any Yanks. After that he drove out by himself in his own car.

On the second visit Louise initially seemed better. They met in a cramped cubicle furnished with two chairs; Louise sat on the edge of hers, her hands folded in her lap, her face polite, withholding. Her English accent was still noticeable, though hard *r*'s surfaced in it from time to time. She was having a good rest, she said; the food was all right and she had met some nice people but she was eager to get back to her work; she worried about who was looking after her students.

"I guess I said some pretty crazy things to you," she smiled.

"Well . . ." Morrison stalled. He was pleased by this sign of her recovery.

"I had it all wrong. I thought I could put the country together by joining the two halves of the city into a circle, using the magnetic currents." She gave a small disparaging laugh, then dropped her voice. "What I hadn't figured out though was that the currents don't flow north and south, like the bridge. They flow east and west, like the river. And I didn't *need* to form the circle out of a bunch of incomplete segments. I didn't even need the baby. I mean," she said in a serious whisper, dropping her accent completely, "I *am* the circle. I have the poles within myself. What I have to do is keep myself in one piece, it *depends* on me."

At the desk he tried to find out what was officially wrong with Louise but they would not tell him anything; it wasn't the policy.

On his next visit she spoke to him almost the whole time in what to his untrained ear sounded like perfectly fluent French. Her mother was a French Protestant, she told him, her father an English Catholic. "*Je peux vous dire tout ceci,*" she said, "*parce que vous êtes américain.* You are outside it." To Morrison this explained a lot; but the next time she claimed to be the daughter of an Italian opera singer and a Nazi general. "Though I also have some Jewish blood," she added hastily. She was tense and kept standing up and sitting down again, crossing and recrossing her legs; she would not look at Morrison directly but addressed her staccato remarks to the centre of his chest.

After this Morrison stayed away for a couple of weeks. He did not think his visits were doing either of them any good, and he had papers to mark. He occupied himself once more with the painting of his apartment and the organ music of the woman downstairs; he shovelled his steps and put salt on them to melt the ice. His landlady, uneasy because she had still not supplied him with a lock, unexpectedly had him to tea, and the tacky plastic grotesqueries of her interior decoration fueled his reveries for a while. The one good thing in her bogus ranch-style bungalow had been an egg, blown and painted in the Ukrainian manner, but she had dismissed it as ordinary, asking him to admire instead a cake of soap stuck with artificial flowers to resemble a flowerpot; she had got the idea out of a magazine. The Korean came up one evening to ask him about life insurance.

But the thought of Louise out there in the windswept institution grounds with nothing and no one she knew bothered him in twinges, like a mental neuralgia, goading him finally into the section of the city that passed for downtown: he would buy her a gift. He selected a small box of water-colour paints: she ought to have something to do. He was intending to mail it, but sooner than he expected he found himself again on the wide deserted entrance driveway.

They met once more in the visitors' cubicle. He was alarmed by the change in her: she had put on weight, her muscles had slackened, her breasts drooped. Instead of sitting rigidly as she had done before, she sprawled in the chair, legs apart, arms hanging; her hair was dull and practically uncombed. She was wearing a short skirt and purple stockings, in one of which there was a run. Trying not to stare at this run and at the white, loose thigh flesh it revealed, Morrison had the first unmistakably physical stirrings of response he had ever felt towards her.

"They have me on a different drug," she said. "The other one was having the wrong effect. I was allergic to it." She mentioned that someone had stolen her hairbrush, but when he offered to bring her another one she said it didn't matter. She had lost interest in the circle and her elaborate system and did not seem to want to talk much. What little she said was about the hospital itself: she was trying to help the doctors, they didn't know how to treat the patients but they wouldn't listen to her. Most of those inside were getting worse rather than better; many had to stay there because no one would take the responsibility of looking after them, even if they were drugged into manageability. They were poor, without relations; the hospital would not let them go away by themselves. She told him about one girl from further north who thought she was a caribou.

She hardly glanced at the water-colour paints, though she thanked him sluggishly. Her eyes, normally wide and vivacious, were puffed shut nearly to slits and her skin appeared to have darkened. She reminded him of someone, though it took him several minutes to remember: it was an Indian woman he had seen early in the fall while he was still searching for a place to have a civilized drink. She had been sitting outside a cheap hotel with her legs apart, taking off her clothes and chanting, "Come on boys, what're you waiting for, come on boys, what're you waiting for." Around her a group of self-conscious, sniggering men had gathered. Morrison, against his will and appalled at her, the men and himself, had joined them. She was naked to the waist when the police got there.

When he rose to say goodbye Louise asked him, as if it was a matter of purely academic interest, whether he thought she would ever get out.

On his way out to the car it struck him that he loved her.

The thought filled him like a goal, a destiny. He would rescue her somehow; he could pretend she was his cousin or sister; he would keep her hidden in the apartment with all his dangerous implements, razors, knives, nail files, locked away; he would feed her, give her the right drugs, comb her hair. At night she would be there in the subzero bedroom for him to sink into as into a swamp, warm and obliterating.

This picture at first elated, then horrified him. He saw that it was only the hopeless, mad Louise he wanted, the one devoid of any purpose or defence. A sane one, one who could judge him, he would never be able to handle. So this was his dream girl then, his ideal woman found at last: a disintegration, mind returning to its component shards of matter, a defeated formless creature on which he could inflict himself like shovel on earth, axe on forest, use without being used, know without being known. Louise's notebook entry, written when she had surely been saner than she was now, had been right about him. Yet in self-defence he reasoned that his desire for her was not altogether evil: it was in part a desire to be reunited with his own body, which he felt less and less that he actually occupied.

Oppressed by himself and by the building, the prison he had just left, he turned when he reached the main road away from the city instead of towards it: he would take his car for a run. He drove through the clenched landscape, recalling with pain the gentle drawl of the accommodating hills east and south, back in that settled land which was so far away it seemed not to exist. Here everything was tightlipped, ungiving, good for nothing, and nothing.

He was halfway to the zoo before he knew he was going there. Louise had said it was kept open all winter.

Not much of the day was left when he reached the entrance: he would be driving back in darkness. He would have to make his visit short, he did not want to be caught inside when they locked the gates. He paid the admission fee to the scarfed and muffled figure in the booth, then took his car along the empty drives, glancing out the side window at the herds of llama, of yak, the enclosure of the Siberian tiger in which only the places a tiger might hide were to be seen.

At the buffalo field he stopped the car and got out. The buffalo were feeding near the wire fence, but at his approach they lifted their heads and glared at him, then snorted and rocked away from him through the haunch-deep snowdunes.

He plodded along the fence, not caring that the wind was up and chilling him through his heavy coat, the blood retreating from his toes. Thin sinister fingers of blown snow were creeping over the road; on the way back he would have to watch for drifts. He imagined the snow rising up, sweeping down in great curves, in waves over the city, each house a tiny centre of man-made warmth, fending it off. By the grace of the power plant and the gas plant: a bomb, a catastrophe to each and the houses would close like eyes. He thought of all the people he barely knew, how they would face it, chopping up their furniture for firewood until the cold overcame. How they were already facing it, the Koreans' fishes fluttering on the clothesline like defiant silver flags, the woman downstairs shrilling "Whispering Hope" off-key into the blizzard, Paul in the flimsy armour of his cheap nationalism, the landlady holding aloft torchlike her bar of soap stuck with artificial flowers. Poor Louise, he saw now what she had been trying desperately to do: the point of the circle, closed and self-sufficient, was not what it included but what it shut out. His own efforts to remain human, futile work and sterile love, what happened when it was all used up, what would he be left with? Black trees on a warm orange wall; and he had painted everything white.

Dizzy with cold, he leaned against the fence, forehead on mittened hand. He was at the wolf pen. He remembered it from his trip with Louise. They had stood there for some time waiting for the wolves to come over to them but they had kept to the far side. Three of them were near the fence now though, lying in its shelter. An old couple, a man and a woman in nearly identical grey coats, were standing near the wolves. He had not noticed them earlier, no cars had passed him, they must have walked from the parking lot. The eyes of the wolves were yellowish grey: they looked out through the bars at him, alert, neutral.

74

"Are they timber wolves?" Morrison said to the old woman. Opening his mouth to speak, he was filled with a sudden chill rush of air.

The woman turned to him slowly: her face was a haze of wrinkles from which her eyes stared up at him, blue, glacial.

"You from around here?" she asked.

"No," Morrison said. Her head swung away; she continued to look through the fence at the wolves, nose to the wind, short white fur ruffled up on edge.

Morrison followed her fixed gaze: something was being told, something that had nothing to do with him, the thing you could learn only after the rest was finished with and discarded. His body was numb; he swayed. In the corner of his eye the old woman swelled, wavered, then seemed to disappear, and the land opened before him. It swept away to the north and he thought he could see the mountains, white-covered, their crests glittering in the falling sun, then forest upon forest, after that the barren tundra and the blank solid rivers, and beyond, so far that the endless night had already descended, the frozen sea.

Under Glass

I'm feeling better. For once the sky is out, there's a breeze, I'm walking through the ellipses and arranged vistas of the park, the trees come solidly up through the earth as though they belong there, nothing wavers. I have confidence in the grass and the distant buildings, they can take care of themselves, they don't need my attention on them to keep them together, my eyes holding them down.

The steam-covered mothers and shrill, hyperthyroid children of yesterday's trip to the zoo are far away, the traces they have left in me are faint as grease smudges and scratchings of twigs on window-panes. That was a risk I shouldn't have taken, it would have been cleverer to have waited, but I managed it. I even made it through the Moonlight Pavilion, darkened tunnels full of screaming, the goggling rodents and shrunken foetal-headed primates deluded by the grey light into going about their lives, so publicly, behind the soundproof panels. I enjoy knowing I can do it without anyone to help.

I pass the 7–B Greenhouse: it glitters, it beckons. Inside are the plants that look like stones, their fleshy lobed leaves knuckle-sized and mottled so that they blend perfectly with the pebbles. I was pleased at first to have discovered them. I think with a kind of horror at myself of the hours I've spent watching them, all of us keeping quite still. Today, however, the greenhouse has no attraction: I walk on two legs, I wear clothes.

In the street outside the station I go shopping. It feels new, my legs ripple as though I've just gotten out of a wheelchair. I buy little brown paper parcels and stow them away inside my serviceable black bag with handles on it like a doctor's. Bread and butter, grapes, greengages which he has probably never had before but we must all try different experiences. Before I zip the bag I rearrange the packages to safeguard the rose, encased in plastic wrap with stem swathed in wet toilet paper. Redundant. It's a gift though and I'm proud of myself for being able, we don't do much of that. I cut it in the garden, which isn't mine. I admire roses but I've never wanted to be one, maybe that's why I'm not worrying much about whether the stem hurts.

What part of a rosebush is the body? Last night I dreamed I had a baby which was the right size and colour. It's a healthy sign, maybe I'll be able to after all, the way other women are supposed to. Usually when I dream of babies they are scrawny as kittens, pale greenish and highly intelligent; they talk in polysyllables and I know they aren't mine but are creatures from another planet sent to take over the earth, or that they are dead. Sometimes they're covered with fur. But last night's was pink and reassuringly illiterate; it cried. He ought to find this promising, he wants to have sons. I've thought about it, I've even gone so far as to read a couple of books on exercises and what they call natural childbirth, though having a gourd or a tomato would surely be more pleasant and useful these days than having a baby, the world has no need of my genes. That's an excuse though.

I put the bag on my knees and keep hold of the handles. It's playing house, we both know I can't cook him anything till he gets his stove repaired, which somehow he postpones; still it's the first domestic thing I've ever done for him. He ought to approve, he's obliged to approve, he'll see it's getting better. I'm feeling so good I even look at other people in the train, their faces and clothes, noticing them, wondering about their lives. See how kind I am, what a cornucopia.

The cement stairway going down to his door smells of piss and antiseptic; I hold my breath as usual. I look in through the letter flap: he isn't up, so I let myself in with my key. His two-room flat is more untidy than last time but it's been worse. Today the dust and litter let my skin alone. I set my black bag on the table and go through to the bedroom.

He's on the bed, asleep in a tangled net of blankets, on his back with his knees up. I'm always afraid to wake him: I remember the stories about men who kill in their sleep with their eyes open, thinking the woman is a burglar or an enemy soldier. You can't be convicted for it. I touch him on the leg and stand back, ready to run, but he wakes immediately and turns his head towards me.

"Hi," he says. "Jesus, I'm hung over."

It's rude of him to be hung over when I've come all this way to see him. "I brought you a flower," I say, determined to be calm and cheerful.

I go out to the other room and unwind the rose from its toilet paper and look for something to put it in. There's a stack of never-used plates in his cupboard, the rest of the space is books and papers. I find a lone glass and fill it with water at the sink. Forks and knives, also unused, are rusting in the drainer. I list to myself the things he needs: a vase, more glasses, a dish towel.

I carry the rose in to him and he sniffs at it dutifully and I set the glass beside the alarm clock on the improvised table, two chairs and a board. He would really like to go back to sleep, but he compromises by pulling me down beside him and involving me in the blankets. His head seeks the hollow between my shoulder and collarbone and he closes his eyes.

"I've missed you," he says. Why should he have missed me, I've only been gone five days? The last time wasn't good, I was nervous, the wallpaper was bothering me and the bright peel-off stick-on butterflies on the cupboard, not his, prior to him. He kisses me: he does have a hangover, his mouth tastes of used wine, tobacco resin and urban decay. He doesn't want to make love, I can tell, I stroke his head understandingly; he nuzzles. I think again of the Moonlight Pavilion, the Slow Loris creeping cautiously through its artificial world, water dishes and withering branches, its eyes large with apprehension, its baby clutched to its fur.

"Want to have lunch?" he says. This is his way of telling me he's in no shape.

"I brought it. Or most of it anyway. I'll go round the corner and get the rest. It's healthier than those greasy hamburgers and chips."

"Great," he says, but he makes no move to get up.

"Have you been taking your vitamin pills?" They were my idea, I was afraid he'd get scurvy, eating the way he does. I always take them myself. I feel him nod ritualistically.

I can't see whether he's telling the truth. I turn over so I'm looking down at him. "Who were you drinking with? Did you go out after you moved the furniture?"

"The furniture was already moved when I got there. She couldn't call to tell me." That's true, he has no phone; our conversations take place in booths. "She wanted to go out and drink instead. I spilled chop suey all over myself," he says with self-pity.

I am supposed to commiserate. "Was it digested or undigested?" I ask.

"I hadn't touched a bite of it."

I'm surprised at her for being so obvious, but then she's always seemed unsubtle, blunt and straightforward, captain of a women's basketball team, no; high-school gym teacher with whistle in mouth. An old friend. No nonsense. Mine had bloomers and skinny legs and made jokes about what she called The Cramps in a way that suggested we weren't supposed to have them. Trampolines, the body contorted, made to perform, the mind barking orders.

"She's been trying to seduce you for months," I say, smiling; the thought amuses me, she looks like a marmot. At this he tries to shrug, but I have him pinned, one arm across the neck. "Did she succeed?"

"By the time we got out of the bar the subway was closed."

I hadn't been serious, but this is suddenly a confession. I want to ignore it but I go on. "You mean she spent the night here?"

"As opposed to trying to get all the way back to her place," he says, "yes." It would be a reason like that. Logical as hell.

What do you think you are, the YWCA? I want to say, but instead I ask the obvious. "I suppose you slept with her." My voice is steady, I'm steady too, I won't let it tip me.

"It was her idea. I was drunk." He thinks both these things are good excuses.

"Why did you tell me?" If he hadn't told me and I'd found out I'd say, *Why didn't you tell me?* I know this while I'm asking it.

"You could have figured it out for yourself, the alarm's set for eight."

"What does that mean?" I say; I don't connect. I'm cold, I get up off the bed and move backwards towards the doorway.

I am sitting in a brand-new hamburger palace; across the table from me is a man eating a cheeseburger. Feeding places are the only chances I have to watch him: the rest of the time I'm looking at the blurs through taxi windows or tracing the unfamiliar wallpaper designs. The colour of his face matches the Formica tabletops: off-white. At other tables are other men, also eating cheeseburgers and being watched by other women. We all have our coats on. The air shimmers with rock music and the smell of exhausted french fries. Though it is winter the room reminds me of a beach, even to the crumpled paper napkins and pop bottles discarded here and there and the slightly gritty texture of the cheeseburgers.

He pushes away his coleslaw.

"You should eat it," I say.

"No no; can't eat vegies," he says. The suppressed dietician in me notes that he is probably suffering from a vitamin A deficiency. I should have been a health inspector, or maybe an organic farmer.

"I'll trade you then," I say. "I'll eat your coleslaw if you'll finish my cheeseburger."

He thinks there's a catch somewhere but decides to risk it. The switch is made and we both examine our halves of the deal. Beyond the plate-glass window slush drifts from the night sky, inside though we are lighted, safe and warm, filtering music through our gills as though it's oxygen.

He finishes my cheeseburger and lights a cigarette. I'm annoyed with him for some reason, though I can't recall which. I thumb my card-file of nasty remarks, choose one: You make love like a cowboy raping a sheep. I've been waiting for the right time to say that, but maybe peace is more important.

Not for him; hunger satisfied, he turns back to an earlier argument. "You're trying to see how much shit I'll take, aren't you?" he says. "Stop treating me like a nine-year-old."

"There's one good way to keep me from treating you like one," I say. What I mean is that he should stop acting like one, but he doesn't bite. In fact he may not even have heard: the music is louder.

"Let's split," he says, and we get up. I check the cashier as we go out: cashiers fill me with dismay, I want them to be happy but they never are. This one is waterlogged and baggy, saturated with too much sound and too many french fries. She is apathetic rather than surly. Fight back, I tell her silently.

We hit the air and walk, not touching. I can't remember what he did but he won't get away with it. He's wearing a long khaki army surplus coat with brass buttons; it's handsome, but right now it only reminds me of my fear of doormen, bus drivers and postal officials, those who use their uniforms as excuses. I steer my course so he will have to go through all the puddles. If I can't win, I tell him, neither can you. I was saner then, I had defences.

"I never get up at eight. She had to go to work." He's conscious now that I'm not going to laugh with him over this one as I have over the others. "If you'd been here it wouldn't have happened," he says, trying to put it off on me.

I see it so clearly, in such an ordinary light, I know what he did, how he moved, what he said even, one warm body attracts another, it's how people behave and I want to be sick. More, I want to take my carefully selected brown paper parcels and shove them down his never-cleaned toilet, which I even—crown of idiocy—had thoughts of cleaning for him, poor thing, no one ever showed him how to do it. Where they belong. So this is what it would be like, me picking up his dirty socks and cigarette butts in my experienced way, woman's greatest joy, safely eight months pregnant so you can't get out of it now, grunting away at the natural childbirth exercises while he's off screwing whatever was propped against him when he hit the mystic number of drinks. A spiritual relationship with you, he said, and merely physical ones with the others. Shove that. What does he think I saw in him in the first place, his remarkable soul?

"I'm going out to do some shopping," I say. I'm too visible here, desert mice with their burrows running down the side of the glass, what an intrusion I thought at the time. "Do you want me to come back?"

This is the call to repentance, he nods without speaking. He really is unhappy but I don't have time to think about that, I have to get out where there are a lot more around me, camouflage. I'm careful not to slam the door, I cross to the market street and dig in among the crowd of shoppers.

It's a room, with bed, dressing table surmounted by mirror, night table plus lamp and telephone, linoleum-patterned drapes covering the windows which in their turn cover the night and a drop of ten stories to molten lights and metal parts, hall opening on bathroom which includes a sink and two taps, hot and cold, closed door. Outside the door is another hall and a line of similar closed doors. It is all correct, all in place though slightly dented around the edges. I've been trying to sleep in the bed, with no success. I'm going back and forth across the floor, raising from the carpet an airport smell of upholstery cleaner. Earlier there was a tray with steak rinds and shreds of old salad on it, but I set it out in the hall a long time ago.

From time to time I open the windows and the room is inundated with traffic noise as though it is part of a city-sized motor; then I close the windows and the room heats again, internal-combustion engine. Sometimes I go into the bathroom and turn the taps on and off, taking drinks of water and sleeping pills, it gives me the illusion of action. I also look at my watch. It's early spring, there are no leaves and no snow; the days have too much sun, it shows the dust on everything, it hurts your eyes. Three hours ago he phoned to say he would be home in half an hour. He speaks of this room where we have never been before and will never be again as home, I suppose because I'm in it. I'm in it and I can't get out, he has the key, where would I go, it's a foreign city. I work out plans: I'll pack now, leave, he'll come back after being—where is he? He could have been in an accident, he's in the hospital, he's dying, no, he would never do it so neatly. The room will be empty. The room is empty now, I'm a place not a person. I'll go into the bathroom, lock the door, lie down in the tub with my arms crossed in the lily position, eyes weighted with invisible pennies. I'll wash down the rest of the sleeping pills and be found draped over something, the bureau, the telephone, in a coma. Their breathing is always described in murder mysteries as "stertorous," I've never known what that meant. He'll come in just as I'm about to fly out the window into the solid hurricane below, my nightgown spread out around me like a huge nylon kite. Hold on to the string, it's tied to my head.

The mechanisms of the room continue their clicking and gurgling, indifferent. I've turned all the knobs on the heating unit but nothing happens, maybe I'm not really here. He ought to be here, he has no right not to be here, this machine is his creation. I get back into the bed for the fifth or sixth time and try to concentrate on the shapes moving across my closed eyelids. Sun, dust, bright colours, headlights, a Persian carpet. There are pictures now, ducks oddly enough, a woman sitting in a chair, a lawn with a country house, Grecian portico and all, clocks made of flowers, a line of dancing cartoon mice, who put them there? Whoever you are, get me out and I promise I'll never never again. Next time it will be just from the neck down, I'll leave his motivations alone.

It was so simple at first, you should have kept it that way, it's the only thing you can handle. Cool it, said the doctor, trying to communicate but coming through like Fred MacMurray in a Walt Disney family picture, take pills. Maybe he's just asserting his freedom, you're too possessive. He's escaping. You've driven him to it, into the phone booth and out comes Superstud. A self-propelling prick with a tiny brain attached to it like a termite's, couple of drinks and he'd stick it into anything. Like night-hunting snakes it has infrared sensors on the front end, in the dark it strikes at anything warm. When the lights went on he was fucking the hot-air register.

That's unfair. What really annoys you is that she got it last night and there wasn't any left for you. Why couldn't he have chosen some other time? He knew I'd be there this morning. He didn't choose it, it just happened. Why can't you see him as a confused human being with problems? Do I ever do anything else? Already I couldn't tell you whether he's my lover or my out-patient. You think you're so magic, you can cure anything. Can't you admit you've failed?

Maybe I'm not a confused human being with problems, maybe I'm something altogether different, an artichoke. None of that.

Actually she's his type, they must have made it fine together, they're both athletic, maybe she keeps time with the whistle, *peep!* they're off.

In a way I admire her, she gets through the days.

When I come back he's dressed and miserable. I move about the room in a parody of domesticity, savaging the bread into sandwiches with his one inadequate knife, sloshing water over the fruit. I open the Pepsi I've brought him.

"Do you have more than one glass?"

He shakes his head. "There's only one."

I bring the soft-headed rose out of the bedroom, throw it into the clothes hamper he uses for trash, rinse out the glass and pour half of the warm Pepsi into it for myself. That's the nearest I can bring myself to physical anger. He starts to eat; I can't. I'm shivering; I get his coat down from the hook and wrap myself up in it.

"Don't look at me like that," he says

"Like what?" I say.

I'm not allowed to be angry, he thinks it's unfair. In fact I'm not angry, I'm flipping through my images, trying to find one that will save me from speaking the unforgiveable, the words that can't be recalled. Tortoises in cement cubicles, the otters in their green-scummed pool, they were eating, bones and the head of something, no, what about the foxes; they were barking, you couldn't hear them but you could see the insides of their mouths. The echidnas, waddling through the sawdust like fat fur-coated madwomen, that's no comfort. Back to the plants, the water-lily house, and in Greenhouse 12, *Victoria amazonica* with her huge plate-shaped leaves six feet across and her spiky blossom, floating in her pond, her harbour, doing nothing at all.

"Look," he says, "I can't stand these silences."

"Then say something."

"Whatever I say you'll think I'm sinister."

"I don't think you're sinister," I say, "I just think you're thoughtless and stupid. Anyone clever would wait until after he'd got the woman moved in with him before starting on that." Part of him, I know, doesn't want me to move in at all, the stove stays broken. Hang on to your defences, I think; you'll be sunk without them.

"I thought it was better to tell the truth right off."

I look at him; he's hurting all right, but I need my mouthful of flesh, I need back some of that blood. He's so unhappy though and it isn't his fault, it's just the way he is, accept me, accept my nervous tics, and he thinks that's all it is, a kind of involuntary muscle spasm.

I want to tell him now what no one's ever taught him, how two people who love each other behave, how they avoid damaging each other, but I'm not sure I know. The love of a good woman. But I don't feel like a good woman right now. My skin is numb, bloodless as a mushroom. It was wrong of me to think I could ever accommodate; he's too human. "I'll walk you to the subway." He can't cope with it, he doesn't believe in talking it through, he wants me out of the way. He won't come near me, touch me, doesn't he know that's all he needs to do? He'll wait for me to cool off, as he puts it. But if I go away like this I won't be back.

Outside I put on my sunglasses, though the sun has gone in. I walk severely, not looking at him, I can't bear to. The outlines are slipping again, it's an effort to press the sidewalk down, it billows under my feet like a mattress. He really is going to take me to the subway and let me disappear without making any effort to stop me. I put my hand on his arm.

"Do you want to talk about it?"

"You just want out," he says, "and you're using this as an excuse."

"That's not true," I say. "If I'd wanted that excuse I could have used it before this." We turn off towards the small park where there is a statue on horseback with a lot of pigeons.

"You're making too much of it," he says. "You always exaggerate."

"Oh, I think I know more or less what happened. You had a few drinks and felt horny, that's all."

"Very perceptive of you," he says. He isn't being ironic, he thinks I've had a genuine though rare insight. He leans forward and takes off my sunglasses so he can see me.

"You can't hide behind those," he says.

The sun gets in and I squint; his face swells, darkens, a paper flower dropped in water. He spreads tendrils; I watch them creeping over my shoulder.

"I wish I didn't love you," I say.

He smiles, his hair scintillating in the parklight, his tie blossoming and receding, his face oriental, inscrutable as an eggplant. I grip the handles on my black bag, force him back to snapshot dimensions.

He kisses my fingers; he thinks we have all been cured. He believes in amnesia, he will never mention it again. It should hurt less each time.

I'm happier though as I go down the stairs to the ticket window. My hands function, exchanging round silver disks for oblong paper. That this can be done, that everyone knows what it means, there may be a chance. If we could do that: I would give him a pebble, a flower, he would understand, he would translate exactly. He would reply, he would give me . . .

I ponder again his need for more glasses and consider buying him a large bath towel. Once on the train though, I find myself being moved gradually, station by station, back towards the 7–B Greenhouse. Soon I will be there, inside are the plants that have taught themselves to look like stones. I think of them; they grow silently, hiding in dry soil, minor events, little zeros, containing nothing but themselves; no food value, to the eye soothing and round, then suddenly nowhere. I wonder how long it takes, how they do it.

The Grave
of the Famous Poet

There are a couple of false alarms before we actually get there, towns we pass through that might be it but aren't, uninformative stores and houses edging the road, no signs. Even when we've arrived we aren't sure; we peer out, looking for a name, an advertisement. The bus pauses.

"This has to be it," I say. I have the map.

"Better ask the driver," he says, not believing me.

"Have I ever been wrong?" I say, but I ask the driver anyway. I'm right again and we get off.

We're in a constricted street of grey flat-fronted houses, their white lace curtains pulled closed, walls rising cliff-straight and lawnless from the narrow sidewalk. There are no other people; at least it isn't a tourist trap. I have to eat, we've been travelling all morning, but he wants to find a hotel first, he always needs a home base. Right in front of us there's a building labelled HOTEL. We hesitate outside it, patting down our hair, trying to look acceptable. When he finally grits up the steps with our suitcase the doors are locked. Maybe it's a pub.

Hoping there may be a place further along, we walk down the hill, following the long stone wall, crossing the road when the sidewalk disappears at the corners. Cars pass us, driving fast as though on their way to somewhere else.

At the bottom of the hill near the beach there's a scattering of shops and a scarred, listing inn. Radio music and hilarious voices from inside.

"It seems local," I say, pleased.

"What does 'Inn' mean here?" he asks, but I don't know. He goes in to see; then he comes out, dispirited. I'm too tired to think up solutions, I'm scarcely noticing the castle on the hill behind us, the sea.

"No wonder he drank," he says.

"I'll ask," I say, aggrieved: it was his idea, he should do the finding. I try the general store. It's full of people, women mostly, with scarves on their heads and shopping baskets. They say there is no hotel; one woman says her mother has some rooms free though, and she gives me directions while the others gaze pityingly, I'm so obviously a tourist.

The house, when we find it, is eighteenth century and enormous, a summer residence when the town was fashionable. It offers Bed and Breakfast on a modest sign. We're glad to have something spelled out for us. The door is open, we go into the hall, and the woman emerges from the parlour as though startled; she has a forties bobby-soxer hairdo with curious frontal lobes, only it's grey. She's friendly to us, almost sprightly, and yes, she has a room for us. I ask, in a lowered voice, if she can tell us where the grave is.

"You can almost see it right from the window," she says, smiling—she knew we would ask that—and offers to lend us a book with a map in it of the points of interest, his house and all. She gets the book, scampers up the wide maroon-carpeted staircase to show us our room. It's vast, chill, high-ceilinged, with floral wallpaper and white-painted woodwork; instead of curtains the windows have inside shutters. There are three beds and numerous dressers and cupboards crowded into the room as though in storage, a chunky bureau blocking the once-palatial fireplace. We say it will be fine.

"The grave is just up the hill, that way," she says, pointing through the window. We can see the tip of a church. "I'm sure you'll enjoy it."

I change into jeans and boots while he opens and closes the

drawers on all the pieces of furniture, searching for ambushes or reading matter. He discovers nothing and we set out.

We ignore the church—he once said it was unremarkable—and head for the graveyard. It must rain a lot: ivy invades everything, and the graveyard is lush with uncut grass, succulent and light green. Feet have beaten animal-trail paths among the tombstones. The graves themselves are neatly tended, most of them have the grass clipped and fresh flowers in the tea-strainer-shaped flower holders. There are three old ladies in the graveyard now, sheaves of flowers in their arms, gladioli, chrysanthemums; they are moving among the graves, picking out the old flowers and distributing the new ones impartially, like stewardesses. They take us for granted, neither approaching nor avoiding us: we are strangers and as such part of this landscape.

We find the right grave easily enough; as the book says, it's the only one with a wooden cross instead of a stone. The cross has been recently painted and the grave is planted with a miniature formal-garden arrangement of moss roses and red begonias; the sweet alyssum intended for a border hasn't quite worked. I wonder who planted it, surely it wouldn't have been her. The old ladies have been here and have left a vase, yellowish glassware of the kind once found in cereal boxes, with orange dahlias and spikes of an unknown pink flower. We've brought nothing and have no ceremonies to perform; we muse for an acceptable length of time, then retreat to the scroll-worked bench up the hill and sit in the sun, listening to the cows in the field across the road and the murmur of the ladies as they stoop and potter below us, their print dresses fluttering in the easy wind.

"It's not such a bad place," I say.

"But dull," he answers.

We have whatever it was we came for, the rest of the day is our own. After a while we leave the graveyard and stroll back down the main street, holding hands absentmindedly, looking in the windows of the few shops: an overpriced antique store, a handicrafts place with pottery and Welsh weaving, a nondescript store that sells everything, including girlie joke magazines and copies of his books. In the window, half-hidden among souvenir cups, maps and faded pennants, is a framed photograph of his face, three-quarters profile. We buy a couple of ice-cream bars; they are ancient and soapy.

We reach the bottom of the winding hill and decide to walk along to his house, which we can see, an indistinct white square separated from us by half a mile of rough beach. It's his house all right, it was marked on the map. At first we have no trouble; there's a wide uneven pathway, broken asphalt, the remains or perhaps the beginning of a road. Above us at the edge of the steep, leaf-covered cliff, what is left of the castle totters down, slowly, one stone a year. For him, turrets are irresistible. He finds a scrabbly trail, a children's entrance up sheer mud.

He goes up sideways, crabwise, digging footholds with the sides of his boots. "Come on!" he shouts down. I'm hesitant but I follow. At the top he reaches his hand to me, but, perpendicular and with the earth beside me, afraid of losing my balance, I avoid it and scramble the last few feet, holding on to roots. In wet weather it would be impossible.

He's ahead, eager to explore. The tunnel through the undergrowth leads to a gap in the castle wall; I follow his sounds, rustlings, the soft thud of his feet. We're in the skeleton of a garden, the beds marked by brick borders now grass-infested, a few rosebushes still attempting to keep order in spite of the aphids, nothing else paying any attention. I bend over a rose, ivory-hearted, browning at the edges; I feel like a usurper. He's already out of sight again, hidden by an archway.

I catch up to him in the main courtyard. Everything is crumbling, stairways, ramparts, battlements; so much has fallen it's hard for us to get our bearings, translate this rubbish back into its earlier clear plan.

"That must have been the fireplace," I say, "and that's the main gate. We must have come round from the back." For some reason we speak in whispers; he tosses a fragment of stone and I tell him to be careful.

We go up the remnants of a stairway into the keep. It's almost totally dark; the floors are earth-covered. People must come here though, there's an old sack, an unidentifiable piece of clothing. We don't stay long inside: I'm afraid of getting lost, though it's not likely, and I would rather be able to see him. I don't like the thought of finding his hand suddenly on me unannounced. Besides, I don't trust the castle; I expect it to thunder down on us at the first loud laugh or false step. But we make it outside safely.

We pass beneath the gateway, its Norman curve still intact. Outside is another, larger courtyard, enclosed by the wall we have seen from outside and broken through; it has trees, recent trees not more than a hundred years old, dark-foliaged as etchings. Someone must come here to cut the grass: it's short, hair-textured. He lies down on it and draws me down beside him and we rest on our elbows, surveying. From the front the castle is more complete; you can see how it could once have been lived in by real people.

He lies down, closing his eyes, raising his hand to shade them from the sun. He's pale and I realize he must be tired too, I've been thinking of my own lack of energy as something he has caused and must therefore be immune from.

"I'd like to have a castle like that," he says. When he admires something he wants to own it. For an instant I pretend that he does have the castle, he's always been here, he has a coffin hidden in the crypt, if I'm not careful I'll be trapped and have to stay with him forever. If I'd had more sleep last night I'd be able to frighten myself this way but as it is I give up and lean back on the grass beside him, looking up at the trees as their branches move in the wind, every leaf sharpened to a glass-clear edge by my exhaustion.

I turn my head to watch him. In the last few days he's become not more familiar to me as he should have but more alien. Close up, he's a strange terrain, pores and hairs; but he isn't nearer, he's further away, like the moon when you've finally landed on it. I move back from him so I can see him better, he misinterprets, thinking I'm trying to get up, and stretches himself over me to prevent me. He kisses me, teeth digging into my lower lip; when it hurts too much I pull away. We lie side by side, both suffering from unrequited love.

This is an interval, a truce; it can't last, we both know it, there have been too many differences, of opinion we called it but it was more than that, the things that mean safety for him mean danger for me. We've talked too much or not enough: for what we have to say to each other there's no language, we've tried them all. I think of the old science-fiction movies, the creature from another galaxy finally encountered after so many years of signals and ordeals only to be destroyed because he can't make himself understood. Actually it's less a truce than a rest, those silent black-and-white comedians hitting each other until they fall down, then getting up after a pause to begin again. We love each other, that's true whatever it means, but we aren't good at it; for some it's a talent, for others only an addiction. I wonder if they ever came here while he was still alive.

Right now though there's neither love nor anger, no resentment, it's a suspension, of fear even, like waiting for the dentist. But I don't want him to die. I feel nothing but I concentrate, somebody's version of God, I will him to exist, right now on the vacant lawn of this castle whose name we don't know in this foreign town we're in only because dead people are more real to him than living ones. Despite the mistakes I want everything to stay the way it is; I want to hold it.

He sits up: he's heard voices. Two little girls, baskets over their arms as though for a picnic or a game, have come into the grounds and are walking towards the castle. They stare at us curiously and decide we are harmless. "Let's play in the tower," one calls and they run and disappear among the walls. For them the castle is ordinary as a backyard.

He gets up, brushing off bits of grass. We haven't visited the house yet but we still have time. We find our break in the wall, our pathway, and slide back down to sea level. The sun has moved, the green closes behind us.

The house is further than it looked from the village. The semi-road gives out and we pick our way along the stoney beach. The tide is out; the huge bay stretches as far as we can see, a solid mud-flat except for the thin silty river that cuts along beside us. The dry part narrows and vanishes, we are stranded below the tide-line, clambering over slippery masses of purplish-brown rock or squelching through the mud, thick as clotted cream. All around us is an odd percolating sound: it's the mud, drying in the sun. There are gulls too, and wind bending the unhealthy-coloured rushes by the bank.

"How the hell did he get back and forth?" he says. "Think of doing this drunk on a dark night."

"There must be a road further up," I say.

We reach the house at last. Like everything else here it has a wall; this one is to keep out the waves at high tide. The house itself is on stilts, jammed up against the cliff, painted stone with a spindly-railed two-decker porch. It hasn't been lived in for many years: one window is broken and the railings are beginning to go. The yard is weed-grown, but maybe it always was. I sit on the wall, dangling my legs, while he pokes around, examining the windows, the outhouse (which is open), the shed once used perhaps for a boat. I don't want to see any of it. Graves are safely covered and the castle so derelict it has the status of a tree or a stone, but the house is too recent, it is still partly living. If I looked in the window there would be a table with dishes not yet cleared away, or a fresh cigarette or a coat just taken off. Or maybe a broken plate: they used to have fights, apparently. She never comes back and I can see why. He wouldn't let her alone.

He's testing the railing on the second-storey porch; he's going to pull himself up by it.

"Don't do that," I say wearily.

"Why not?" he says. "I want to see the other side."

"Because you'll fall and I don't want to have to scrape you off the rocks."

"Don't be like that," he says.

How did she manage? I turn my head away, I don't want to watch. It will be such an effort, the police, I'll have to explain what I was doing here, why he was climbing and fell. He should be more considerate. But for once he thinks better of it.

There is another road, we discover it eventually, along the beach and up an asphalt walk beside a neat inhabited cottage.

Did they see us coming, are they wondering who we are? The road above is paved, it has a railing and a sign with the poet's name on it, wired to the fence.

"I'd like to steal that," he says.

We pause to view the house from above. There's an old lady in a garden-party hat and gloves, explaining things to an elderly couple. "He always kept to himself, he did," she is saying. "No one here ever got to know him really." She goes on to detail the prices that have been offered for the house: America wanted to buy it and ship it across the ocean, she says, but the town wouldn't let them.

We start back towards our room. Halfway along we sit down on a bench to scrape the mud from our boots; it clings like melted marshmallow. I lean back; I'm not sure I can make it to the house, whatever reserves my body has been drawing on are almost gone. My hearing is blurred and it's hard to breathe.

He bends over to kiss me. I don't want him to, I'm not calm now, I'm irritated, my skin prickles, I think of case histories, devoted wives who turn kleptomaniac two days a month, the mother who threw her baby out into the snow, it was in *Reader's Digest*, she had a hormone disturbance, love is all chemical. I want it to be over, this long abrasive competition for the role of victim; it used to matter that it should finish right, with grace, but not now. One of us should just get up from the bench, shake hands and leave, I don't care who is last, it would sidestep the recriminations, the totalling up of scores, the reclaiming of possessions, your key, my book. But it won't be that way, we'll have to work through it, boring and foreordained though it is. What keeps me is a passive curiosity, it's like an Elizabethan tragedy or a horror movie, I know which ones will be killed but not how. I take his hand and stroke the back of it gently, the fine hairs rasping my fingertips like sandpaper.

We'd been planning to change and have dinner, it's almost six, but back in the room I have only strength enough to pull off my boots. Then with my clothes still on I crawl into the enormous, creaking bed, cold as porridge and hammock-saggy.

I float for an instant in the open sky on the backs of my eyelids, free-fall, until sleep rushes up to meet me like the earth.

I wake up suddenly in total darkness. I remember where I am. He's beside me but he seems to be lying outside the blankets, furled in the bedspread. I get stealthily out of the bed, grope to the window and open one of the wooden shutters. It's almost as dark outside, there are no streetlights, but by straining I can read my watch: two o'clock. I've had my eight hours and my body thinks it's time for breakfast. I notice I still have my clothes on, take them off and get back in bed, but my stomach won't let me sleep. I hesitate, then decide it won't do him any harm and turn on the bedside lamp. On the dresser there's a crumpled paper bag; inside it is a Welsh cake, a soft white biscuit with currants in it. I bought it yesterday near the train station, asking in bakeries crammed with English buns and French pastries, running through the streets in a crazed search for local colour that almost made us late for the bus. Actually I bought two of them. I ate mine yesterday, this one is his, but I don't care; I take it out of the bag and devour it whole.

In the mirror I'm oddly swollen, as though I've been drowned, my eyes are purple-circled, my hair stands out from my head like a second-hand doll's, there's a diagonal scarlike mark across my cheek where I've been sleeping on my face. This is what it does to you. I estimate the weeks, months, it will take me to recuperate. Fresh air, good food and plenty of sun.

We have so little time and he just lies there, rolled up like a rug, not even twitching. I think of waking him, I want to make love, I want all there is because there's not much left. I start to think what he will do after I'm over and I can't stand that, maybe I should kill him, that's a novel idea, how melodramatic; nevertheless I look around the room for a blunt instrument; there's nothing but the bedside lamp, a grotesque woodland nymph with metal tits and a light bulb coming out of her head. I could never kill anyone with that. Instead I brush my teeth, wondering if he'll ever know how close he came to being murdered, resolving anyway never to plant flowers for him, never to come back, and slide in among the chilly furrows and craters of the bed. I intend to watch the sun rise but I fall asleep by accident and miss it.

Breakfast, when the time for it finally comes, is shabby, decorous, with mended linens and plentiful but dinted silver. We have it in an ornate, dilapidated room whose grandiose mantelpiece now supports only china spaniels and tinted family photos. We're brushed and combed, thoroughly dressed; we speak in subdued voices.

The food is the usual: tea and toast, fried eggs and bacon and the inevitable grilled tomato. It's served by a different woman, grey-haired also but with a corrugated perm and red lipstick. We unfold our map and plan the route back; it's Sunday and there won't be a bus to the nearest railway town till after one, we may have trouble getting out.

He doesn't like fried eggs and he's been given two of them. I eat one for him and tell him to hack the other one up so it will look nibbled at least, it's only polite. He is grateful to me, he knows I'm taking care of him, he puts his hand for a moment over mine, the one not holding the fork. We tell each other our dreams: his of men with armbands, later of me in a cage made of frail slatlike bones, mine of escaping in winter through a field.

I eat his grilled tomato as an afterthought and we leave.

Upstairs in our room we pack; or rather I pack, he lies on the bed.

"What're we going to do till the bus comes?" he says. Being up so early unsettles him.

"Go for a walk," I say.

"We went for a walk yesterday," he says.

I turn around and he's holding out his arms, he wants me to come and lie down beside him. I do and he gives me a perfunctory initial kiss and starts to undo my buttons. He's using only his left hand, the right one is underneath me. He's having trouble. I stand up and take off, reluctantly, the clothes I've so recently put on. It's time for sex; he missed out on it last night.

He reaches up and hauls me in among the tangled sheets. I tense; he throws himself on me with the utilitarian urgency of a man running to catch a train, but it's more than that, it's different, he's biting down on my mouth, this time he'll get blood if it kills him. I pull him into me, wanting him to be with me, but for the first time I feel it's just flesh, a body, a beautiful machine, an animated corpse, he isn't in it any more, I want him so much and he isn't here. The bedsprings mourn beneath us.

"Sorry about that," he says.

"It's all right."

"No, shit, I really am sorry. I don't like it when that happens."

"It's all right," I say. I smooth his back, distancing him: he's back by the deserted house, back lying on the grass, back in the graveyard, standing in the sun looking down, thinking of his own death.

"We better get up," I say, "she might want to make up the room."

We're waiting for the bus. They lied to me in the general store, there is a hotel, I can see it now, it's just around the corner. We've had our quarrel, argument, fight, the one we were counting on. It was a routine one, a small one comparatively, its only importance the fact that it is the last. It carries the weight of all the other, larger things we said we forgave each other for but didn't. If there were separate buses we'd take them. As it is we wait together, standing a little apart.

We have over half an hour. "Let's go down to the beach," I say. "We can see the bus from there; it has to go the other way first." I cross the road and he follows me at a distance.

There's a wall; I climb it and sit down. The top is scattered with sharp flakes of broken stone, flint possibly, and bleached thumbnail-sized cockleshells, I know what they are because I saw them in the museum two days ago, and the occasional piece of broken glass. He leans against the wall near me, chewing on a cigarette. We say what we have to say in even, conversational voices, discussing how we'll get back, the available trains. I wasn't expecting it so soon.

After a while he looks at his watch, then walks away from me towards the sea, his boots crunching on the shells and pebbles. At the edge of the reed bank by the river he stops, back to me, one leg slightly bent. He holds his elbows, wrapped in his clothes as though in a cape, the storm breaks, his cape billows, thick leather boots sprout up his legs, a sword springs to attention in his hand. He throws his head back, courage, he'll meet them alone. Flash of lightning. Onward.

I wish I could do it so quickly. I sit calmed, frozen, not yet sure whether I've survived, the words we have hurled at each other lying spread in fragments around me, solidified. It's the pause during the end of the world; how does one behave? The man who said he'd continue to tend his garden, does that make sense to me? It would if it were only a small ending, my own. But we aren't more doomed than anything else, it's dead already, at any moment the bay will vaporize, the hills across will lift into the air, the space between will scroll itself up and vanish; in the graveyard the graves will open to show the dry puff-ball skulls, his wooden cross will flare like a match, his house collapse into itself, cardboard and lumber, no more language. He will stand revealed, history scaling away from him, the versions of him I made up and applied, stripped down to what he really is for a last instant before he flames up and goes out. Surely we should be holding each other, absolving, repenting, saying goodbye to each other, to everything because we will never find it again.

Above us the gulls wheel and ride, crying like drowning puppies or disconsolate angels. They have black rims around their eyes; they're a new kind, I've never seen any like that before. The tide is going out; the fresh wet mud gleams in the sun, miles of it, a level field of pure glass, pure gold. He stands outlined against it: a dark shape, faceless, light catching the edges of his hair.

I turn aside and look down at my hands. They are covered

with greyish dust: I've been digging among the shells, gathering them together. I arrange them in a border, a square, each white shell overlapping the next. Inside I plant the flints, upright in tidy rows, like teeth, like flowers

Hair Jewellery

There must be some approach to this, a method, a technique, that's the word I want, it kills germs. Some technique then, a way of thinking about it that would be bloodless and therefore painless; devotion recollected in tranquillity. I try to conjure up an image of myself at that time, also one of you, but it's like conjuring the dead. How do I know I'm not inventing both of us, and if I'm not inventing then it really is like conjuring the dead, a dangerous game. Why should I disturb those sleepers, sleepwalkers, as they make their automaton rounds through the streets where we once lived, fading from year to year, their voices thinning to the sound of a thumb drawn across a wet window: an insect squeak, transparent as glass, no words. You can never tell with the dead whether it is they who wish to return or the living who want them to. The usual explanation is that they have something to tell us. I'm not sure I believe it; in this case it's more likely that I have something to tell them.

Be careful, I want to write, *there is a future*, God's hand on the temple wall, clear and unavoidable in the new snow, just in front of them where they are walking—I see it as December—along the brick sidewalk in Boston, city of rotting dignities, she in her wavering high heels, getting her feet wet from sheer vanity. Boots were ugly then, heavy shapeless rubber like rhinoceros paws, flight boots they called them, or furred at the tops like old ladies' or bedroom slippers, with stringy bows; or there were those plastic wedge-shaped rain boots, they would yellow quickly and become encrusted with dirt on the inside, they looked like buried teeth.

That's my technique, I resurrect myself through clothes. In fact it's impossible for me to remember what I did, what happened to me, unless I can remember what I was wearing, and every time I discard a sweater or a dress I am discarding a part of my life. I shed identities like a snake, leaving them pale and shrivelled behind me, a trail of them, and if I want any memories at all I have to collect, one by one, those cotton and wool fragments, piece them together, achieving at last a patchwork self, no defence anyway against the cold. I concentrate, and this particular lost soul rises miasmic from the Crippled Civilians Clothing Donation Box in the Loblaws parking lot in downtown Toronto, where I finally ditched that coat.

The coat was long and black. It was good quality—good quality mattered then, and the women's magazines had articles about basic wardrobes and correct pressing and how to get spots out of camel's hair—but it was far too big for me, the sleeves came to my knuckles, the hem to the tops of my plastic rain boots, which did not fit either. When I bought it I meant to alter it, but I never did. Most of my clothes were the same, they were all too big, perhaps I believed that if my clothes were large and shapeless, if they formed a sort of tent around me, I would be less visible. But the reverse was true; I must have been more noticeable than most as I billowed along the streets in my black wool shroud, my head swathed in, was it a plaid angora scarf, also good quality; at any rate, my head swathed.

I bought these clothes, when I bought clothes at all—for you must remember that, like you, I was poor, which accounts for at least some of our desperation—in Filene's Basement, where good quality clothes that failed to sell at the more genteel levels were disposed of at slashed prices. You often had to try them on in the aisles, as there were few dressing rooms, and the cellar, for it was a cellar, low-ceilinged, dimly lit, dank with the smell of anxious armpits and harassed feet, was filled on bargain days with struggling women in slips and bras, stuffing themselves into torn and soiled designer originals to the sound of heavy breathing and a hundred sticking zippers. It is customary to laugh at bargain-hunting women, at their voraciousness, their hysteria, but Filene's Basement was, in its own way, tragic. No one went there who did not aspire to a shape-change, a transformation, a new life, but the things never did quite fit.

Under the black coat I wear a heavy tweed skirt, grey in colour, and a brown sweater with only one not very noticeable hole, valued by me because it was your cigarette that burned it. Under the sweater I have a slip (too long), a brassiere (too small), some panties with little pink roses on them, also from Filene's Basement, only twenty-five cents, five for a dollar, and a pair of nylon stockings held up by a garter belt which, being too large, is travelling around my waist, causing the seams at the backs of my legs to spiral like barbers' poles. I am lugging a suitcase which is far too heavy—no one carried packsacks then except at summer camp—as it contains another set of my weighty, oversized clothes as well as six nineteenth-century Gothic novels and a sheaf of clean paper. On the other side, counterbalancing the suitcase, are my portable typewriter and my Filene's Basement handbag, gargantuan, bottomless as the tomb. It is February, the wind whips the black coat out behind me, my plastic rain boots skid on the ice of the sidewalk, in a passing store window I see a woman thick and red and bundled. I am hopelessly in love and I am going to the train station to escape.

If I had been richer it would have been the airport. I would have gone to California, Algiers, somewhere oily and alien and above all warm. As it was, I had just enough money for a return ticket and three days in Salem, the only other place both accessible and notable being Walden Pond, which was not much good in winter. I had already justified the trip to myself: it would be more educational to go to Salem than to Algiers, for I was supposed to be "doing work" on Nathaniel Hawthorne. "Doing work," they called it; they still call it that. I would be able to soak up atmosphere; perhaps from this experience, to which I did not look forward, the academic paper required for my survival as a scholar would emerge, like a stunted dandelion from a crack in the sidewalk. Those dismal streets, that Puritanical melancholy combined with the sodden February sea winds would be like a plunge into cold water, shocking into action my critical faculties, my talent for word-chopping and the construction of plausible footnotes which had assured so far the trickle of scholarship money on which I subsisted. For the past two months these abilities had been paralyzed by unrequited love. I thought that several days away from you would give me time to think things over. In my subsequent experience, this does no good at all.

Unrequited love was, at that period of my life, the only kind I seemed to be capable of feeling. This caused me much pain, but in retrospect I see it had advantages. It provided all the emotional jolts of the other kind without any of the risks, it did not interfere with my life, which, although meagre, was mine and predictable, and it involved no decisions. In the world of stark physical reality it might call for the removal of my ill-fitting garments (in the dark or the bathroom, if possible: no woman wants a man to see her safety pins), but it left undisturbed their metaphysical counterparts. At that time I believed in metaphysics. My Platonic version of myself resembled an Egyptian mummy, a mysteriously wrapped object that might or might not fall into dust if uncovered. But unrequited love demanded no stripteases.

If, as had happened several times, my love was requited, if it became a question of the future, of making a decision that would lead inevitably to the sound of one's beloved shaving with an electric razor while one scraped congealed egg from his breakfast plate, I was filled with panic. My academic researches had made me familiar with the moment at which one's closest friend and most trusted companion grows fangs or turns into a bat; this moment was expected, and held few terrors for me. Far more disconcerting was that other moment, when the scales would fall from my eyes and my current lover would be revealed not as a demigod or a monster, impersonal and irresistible, but as a human being. What Psyche saw with the candle was not a god with wings but a pigeon-chested youth with pimples, and that's why it took her so long to win her way back to true love. It is easier to love a daemon than a man, though less heroic.

You were, of course, the perfect object. No banal shadow of lawn mowers and bungalows lurked in your melancholy eyes, opaque as black marble, recondite as urns, you coughed like Roderick Usher, you were, in your own eyes and therefore in mine, doomed and restless as Dracula. Why is it that doleful-ness and a sense of futility are so irresistible to young women? I watch this syndrome among my students: those febrile young men who sprawl on the carpets which this institution of higher learning has so thoughtfully provided for them, grubby and slack as hookworm victims, each with some girl in tow who buys cigarettes and coffee for him and who receives in turn his outpourings of spleen, his condemnations of the world and his mockery of her in particular, of the way she dresses, of the rec-reation room and two television sets owned by her parents, who may be in fact identical to his, of her friends, of what she reads, of how she thinks. Why do they put up with it? Perhaps it makes them feel, by contrast, healthful and life-giving; or perhaps these men are their mirrors, reflecting the misery and chaps they contain but are afraid to acknowledge.

Our case was different only in externals; the desperation, I'm sure, was identical. I had ended up in academia because I did not want to be a secretary, or, to put it another way, be-cause I did not want always to have to buy my good-quality clothes in Filene's Basement; you, because you did not want to be drafted, and at that time the university dodge still worked. We were both from small, unimportant cities, whose Rotary Club denizens, unaware of our actual condition, believed that their minute bursaries were helping us to pursue arcane but glamourous careers which would in some vague way reflect credit on the community. But neither of us wanted to be a professional scholar, and the real ones, some of whom had brush-cuts and efficient briefcases and looked like junior executives of shoe companies, filled us with dismay. Instead of "doing work" we would spend our time drinking draft beer in the cheapest of the local German restaurants, ridiculing the pomposity of our seminars and the intellectual mannerisms of our fellow students. Or we would wander through the stacks of the library, searching for recondite titles no one could possibly have heard of so we could drop them into the next literary debate in that reverential tone soon mastered by every future departmental chairman, and watch the ripples of dismay spread through the eyes of our fellow inmates. Sometimes we would sneak into the Music Department, co-opt a vacant piano and sing maudlin Victorian favourites or bouncy choruses from Gilbert and Sullivan, or a plaintive ballad by Edward Lear from which we had been compelled, earlier in the year, to extract the Freudian symbols. I associate it with a certain brown corduroy skirt which I had made myself, the hem of which was stapled in several places because I had not had the moral energy to sew it.

> On the coast of Coromandel,
> Where the early pumpkins blow
> In the middle of the woods
> Lived the Yonghy-Bonghy-Bo . . .

> Two old chairs, and half a candle
> One old jug without a handle,
> These were all his worldly goods
> In the middle of the woods . . .

The mutilated candle and the broken jug had caused much snide merriment at the seminar, but for us they held a compelling pathos. The state of affairs in Coromandel, its squalor and hopelessness, seemed too apt a comment on our own.

Our problem, I thought, was that neither the world around us nor the future stretching before us contained any image of what we might conceivably become. We were stranded in the present as in a stalled, otherwise empty subway train, and in this isolation we clutched morosely at each other's shadows. That at any rate was my analysis as I lugged my suitcase through the icy twilight towards the only hotel in Salem that was open, or so the conductor had told me. I have trouble seeing this, but I think the railroad station was condensed and dark, lit by a muddy orange light like the subway stations in Boston, and it too had the smell of weak disinfectant unsuccessfully applied to a layer of dried urine so old as to be almost respectable. It did not remind me of Puritans or witches or even of overstuffed shipbuilders, but of undernourished mill-workers with lung trouble, a later generation.

The hotel, too, smelt of decay and better days. It was being repainted, and the painters' canvas cloths and stepladders almost blocked the corridors. The hotel was open only because of the renovations; otherwise, said the desk clerk, who seemed also to be the bellboy, the manager and possibly the owner, he would have shut it down and gone to Florida. "People only come here in the summer," he said, "to see the House of the Seven Gables and that." He resented my being there at all, and more especially for refusing to give a satisfactory explanation. I told him I had come to look at the tombstones but he did not believe this. As he hauled my suitcase and my typewriter towards the windswept cupboard in which he was about to deposit me, he kept looking back over my shoulder as though there ought to have been a man behind me. Illicit sex, he knew, was the only conceivable reason for Salem in February. He was right, of course.

The bed was narrow and hard as a mortuary slab, and I soon discovered that although there was a brisk sea breeze blowing through the closed window, the management was aware of it and had compensated; each fresh onslaught of central heating was announced by the sound of hammers and leaden gongs from the radiator.

Between my fits of sleep I thought about you, rehearsing our future, which I knew would be brief. Of course we would sleep together, though this topic had not yet been discussed. In those days, as you recall, it had to be discussed first, and so far we had not progressed beyond a few furtive outdoor gropings and one moment when, under a full moon on one of those deserted brick streets, you had put your hand on my throat and announced that you were the Boston Strangler; a joke which, for one with my literary predilections, amounted to a seduction. But though sex was a necessary and even a desirable ritual, I dwelt less on it than on our parting, which I visualized as sad, tender, inevitable and final. I rehearsed it in every conceivable location: doorways, ferry-boat docks, train, plane and subway stations, park benches. We would not say much, we would look at each other, we would *know* (though precisely what we would know I wasn't sure); then you would turn a corner and be lost forever. I would be wearing a trench coat, not yet purchased, though I had seen the kind of thing I wanted in Filene's Basement the previous autumn. The park bench scene—I set it in spring, to provide a contrast to the mood—was so affecting that I cried, though since I had a horror of being overheard, even in an empty hotel, I timed it to coincide with the radiator. Futility is so attractive to the young, and I had not yet exhausted its possibilities.

By the next morning I was tired of brooding and snivelling. I decided to seek out the main derelict graveyard, which might provide me with a quaint seventeenth-century tombstone epitaph suitable for my Hawthorne paper. In the hall the workmen were hammering and painting; as I walked down the corridor they stared after me like frogs in a pond. The desk clerk grudgingly relinquished a Chamber of Commerce tourist brochure, which had a map and a short list of the points of interest.

There was no one in the streets outside, and very few cars. The houses, filmed with soot, their paint peeled by the salty air, seemed deserted, though in several of the front windows behind the greying lace curtains I could see the shadowy outline of a face. The sky was grey and furrowed, like the inside of a mattress, and there was a high wind blowing. I skidded over the sidewalks in my slippery boots, the wind pushing my black coat like a sail, making good progress until I turned a corner and the wind was no longer behind me. Soon after that I gave up the graveyard idea.

Instead I turned into a small restaurant; I had not yet had breakfast—the hotel had been surly about it—and I wanted to eat and to consider what to do next. I ordered an egg sandwich and a glass of milk and studied the brochure. The waitress and the proprietor, who were the only other people in the room, retreated to the far end and stood with folded arms, watching me suspiciously while I ate as though expecting me to leap up and perform some act of necromancy with the butter knife. Meanwhile, the House of the Seven Gables was closed for the winter. It had nothing to do with Hawthorne anyway; it was just an old house that had avoided being torn down, and which people now paid money to see because it had been given the name of a novel. No genuine author's sweat on the banisters. I think this was the moment at which I started to become cynical about literature.

The only other point of interest, according to the Chamber of Commerce, was the library. Unlike everything else it was open in February, and was apparently world-famous for its collection of genealogies. The last thing I wanted was a visit to the library, but returning to the hotel with its noise and chemical smells was pointless, and I couldn't stay in the restaurant all day.

The library was empty, except for a middle-aged man in a felt hat who was looking doggedly at the rows of genealogies, palpably killing time. An official woman with a bun and a scowl was sitting behind a blunt desk doing crossword puzzles. The library served also as a museum of sorts. There were several ship's figureheads, maidens with rigid eyes, wooden men, ornate fish and lions, their gilt worn thin; and, displayed in glass cases, a collection of Victorian hair jewellery; brooches and rings, each with a crystal front protecting a design of woven hair; flowers, initials, wreaths or weeping willows. The more elaborate ones had hair of different colours. Though originally they must have shone, the strands by now had aged to the texture of something you find under a chair cushion. It struck me that Donne had been wrong about the circlet of bright hair about the bone. A hand-lettered card explained that many of these pieces were memorial jewellery, intended for distribution to the mourners at funerals.

"The funeral ones," I said to the woman at the desk. "I mean, how did they . . . did they cut the hair off before or after?"

She looked up from her puzzle. She did not understand at all what I was talking about.

"Before or after the person died," I said. If it was before, it seemed to me a callous thing to do. If after, how did they have time to weave all those willow trees before the funeral? And why would they want to? I could not imagine wearing at my throat one of those heavy brooches, like a metal pillow, stuffed with the gradually dimming tresses of one I loved. It would be like a dried hand. It would be like a noose.

"I'm sure I don't know," she said with distaste. "This is a travelling exhibition."

The man in the felt hat was lying in wait for me outside the door. He asked me to join him for a drink. He must have been staying at the hotel.

"No, thank you," I said, adding, "I'm with someone." I said this to mollify him—women always feel compelled to mollify men by whom they are declining to be picked up—but as I said it I realized I had come here not to get away from you, as I had thought, but to be with you, more completely than your actual presence would allow. In the flesh your irony was impenetrable, but alone I could wallow uninterrupted in romantic doom. I've never understood why people consider youth a time of freedom and joy. It's probably because they have forgotten their own. Surrounded now by the doleful young, I can only feel grateful for having escaped, hopefully forever (for I no longer believe in reincarnation), from the intolerable bondage of being twenty-one.

I had told you I was going away for three days, but undiluted fantasy was too much for me. Salem was a vacuum and you were expanding to fill it. I knew whose hair that was in the massive black and gold *memento mori* in the second row of brooches, I knew who I had heard in the vacant hotel room to the left of mine, breathing almost inaudibly between the spasms of the radiator. Luckily there was an afternoon train; I took it, and fled back to the present.

I called you from the Boston train station. You accepted my early return with your usual fatalism, expressing neither glee nor surprise. You were supposed to be doing work on ambiguity in Tennyson's "Locksley Hall," which, you informed me, was clearly out of the question. Ambiguity was big in those days. We went for a walk instead. It was milder and the snow was turning to mush; we ended up at the Charles River, where we rolled snowballs and pitched them into the water. After that we constructed a damp statue of Queen Victoria, complete with jutting bosom, monumental bustle and hooked nose, then demolished it with snowballs and chunks of ice, sniggering at intervals with what I then thought was liberated abandon but now recognize as hysteria.

And then, and then. What did I have on? My coat, of course, and a different skirt, a sickly greenish plaid; the same sweater with the burnt hole in it. We slithered together through the partially frozen slush beside the river, holding each other's chilly hands. It was evening and getting colder. From time to time we stopped, to jump up and down and kiss each other, in order to keep warm. On the oily surface of the Charles were reflected, like bright mirages, the towers and belfries from which the spring examination hopeless ones would later hurl themselves, as they did every year; in its sludgy depths floated the literary suicides, Faulkner's among them, encrusted with crystalline words and glittering like eyes; but we were reckless, we sang in mockery of them, a ragged duet:

> Two old chairs, and half a candle,
> One old jug without a handle, . . .

For once you were laughing. I renounced my carefully constructed script, the ending I had planned for us. The future opened like a wide-screen vista, promising and dangerous, any direction was possible. I felt as if I was walking along the edge of a high bridge. It seemed to us—at least it seemed to me—that we were actually happy.

When the cold was finally too much for us and you had begun to sneeze, we went to one of the cheap restaurants where, it was rumoured, you could live for nothing by eating the free packets of ketchup, relish and sugar and drinking the cream out of the cream-jugs when no one was looking. There we debated the advisability of sleeping together, the pros and cons and, quite soon after that, the ways and means. It was not done lightly, especially by female graduate students, who were supposed to be like nuns, dedicated and unfleshly. Not that in those monastic surroundings they had much chance to be anything else, as the male ones mostly went to the opera together in little groups and had sherry parties to which they invited only each other. We both lived in residence; we both had cellmates who were always in the room, biting their nails and composing bibliographies. Neither of us had a car, and we were sure the local hotels would reject us. It would have to be somewhere else. We settled on New York at Easter Break.

The day before the trip I went to Filene's Basement and bought, after some deliberation, a red nylon baby-doll nightgown, only one size too big and with a shoulder strap that could easily be sewed back on. I lingered over a mauve one with Carmen-like flounces, but I could wear only one at a time and the money would be needed for other things. On Good Friday I took the bus down to New York. You had left several days earlier, but I had stayed to finish an overdue essay on Mrs. Radcliffe's *The Italian*. You yourself had three overdue papers by that time, but you no longer seemed to care. You had been spending a lot of time taking showers, which had annoyed your roommate; you had also been suffering from extended nightmares, which featured, as I recall, elephants, alligators and other large animals rolling down hills in wheelchairs, and people being nailed to crosses and incinerated. I viewed these as evidence of your sensitivity.

The plan was that you would stay at the apartment of an

old friend from your hometown, while I was to get a single hotel room. This would defeat suspicion, we hoped; also it would be less expensive.

At that time I had never been to New York and I was not prepared for it. At first it made me dizzy. I stood in the Port Authority in my long black coat, with my heavy suitcase and my bottomless purse, looking for a phone booth. The crowd was like a political demonstration, though at that time I had never seen a real one. Women jostled each other and spat insults as if they were slogans, hauling grumpy children in their wake; there was a lineup of seedy old men on the benches, and the floor was dotted with gum, candy wrappers and cigarette stubs. I'm not sure but I think there were pinball machines; can that be possible? I wished now that I had asked you to meet the bus, but such dependencies were not part of our understanding.

As I headed for what I guessed was the exit, a black man grabbed hold of my suitcase and began to pull. He had a fresh cut on his forehead from which the blood was running, and his eyes were filled with such desperation that I almost let go. He was not trying to steal my suitcase, I realized after a minute; he just wanted to carry it to a taxi for me.

"No thank you," I said. "No money."

He glanced with scorn at my coat—it was, after all, good quality—and did not let go. I pulled harder and he gave up. He shouted something after me that I didn't understand; those words had not yet become common currency.

I knew the address of the hotel, but I didn't know how to get there. I began to walk. The sun was out and I was sweating, from fright as well as heat. I found a telephone booth: the phone had been eviscerated and was a tangle of wires. The next one was intact, but when I called you there was no answer. This was strange, as I'd told you what time I was arriving.

I leaned against the side of the phone booth, making an effort not to panic. New York had been designed like a barred window, so by looking at the street signs and counting, I should be able to deduce the location of the hotel. I did not want to ask anyone: the expressions of blank despair or active malice made me nervous, and I had passed several people who were talking out loud to themselves. New York, like Salem, appeared to be falling to pieces. A rich person might have seen it as potential urban renewal, but the buildings with chunks missing, the holes in the sidewalks, did not reassure me.

I set out to drag my suitcase to the hotel, stopping at every phone booth to dial your number. In one of these I left your copy of *The Education of Henry Adams,* by mistake. It was just as well, as it was the only thing of yours I had; it would have been unlucky to have kept it.

The hotel clerk was nearly as suspicious of me as the one in Salem had been. I had ascribed the distrust of me there to small-town xenophobia, but it occurred to me now for the first time that it might be the way I was dressed. With my cuffs down to my knuckles, I did not look like someone with a credit card.

I sat in my room, which was really very much like the one in Salem, wondering what had happened to you, where you were. I phoned every half hour. There was not much I could do while waiting. I unpacked the red nightgown with the broken strap, only to find I'd forgotten the needle and thread with which I'd intended to repair it; I didn't even have a safety pin. I wanted to take a bath, but the handle of my door kept turning, and although I had fastened the chain I did not want to take the chance. I even kept my coat on. I began to think that you had given me the wrong number, or, worse, that you were something I had invented.

Finally at about seven o'clock someone answered the phone at your end. It was a woman. When I asked for you she laughed, not pleasantly.

"Hey, Voice of Doom," I heard her say. "Some chick wants you." When you came on your voice was even more remote than usual.

"Where are you?" I said, trying not to sound like a nagging wife. "I've been trying to get hold of you since two-thirty."

"It's my friend," you said. "She swallowed a bottle of sleeping pills this morning. I had to walk her around a lot."

"Oh," I said. I'd had the impression that the friend was male. "Couldn't you have taken her to a hospital or something?"

"You don't take people to hospitals here unless you really have to."

"Why did she do it?" I asked.

"Who knows?" you said, in the voice of someone annoyed at being involved, however peripherally. "To pass the time, I guess." In the background the woman said something that sounded like "You shit."

The soles of my feet turned cold, my legs went numb. I had realized suddenly that she was not just an old friend, as you had told me. She had been a lover, she was still a lover, she was serious, she had taken the pills because she found out I was arriving that day and she was trying to stop you; yet all this time you were calmly writing down the room number, the phone number, that I was just as calmly giving you. We arranged to meet the next day. I spent the night lying on the bed with my coat on.

Of course you failed to arrive, and by that time I had thought twice about phoning. You did not even return to Boston. In May I got a cryptic note from you on a postcard with a picture of the Atlantic City boardwalk on the front:

I ran off to join the Navy but they wouldn't have me, they didn't think Ancient Greek was a good enough qualification. I got a job in a hash joint by lying about my literacy. It's better than jumping off the bell tower. Give my regards to Coromandel. Ever yours, Bo.

As usual, I couldn't decide whether or not you were sneering.

Of course I mourned; not so much for your departure, as that had been, I now saw, a foregone conclusion, but for its suddenness. I had been deprived of that last necessary scene, the park bench, the light spring wind, the trench coat (which I was destined never to buy), your vanishing figure. Even after I realized that our future would have contained neither the dreaded bungalow and electric razor nor those vague, happy possibilities I had once imagined, but, inevitable as a rhymed couplet, an emptied bottle of sleeping pills whose effects you might not have helped me walk off, I continued to mourn.

Because you had not left in the proper way it seemed as though you had never left at all. You hung around, like a miasma or the smell of mice, waiting to deflate my attempts at optimism—for out of sheer fright I soon began to make them—with your own jaundiced view of my behaviour. As if you were my darker twin or an adept in sinister telepathy I could sense on every occasion what your opinion would be. When I became engaged (seven months later, to an architect who designed, and continues to design, apartment buildings), you let me know you had expected other things of me. The actual wedding, and yes, I had all the trimmings including a white gown, filled you with scorn. I could see you in your dingy room, surrounded by empty sardine tins and lint-covered socks, living on nothing but your derision and your refusal to sell out, as I was so palpably doing. (To what? To whom? Unlike later generations, we were never able to pinpoint the enemy.)

My two children did not impress you, nor did the academic position which I subsequently achieved. I have become, in a minor way, an authority on women domestic novelists of the nineteenth century. I discovered after my marriage that I really had more in common with them than I did with Gothic romances; I suppose this insight into my true character signifies maturity, a word you despise. The most prominent of my subjects is Mrs. Gaskell, but you may have heard of Mrs. J. H. Riddell as well; she wrote also under the pen name of F. G. Trafford. I gave quite a creditable paper on her *George Geith of Fen Court*, which was later published in a reputable journal. Needless to say I have tenure, as my department, averse to women for many years, has recently been under some pressure to justify its hiring policies. I am a token, as you never tire of pointing out. I dress well, too, as befits a token. The drab, defiantly woollen wardrobe you may remember vanished little by little into the bins of the Salvation Army as I grew richer, and was replaced by a moderately chic collection of pantsuits and brisk dresses. My male colleagues think of me as efficient and rather cold. I no longer have casual affairs, as I hate mementoes that cannot be thrown away. My coats no longer flap, and when I attend academic conferences nobody stares.

It was at one of these, the big one, the central flesh market and hiring fair, that I saw you last. Curiously enough, it was held in New York that year. I was giving a paper on Amelia Edwards and other female journalists of the period. When I saw your name on the agenda I thought it must be someone else. But it was you, all right, and you spent the entire session discussing whether or not John Keats had had syphilis. You had done a considerable amount of research on the medical uses of mercury in the early part of the century, and your last paragraph was a masterpiece of inconclusion. You had gained weight, in fact you looked healthy, you looked as if you played golf. Though I watched in vain for a sardonic smile: your delivery was deadpan.

Afterwards I went up to congratulate you. You were surprised to see me; you had never thought of me, you said, ending up quite like this, and your possibly dismayed gaze took in my salon haircut, my trim-fitting red jump suit, my jaunty boots. You yourself were married, with three children, and you hastily showed me wallet snapshots, holding them out like protective talismans. I matched them with my own. Neither of us suggested having a drink. We wished each other well; we were both disappointed. You had wanted me, I saw now, to die young of consumption or some equally operatic disease. Underneath it all you too were a romantic.

That should have been that, and I can't understand why it isn't. It is absolutely true that I love my husband and children. In addition to attending faculty meetings, where I crochet afghan squares during discussions of increments and curricula, I cook them nourishing meals, arrange birthday parties and make my own bread and pickles, most of the time. My husband admires my achievements and is supportive, as they say, during my depressions, which become rarer. I have a rich and rewarding sex life, and I can already hear you ridiculing the adjectives, but it is rich and rewarding in spite of you. And you have done no better than I have.

But when I returned from the conference to the house where I live, which is not a bungalow but a two-storey colonial and in which, ever since I moved in, you have occupied the cellar, you were not gone. I expected you to have been dispelled, exorcised: you had become real, you had a wife and three snapshots, and banality is after all the magic antidote for unrequited love. But it was not enough. There you were, in your accustomed place, over by the shelf to the right of the cellar stairs where I keep the preserves, standing dusty and stuffed like Jeremy Bentham in his glass case, looking at me not with your former scorn, it's true, but with reproach, as if I had let it happen, as if it was my fault. Surely you don't want it back, that misery, those decaying buildings, that seductive despair and emptiness, that fear? Surely you don't want to be stuck on that slushy Boston street forever. You should have been more careful. I try to tell you it would have ended badly, that it was not the way you remember, you are deceiving yourself, but you refuse to be consoled. *Goodbye,* I tell you, waiting for your glance, pensive, regretful. You are supposed to turn and walk away, past the steamer trunks, around the corner into the laundry room, and vanish behind the twinset washer-dryer; but you do not move.

When It Happens

Mrs. Burridge is putting up green tomato pickles. There are twelve quarts in each lot with a bit left over, and that is the end of the jars. At the store they tell her there's a strike on at the factory where they get made. She doesn't know anything about that but you can't buy them anywhere, and even before this they were double what they were last year; she considers herself lucky she had those in the cellar. She has a lot of green tomatoes because she heard on the weather last night there was going to be a killer frost, so she put on her parka and her work gloves and took the lantern out to the garden in the pitch-dark and picked off all the ones she could see, over three bushels. She can lift the full baskets herself but she asked Frank to carry them in for her; he grumbles, but he likes it when she asks. In the morning the news said the growers had been hit and that would shoot the price up, not that the growers would get any of it themselves, everyone knows it's the stores that make the money.

She feels richer than she did yesterday, but on the other hand there isn't that much you can do with green tomatoes. The pickles hardly made a dint in them, and Frank has said, as he does every year, that they will never eat twenty-four quarts of green tomato pickle with just the two of them and the children gone. Except when they come to visit and eat me out of house and home, Mrs. Burridge adds silently. The truth is she has always made two batches and the children never liked it anyway, it was Frank ate them all and she knows perfectly well he'll do it again, without even noticing. He likes it on bread and cheese when he's watching the hockey games, during every commercial he goes out to the kitchen and makes himself another slice, even if he's just had a big meal, leaving a trail of crumbs and bits of pickle from the counter across the floor and over the front-room rug to his big chair. It used to annoy Mrs. Burridge, especially the crumbs, but now she watches him with a kind of sadness; she once thought their life together would go on forever but she has come to realize this is not the case.

She doesn't even feel like teasing him about his spare tire any more, though she does it all the same because he would miss it if she stopped. "There you go," she says, in the angular, prodding, metallic voice she cannot change because everyone expects it from her, if she spoke any other way they would think she was ill, "you keep on munching away like that and it'll be easy for me to get you out of bed in the mornings, I'll just give you a push and you'll roll all the way down the stairs like a barrel." And he answers in his methodical voice, pretending to be lazy even though he isn't, "You need a little fun in life," as though his pickles and cheese are slightly disreputable, almost like an orgy. Every year he tells her she's made too much but there would be a fuss all right if he went down to the cellar one day and there wasn't any left.

Mrs. Burridge has made her own pickles since 1952, which was the first year she had the garden. She remembers it especially because her daughter Sarah was on the way and she had trouble bending down to do the weeding. When she herself was growing up everyone did their own pickles, and their own canning and preserving too. But after the war most women gave it up, there was more money then and it was easier to buy things at the store. Mrs. Burridge never gave it up, though most of her friends thought she was wasting her time, and now she is glad she didn't, it kept her in practice while the others were having to learn all over again. Though with the sugar going up the way it is, she can't understand how long anyone is going to be able to afford even the homemade things.

On paper Frank is making more money than he ever has; yet they seem to have less to spend. They could always sell the farm, she supposes, to people from the city who would use it as a weekend place; they could get what seems like a very high price, several of the farms south of them have gone that way. But Mrs. Burridge does not have much faith in money; also it is a waste of the land, and this is her home, she has it arranged the way she wants it.

When the second batch is on and simmering she goes to the back door, opens it and stands with her arms folded across her stomach, looking out. She catches herself doing this four or five times a day now and she doesn't quite know why. There isn't much to see, just the barn and the back field with the row of dead elms Frank keeps saying he's going to cut down, and the top of Clarke's place sticking over the hill. She isn't sure what she is looking for but she has the odd idea she may see something burning, smoke coming up from the horizon, a column of it or perhaps more than one column, off to the south. This is such a peculiar thought for her to have that she hasn't told it to anyone else. Yesterday Frank saw her standing at the back door and asked her about it at dinner; anything he wants to talk to her about he saves up till dinner, even if he thinks about it in the morning. He wondered why she was at the back door, doing nothing at all for over ten minutes, and Mrs. Burridge told him a lie, which made her very uneasy. She said she heard a strange dog barking, which wasn't a good story because their own dogs were right there and they didn't notice a thing. But Frank let it pass; perhaps he thinks she is getting funny in her old age and doesn't want to call attention to it, which would be like him. He'll track mud all over her nice shiny kitchen floor but he'd hate to hurt anyone's feelings. Mrs. Burridge decides, a little wistfully, that despite his pigheadedness he is a kind and likeable man, and for her this is like renouncing a cherished and unquestionable belief, such as the flatness of the earth. He has made her angry so many times.

When the pickles are cool she labels them as she always does with the name and the date and carries them down the cellar stairs. The cellar is the old kind, with stone walls and a dirt floor. Mrs. Burridge likes to have everything neat—she still irons her sheets—so she had Frank build her some shelves right after they were married. The pickles go on one side, jams and jellies on the other, and the quarts of preserves along the bottom. It used to make her feel safe to have all that food in the cellar; she would think to herself, Well, if there's a snowstorm or anything and we're cut off, it won't be so bad. It doesn't make her feel safe any more. Instead she thinks that if she has to leave suddenly she won't be able to take any of the jars with her, they'd be too heavy to carry.

She comes back up the stairs after the last trip. It's not as easy as it used to be, her knee still bothers her as it has ever since she fell six years ago, she tripped on the second-last step. She's asked Frank a million times to fix the stairs but he hasn't done it, that's what she means by pig-headed. If she asks him more than twice to do something he calls it nagging, and maybe it is, but who's going to do it if he won't? The cold vacant hole at the back of this question is too much for her.

She has to stop herself from going to the back door again. Instead she goes to the back window and looks out, she can see almost the same things anyway. Frank is going towards the barn, carrying something, it looks like a wrench. The way he walks, slower than he used to, bent forward a little—from the back he's like an old man, how many years has he been walking that way?—makes her think, He can't protect me. She doesn't think this on purpose, it simply occurs to her, and it isn't only him, it's all of them, they've lost the power, you can tell by the way they walk. They are all waiting, just as Mrs. Burridge is, for whatever it is to happen. Whether they realize it or not. Lately when she's gone to the Dominion Store in town she has seen a look on the faces of the women there, she knows most of them, she wouldn't be mistaken—an anxious, closed look, as if they are frightened of something but won't talk about it. They're wondering what they will do, perhaps they think there's nothing they can do. This air of helplessness exasperates Mrs. Burridge, who has always been practical.

For weeks she has wanted to go to Frank and ask him to teach her how to use the gun. In fact he has two guns, a shotgun and a twenty-two rifle; he used to like going after a few ducks in the fall, and of course there are the groundhogs, they have to be shot because of the holes they make in the fields. Frank drives over on the tractor five or six times a year. A lot of men get injured by overturning tractors. But she can't ask him because she can't explain to him why she needs to know, and if she doesn't explain he will only tease. "Anyone can shoot a gun," he'll say, "all you have to do is pull the trigger . . . oh, you mean you want to hit something, well now, that's different, who you planning to kill?" Perhaps he won't say that; perhaps this is only the way he talked twenty years ago, before she stopped taking an interest in things outside the house. But Mrs. Burridge will never know because she will never ask. She doesn't have the heart to say to him, *Maybe you'll be dead. Maybe you'll go off somewhere when it happens, maybe there will be a war.* She can remember the last war.

Nothing has changed outside the window, so she turns away and sits down at the kitchen table to make out her shopping list. Tomorrow is their day for going into town. She tries to plan the day so she can sit down at intervals; otherwise her feet start swelling up. That began with Sarah and got worse with the other two children and it's never really gone away. All her life, ever since she got married, she has made lists of things that have to be bought, sewed, planted, cooked, stored; she already has her list made for next Christmas, all the names and the gift she will buy for each, and the list of what she needs for Christmas dinner. But she can't seem to get interested in it, it's too far away. She can't believe in a distant future that is orderly like the past, she no longer seems to have the energy; it's as if she is saving it up for when she will have to use it.

She is even having trouble with the shopping list. Instead of concentrating on the paper—she writes on the backs of the used-up days off the page-a-day calendar Frank gives her every New Year's—she is gazing around the kitchen, looking at all the things she will have to leave behind when she goes. That will be the hardest part. Her mother's china, her silver, even though it is an old-fashioned pattern and the silver is wearing off, the egg timer in the shape of a chicken Sarah gave her when she was twelve, the ceramic salt and pepper shakers, green horses with perforated heads, that one of the other children brought back from the Ex. She thinks of walking up the stairs, the sheets folded in the chest, the towels stacked neatly on the shelves, the beds made, the quilt that was her grandmother's, it makes her want to cry. On her bureau, the wedding picture, herself in a shiny satin gown (the satin was a mistake, it emphasized her hips), Frank in the suit he has not worn since except to funerals, his hair cut too short on the sides and a surprising tuft at the top, like a woodpecker's. The children when they were babies. She thinks of her girls now and hopes they will not have babies; it is no longer the right time for it.

Mrs. Burridge wishes someone would be more precise, so she could make better plans. Everyone knows something is going to happen, you can tell by reading the newspapers and watching the television, but nobody is sure what it will be, nobody can be exact. She has her own ideas about it though. At first it will simply become quieter. She will have an odd feeling that something is wrong but it will be a few days before she is able to pin it down. Then she will notice that the planes are no longer flying over on their way to the Malton Airport, and that the noise from the highway two miles away, which is quite distinct when the leaves are off the trees, has almost disappeared. The television will be non-committal about it; in fact, the television, which right now is filled with bad news, of strikes, shortages, famines, layoffs and price increases, will become sweet-tempered and placating, and long intervals of classical music will appear on the radio. About this time Mrs. Burridge will realize that the news is being censored as it was during the war.

Mrs. Burridge is not positive about what will happen next; that is, she knows what will happen but she is not positive about the order. She expects it will be the gas and oil: the oil delivery man will simply not turn up at his usual time, and one morning the corner filling station will be closed. Just that, no explanations, because of course they—she does not know who "they" are, but she has always believed in their existence—they do not want people to panic. They are trying to keep things looking normal, possibly they have already started on this program and that is in fact why things still do look normal. Luckily she and Frank have the diesel fuel tank in the shed, it is three-quarters full, and they don't use the filling station anyway, they have their own gas pump. She has Frank bring in the old wood stove, the one they stored under the barn when they had the furnace and the electricity put in, and for once she blesses Frank's habit of putting things off. She was after him for years to take that stove to the dump. He cuts down the dead elms, finally, and they burn them in the stove.

The telephone wires are blown down in a storm and no one comes to fix them; or this is what Mrs. Burridge deduces. At any rate, the phone goes dead. Mrs. Burridge doesn't particularly mind, she never liked using the phone much anyway, but it does make her feel cut off.

About now men begin to appear on the back road, the gravel road that goes past the gate, walking usually by themselves, sometimes in pairs. They seem to be heading north. Most of them are young, in their twenties, Mrs. Burridge would guess. They are not dressed like the men around here. It's been so long since she has seen anyone *walking* along this road that she becomes alarmed. She begins leaving the dogs off their chains, she has kept them chained at night ever since one of them bit a Jehovah's Witness early one Sunday morning. Mrs. Burridge doesn't hold with the Witnesses—she is United —but she respects their perseverance, at least they have the courage of their convictions which is more than you can say for some members of her own church, and she always buys a *Watchtower*. Maybe they have been right all along.

It is about this time too that she takes one of the guns, she thinks it will be the shotgun as she will have a better chance of hitting something, and hides it, along with the shells, under a piece of roofing behind the barn. She does not tell Frank; he will have the twenty-two. She has already picked out the spot.

They do not want to waste the little gasoline they still have left in the pump so they do not make unnecessary trips. They begin to eat the chickens, which Mrs. Burridge does not look forward to. She hates cleaning and plucking them, and the angriest she ever got at Frank was the time he and Henry Clarke decided to go into turkey farming. They did it too, despite all she had to say against it, and she had to cope with the turkeys escaping and scratching in the garden and impossible to catch, in her opinion they were the stupidest birds in God's creation, and she had to clean and pluck a turkey a week until luckily the blackhead wiped out a third of the flock, which was enough to discourage them, they sold off the rest at a loss. It was the only time she was actually glad to see Frank lose money on one of his ventures.

Mrs. Burridge will feel things are getting serious on the day the electricity goes off and does not come back on. She knows, with a kind of fatalism, that this will happen in November, when the freezer is full of the vegetables but before it is cold enough to keep the packages frozen outside. She stands and looks at the Pliofilm bags of beans and corn and spinach and carrots, melting and sodden, and thinks, Why couldn't they have waited till spring? It is the waste, of food and also of her hard work, that aggravates her the most. She salvages what she can. During the Depression, she remembers, they used to say those on farms were better off than those in the city, because at least they had food; if you could keep the farm, that is; but she is no longer sure this is true. She feels beleaguered, isolated, like someone shut up inside a fortress, though no one has bothered them, in fact no one has passed their way for days, not even the solitary walking men.

With the electricity off they can no longer get the television. The radio stations, when they broadcast at all, give out nothing but soothing music, which Mrs. Burridge does not find soothing in the least.

One morning she goes to the back door and looks out and there are the columns of smoke, right where she's been expecting to see them, off to the south. She calls Frank and they stand watching. The smoke is thick and black, oily, as though something has exploded. She does not know what Frank is thinking; she herself is wondering about the children. She has had no news of them in weeks, but how could she? They stopped delivering mail some time now.

Fifteen minutes later, Henry Clarke drives into the yard in his half-ton truck. This is very unusual as no one has been driving anywhere lately. There is another man with him, and Mrs. Burridge identifies him as the man three farms up who moved in four or five years ago. Frank goes out and talks with them, and they drive over to the gas pump and start pumping the rest of the precious gas into the truck. Frank comes back to the house. He tells her there's a little trouble down the road, they are going along to see about it and she isn't to worry. He goes into the back room, comes out with the twenty-two, asks her where the shotgun is. She says she doesn't know. He searches for it, fruitlessly—she can hear him swearing, he does not swear in her presence—until he gives up. He comes out, kisses her goodbye, which is unusual too, and says he'll be back in a couple of hours. She watches the three of them drive off in Henry Clarke's truck, towards the smoke, she knows he will not come back. She supposes she ought to feel more emotional about it, but she is well prepared, she has been saying goodbye to him silently for years.

She re-enters the house and closes the door. She is fifty-one, her feet hurt, and she does not know where she can go, but she realizes she cannot stay here. There will now be a lot of hungry people, those that can make it this far out of the cities will be young and tough, her house is a beacon, signalling warmth and food. It will be fought over, but not by her.

She goes upstairs, searches in the cupboard, and puts on her heavy slacks and her two thickest sweaters. Downstairs she

127

gathers up all the food that will be light enough for her to carry: raisins, cooking chocolate, dried prunes and apricots, half a loaf of bread, some milk powder which she puts into a quart freezer bag, a piece of cheese. Then she unearths the shotgun from behind the barn. She thinks briefly of killing the livestock, the chickens, the heifers and the pig, so no one will do it who does not know the right way; but she herself does not know the right way, she has never killed anything in her life, Frank always did it, so she contents herself with opening the henhouse door and the gate into the back field. She hopes the animals will run away but she knows they probably will not.

She takes one last look around the house. As an afterthought, she adds her toothbrush to the bundle: she does not like the feel of unbrushed teeth. She does not go down into the cellar but she has an image of her carefully sealed bottles and jars, red and yellow and purple, shattered on the floor, in a sticky puddle that looks like blood. Those who come will be wasteful, what they cannot eat themselves they will destroy. She thinks about setting fire to the house herself, before anyone else can do it.

Mrs. Burridge sits at her kitchen table. On the back of her calendar page, it's for a Monday, she has written *Oatmeal*, in her evenly spaced public-school handwriting that always got a star and has not changed very much since then. The dogs are a problem. After some thought she unchains them, but she does not let them past the gate: at a crucial moment they might give her away. She walks north in her heavy boots, carrying her parka because it is not yet cold enough to put it on, and her package of food and the shotgun which she has taken care to load. She passes the cemetery where her father and mother and her grandmother and grandfather are buried; the church used to be there but it burned down sixteen years ago and was rebuilt closer to the highway. Frank's people are in the other cemetery, his go back to the great-grandfather but they are Anglican, not that he kept it up. There is no one else on the road; she feels a little foolish. What if she is wrong and Frank comes back after all, what if nothing, really, is the matter? *Shortening*, she writes. She intends to make a lemon meringue pie for Sunday, when two of the children are coming up from the city for dinner.

It is almost evening and Mrs. Burridge is tired. She is in a part of the country she cannot remember, though she has stayed on the same road and it is a road she knows well; she has driven along it many times with Frank. But walking is not the same as driving. On one side there is a field, no buildings, on the other a woodlot; a stream flows through a culvert under the road. Mrs. Burridge kneels down to drink: the water is ice-cold and tastes of iron. Later there will be a frost, she can feel it. She puts on her parka and her gloves, and turns into the forest where she will not be seen. There she will eat some raisins and cheese and try to rest, waiting for the moon to rise so she can continue walking. It is now quite dark. She smells earth, wood, rotting leaves.

Suddenly her eye is caught by a flicker of red, and before she can turn back—how can this happen so quickly?—it takes shape, it is a small fire, off to the right, and two men are crouching near it. They have seen her, too: one of them rises and comes towards her. His teeth bare, he is smiling; he thinks she will be easy, an old woman. He says something but she cannot imagine what it is, she does not know how people dressed like that would talk.

They have spotted her gun, their eyes have fastened on it, they want it. Mrs. Burridge knows what she must do. She must wait until they are close enough and then she must raise the gun and shoot them, using one barrel for each, aiming at the faces. Otherwise they will kill her, she has no doubt about that. She will have to be fast, which is too bad because her hands feel thick and wooden; she is afraid, she does not want the loud noise or the burst of red that will follow, she has never killed anything in her life. She has no pictures beyond this point. You never know how you will act in a thing like that until it actually happens.

Mrs. Burridge looks at the kitchen clock. On her list she writes *Cheese*, they are eating more cheese now than they used to because of the price of meat. She gets up and goes to the kitchen door.

A Travel Piece

Annette is wiped right out. She never used to be this wiped out after a job; she supposes it's the medication. Any kind of a pill is a drain on the system, she doesn't like taking them but there you are.

She chews on one of the vacu-packed peanuts, thumbing through the travel brochure from the seat pocket, letting her mind drift among the coloured pictures. Thirty-six vacations in the sun, described in glowing terms, with the prices, all-inclusive it says but of course there are extras. *A gem of an island almost undiscovered by tourists, with brilliant white sand beaches and blue-green lagoons complemented by the friendliness of the people.* Annette is returning from just such an island and she too writes pieces like this, but hers are not advertisements, they're for the newspaper and, when she gets lucky, for the glossy magazines as well, so the things she writes have to be less bland: little anecdotes, the personal touch, details on where to eat and how good the service is, jokes told by the barman if any, where to go shopping for bargains, all those straw hats and curios, out-of-the-way things you might do, such as climbing an extinct volcano or cooking a parrot-fish on a coral reef, if you had the energy and the desire. Increasingly she doesn't, but she puts herself through the paces anyway, she would consider it cheating to recommend these things without having done them. This is what makes her a good travel writer, among other things; and she has a knack for discovering local oddities, she knows what to look for, she has an eye for detail.

She's learned though that she has to strike the right balance between what she manages to notice, spontaneously and candidly—and she always takes a camera with her, just in case, though for the glossies they usually send down their own photographer—and what she chooses to leave out. For instance, by lifting her head slightly she can read: LIFE JEST INDER FRONT OF YOUR SEAT. It says LIFE JEST because the lettering, which is embroidered right into the cloth of the pocket, has been worn away by the outgoing and incoming thighs of countless passengers. It would strike a humorous note but she can't use it; the airline company would resent the implication that its planes were falling to pieces and that would be it for the complimentary tickets.

People, she found, did not want any hint of danger in the kind of articles it was her business to write. Even the ones who would never go to the places she described, who could not afford it, did not want to hear about the danger or even unpleasantness; it was as if they wanted to believe that there was somewhere left in the world where all was well, where unpleasant things did not happen. An unspoiled Eden; that had been a useful phrase. Once, it seemed a long time ago, staying home meant safety, though tedium as well, and going to the places that were her specialty—the Caribbean, the northern half of South America, Mexico—meant adventure, threat, pirates, brigands, lawlessness. Now it was the reverse, home was the dangerous place and people went on vacation to snatch a few weeks of uneventfulness. If small black beads of oil were appearing on the white sand beaches, if the barman's niece had stabbed her husband, if things were stolen or it rained, they did not want to know about it; if they felt like disasters or crimes they could read about them in the other pages of the newspaper. So she did not report such things and she tried her best not to notice them. There was that pig on the beach in

Mexico, being killed by a man who didn't know how to do it properly, because some tourist had wanted a Polynesian feast. That was the sort of thing you had to filter out. Her job was to be pleased, and she did this well, she was evenly tanned and in trim physical shape, she had direct blue eyes and a white smile and was good at asking interested, polite questions and coping with minor emergencies, such as lost suitcases, cheerfully and without becoming irritated. She seldom had trouble; there was something about her, an air of professionalism, she was too thorough to be an ordinary tourist; those in the industry sensed it would be bad for business to upset her.

So she went her way undisturbed among the green trees, along the white beaches, between the blue sky and the indecently blue ocean, which more and more lately had come to seem like a giant screen, flat and with pictures painted on it to create the illusion of solidity. If you walked up to it and kicked it, it would tear and your foot would go right through, into another space which Annette could only visualize as darkness, a night in which something she did not want to look at was hiding. Things were being kept from her, she had begun to feel, especially in lobbies and in cars taking her to and from airports; people were watching her, as if they were aware of this. It was the constant surveillance that was exhausting her, and the effort she had been making not to find out.

She attempted once to describe these feelings to her husband, but the attempt was not a success. Her capacity for being easily pleased, delighted even, had pervaded their marriage as well as her job, and he reacted at first with a kind of restrained, offended outrage, as if she had complained to the maître d' about a wine. Very well, madam, it shall be replaced, and a look that says: Stupid bitch. Jeff seemed hurt that she was not totally and altogether happy, that she had been coming home from her trips too tired to go out for special little dinners with him, that she crawled into bed and remained there between her mock vacations, emerging only long enough to plod through the required exercises at the typewriter. When she said, "Sometimes I feel I'm not alive," he took it as a comment on his love-making, and she had to spend half an hour reassuring him, telling him that wasn't what she meant; she'd been talking about her job. But his view of her job was that it was a lucky accident, she was a very fortunate girl to have a job like that. He himself was interning at a hospital—she'd put him through medical school on her own salary—and he felt abused and overworked. He could not understand why she wanted to stay home more; finally he swiped the pills for her, telling her they would steady her nerves. Which they have, she supposes, but then her nerves have not been unsteady, quite the contrary. It's the unbroken calm, both within and without, that is getting to her. Real events happen to other people, she thinks, why not me? And then there's her conviction that they are happening, all around her, but that they're being kept from her.

Once she took Jeff along with her, to Bermuda, though they couldn't really afford it as his way had to be paid, of course. She thought it would be good for them, he would see what she really did and stop idealizing her; she felt that perhaps he had married her because of her tan, he found her glamourous. And it would be fun to get away together. But it hadn't been. All he'd wanted to do was lie in the sun and he'd refused to eat the pumpkin soup, he was a meat and potatoes man. "Relax," he kept telling her, "why don't you just lie down beside me and relax?" He hadn't understood why she needed to go shopping, to explore the markets, to visit all the possible beaches and restaurants. "It's my job," she told him, to which he replied, "Some job, I should have a job like that." "You're not suited for it," she said, thinking of the fuss he had made over the fried plantain. He could not understand that being pleased was hard work, and he thought she was being too friendly with the taxi drivers.

The plane starts to tilt down as Annette is finishing her martini. Jeff told her she should go easy on mixing the pills and liquor, but one wouldn't hurt, so dutifully she ordered only one. For a minute or two no one notices; then the stewardesses are at their posts and a blurred, alarmed voice is coming through the intercom, but as usual it's inaudible, and half of it is in French anyway. Hardly anyone is screaming. Annette takes off her high-heeled shoes, Cuban actually, they're better for walking, slips them under the seat, and rests her forehead on her knees, protecting it with her arms. She's following the instructions on the card tucked into the seat pocket; there's a diagram on it too, about how to blow up the life vest by pulling the knobs. When the girls went through their routine at the beginning of the flight she didn't watch; she hasn't watched for a long time.

By twisting her head to the right she can see the card sticking out of the pocket of the seat next to her, and the edge of the vomit bag as well; they don't say *vomit* but *discomfort*, which fits. Next to the vomit bag is a man's knee. Nothing seems to be happening so Annette looks up to see what's going on. A lot of the people don't have their heads down on their knees the way they've been told, they're sitting bolt upright, just staring, as if they're watching a movie. The man next to Annette is white as a sheet. She asks him if he wants a Rolaid, but he doesn't, so she eats one herself. She carries a small arsenal of patent medicines with her on these trips, laxatives, cold remedies, vitamin C, aspirins; everything you can get she's had a dose of at one time or another.

The plane is going down in a long glide, it's a lot easier than she would have expected. There's a faint smell of burning rubber, that's all, no explosions; she feels hardly any discomfort, though her ears are popping. The descent is silent too because the engines aren't working, and except for one woman who is still screaming half-heartedly and another who is crying, none of the passengers is making much noise.

"Where you from?" the man beside her says, abruptly, perhaps it's the only thing he can think of to say to a woman on an airplane, no matter what the circumstances; but before Annette can answer there's a jolt that knocks her teeth together, it isn't at all like hitting water. More like a slightly bumpy runway, as if the sea is hard, like cement.

It must have damaged the loudspeakers though, because the blurred voices have stopped. The passengers crowd into the aisles, released, their mingled voices rising excitedly, like children let out of school. Annette thinks they are being remarkably calm, though real panic, with stampeding feet and people being trampled on, is difficult when the aisle is so narrow. She always notes the locations of the emergency exits and tries to sit near one but she has not managed it this time, so she decides to wait in her seat until the jam is over. The back door appears to be stuck so everyone is shoving to the front. The man sitting beside her is trying to elbow his way into the lineup, which is like a supermarket queue, they even have bundles. Annette folds her hands and looks out through the oval porthole window but all she can see is the surface of the ocean, flat as a parking lot; there isn't even any smoke or flames.

When the aisle is clearer she stands up, lifts the seat as the instruction card has told her and takes out the life vest. She has noticed that many people in their rush to get out have been forgetting to do this. She collects her coat from the overhead rack, which is still crammed with other coats, abandoned by their owners. The sun is shining as brightly as ever, but it may cool off at night. She has the coat with her because when she steps off the plane at the other end it will still be winter. She picks up her camera bag and her large purse, which doubles as a flight bag; she's familiar with the advantages of travelling light, she once did a fashion piece on crushable dresses.

Between the First Class cabin at the front and the Tourist Class is the tiny kitchen. As she goes through it, at the tail end of the line, Annette sees a rack of lunch trays, with plastic-wrapped sandwiches and desserts with snap-on lids. The drink trolley is there too, parked out of the way. She takes several of the sandwiches, three bottles of ginger ale and a handful of vacu-packed peanuts and stuffs them into her purse. She does this as much because she is hungry as for any other reason, but she is thinking, too, that they may need provisions. Though they will certainly be picked up soon, the plane must have sent out a distress signal. They will be rescued by helicopters. Still, it will be nice to have some lunch. She considers momentarily taking a bottle of liquor too, from the drink trolley, but rejects this as a bad idea. She remembers having read magazine articles about delirious sailors.

When she gets to the chute leading down from the open doorway she hesitates. The blue watery surface below her is dotted with round orange disks. Some of them have already made considerable headway, or have they been blown? From a distance the scene looks delightful, with the orange circles twirling on the sea like wading pools filled with happy children. Though she's a little disappointed; she knows this is an emergency but so far everything has been so uneventful, so orderly. Surely an emergency ought to feel like one.

She would like to take a picture of the scene, with the orange against the blue, two of her favourite colours. But someone at the bottom is calling to her to hurry up, so she sits on the chute, placing her knees together so her skirt won't blow up, holds her purse, her camera and her folded coat firmly on her lap, and pushes off. It's like going down a slide, the kind they used to have in parks.

Annette finds it odd that she should be the last one off the plane. Surely the captain and the stewardesses ought to have remained on board until all the passengers were safely off, but there is no sign of them. She doesn't have much time to think about this however, because the round boat is in a state of confusion, there seem to be a lot of people on it and someone is shouting orders. "Row," the voice says, "we've got to get away from here . . . the suction!"

Annette wonders what he is talking about. There are only two paddles in any case so she settles herself out of the way and watches while a couple of men, the owner of the voice and a younger man, paddle at either side of the boat as if their lives depended on it. The boat moves up and down with the waves, which are not large, it rotates—one of the men must be stronger than the other, Annette thinks—and it moves gradually away from the plane, in the direction of the afternoon sun. Annette feels as though she's being taken for a boat-ride; she leans back against the swelling rubber side of the boat and enjoys it. Behind them, the plane settles imperceptibly lower. Annette thinks it would be a good idea to get a picture of it, for use when they are rescued and she can write up the story, and she opens her camera bag, takes out her camera and adjusts the lens; but when she squirms around so she can get a better view, the plane is gone. She thinks it ought to have made a noise of some kind, but they are quite a distance from where it was.

"No sense in getting too far away from the crash site," says the man who has been giving the orders. There's something military about him, Annette decides; maybe it's the trimmed moustache or the fact that he's older. He and the other man ship their paddles and he begins to roll a cigarette, taking the papers and tobacco from his breast pocket. "I suggest we introduce ourselves," he says; he's used to directing.

There are not as many people in the boat as Annette at first supposed. There's the two men, the one who says he's in insurance (though Annette doubts this), and the younger one, who has a beard and claims to teach at a free school; the older man's wife, who is plump and kind-looking and keeps saying "I'm all right," although she isn't, she's been crying quietly to herself ever since they've been in the boat; an overly tanned woman of forty-five or so who gives no clue as to her occupation and a boy who says he's a university student. When it comes to Annette's turn she says, "I write a food column for one of the newspapers." In fact she did this for a couple of months, before she got onto the travel page, so she knows enough about it to be able to back it up. Still, she is surprised at herself for lying and can't imagine why she did. The only reason she can think of is that she hasn't believed the stories of any of the others, except the plump, crying woman, who could not possibly be anything other than what she so obviously is.

"We've been damn lucky," says the older man, and they all agree.

"What are we supposed to do now?" says the tanned woman.

"Just sit around and wait to be rescued, I guess," the bearded schoolteacher says, with a nervous laugh. "It's an enforced vacation."

"It'll just be a matter of hours," says the older man. "They're more efficient about these things than they used to be."

Annette volunteers the information that she has some food and they all congratulate her for being so resourceful and fore-sighted. She provides the wrapped sandwiches and they divide them up equally; they pass around one of the bottles of ginger ale to wash them down. Annette doesn't say anything about the peanuts or the other two bottles of ginger ale. She does say, however, that she has some seasick pills if anyone needs one.

She's about to toss the plastic sandwich trays overboard, but the older man stops her. "No, no," he says, "can't throw those away. They might come in handy." She can't imagine what for, but she does as he says.

The plump woman has stopped crying and has become quite talkative; she wants to know all about the food column. In fact they are now a festive bunch, chattering away as if they are on a huge sofa in a recreation room, or in the waiting room of an airport where the flights have been temporarily held up. There's the same atmosphere of time being passed, from necessity but with superficial cheer. Annette is bored. For a moment she thought something real had happened to her but there is no danger here, it is as safe in this lifeboat as everywhere else, and the piece she would write about it would come out sounding the same as her other pieces. *For exploring the Caribbean, a round orange lifeboat strikes an unusual note. The vistas are charming, and you have a body-to-body contact with the sea which is simply not possible in any other kind of boat. Take some sandwiches and plan to stay out for lunch!*

The sun sets in its usual abrupt, spectacular fashion, and it's not until then that they begin to get worried. No helicopters have appeared, and none of the other lifeboats are in sight. Perhaps they paddled away too quickly. They haven't even heard any sounds of distant rescue operations. But, "They'll be along, all right," the older man says, and his wife suggests they have a singsong. She begins with "You Are My Sunshine," warbling in a church soprano, and continues through a repertoire of once-popular favourites: "On Top of Old Smokey," "Good Night, Irene." The others join in, and Annette is momentarily amazed by the numbers of words to these songs that she herself can remember. She goes to sleep during one of the choruses, her winter coat pulled over her; she's glad she brought it.

She awakens feeling groggy and clogged. She can't believe they're all still in the boat, it's beginning to get annoying, and she is boiling hot under her coat. The rubber of the lifeboat is hot too and there's no wind, the sea is as flat as the palm of your hand with only a sickening ground-swell. The others are sprawled listlessly around the boat's circumference, their legs in awkward tangles here and there. Annette thinks to herself they'd be better off with fewer people in the boat, but immediately censors this. The two women are still asleep; the plump one, the singer, lies with her mouth open, snoring slightly. Annette rubs her eyes; the lids feel dry and gritty. She seems to remember getting up in the night and squatting perilously over the edge of the boat; someone else must have made this effort and failed, or not made it at all, for there is a faint smell of urine. She is very thirsty.

The older man is awake, smoking in silence; so is the one with the beard. The student is drowsing still, curled in a heap, like a puppy.

"What should we do?" Annette asks.

"Stick it out till they come for us," says the older man. He doesn't look so military any more with his day's growth of stubble.

"Maybe they won't come," says the bearded man. "Maybe we're in the Bermuda whatchamacallit. You know, where those ships and planes vanish without a trace. What made the plane go down, anyway?"

Annette looks at the sky, which is more like a flat screen than ever. Maybe this is what has happened, she thinks, they've gone through the screen to the other side; that's why the rescuers can't see them. On this side of the screen, where she thought there would be darkness, there is merely a sea like the other one, with thousands of castaways floating around in orange lifeboats, lost and waiting to be rescued.

"The main thing," says the older man, "is to keep your mind occupied." He flicks his cigarette butt into the water. Annette expects to see a shark emerge and snap it up, but none does. "First off, we'll all get sunstroke if we aren't careful." He's right, they are all quite red.

He wakes the others and puts them to work constructing a shade, which they make from Annette's winter coat and the men's suit jackets, the buttons of one inserted into the buttonholes of the next. They prop it up with the paddles, lashing it on with neckties and stockings, and sit under it, with a fleeting sense of accomplishment. It's hot and stuffy, but it is out of the sun. Again at his suggestion the men turn out their pockets and the women empty their purses, "to see what we've got to work with," the older man says. Annette has forgotten everyone's name and suggests they introduce themselves again, which they do. Bill and Verna, Julia, Mike and Greg. Julia has a pounding headache and takes several of Annette's aspirins-with-codeine. Bill is going through the assortment of handkerchiefs, keys, compacts, lipsticks, travel-sized bottles of hand lotion, pills and chewing gum. He has appropriated the two remaining bottles of ginger ale and the peanuts which he says will have to be rationed. For breakfast he lets them each have a Chiclet and a cough drop, to suck on. After that they take turns brushing their teeth, with Annette's toothbrush. She's the only one who has travelled light and thus has all her toiletries with her. The others used suitcases, which of course went down in the hold of the plane.

"If it rains," Bill says, "this boat is perfect for catching water"; but it does not look like rain.

Bill has a lot of good ideas. In the afternoon he spends some time fishing, with a hook made from a safety-pin and a line of dental floss. He catches nothing. He says they could attract sea-gulls by flashing Annette's camera lens at them, if there were any sea-gulls. Annette is lethargic, although she keeps prodding herself, reminding herself that this is important, this may be the real thing, now that they have not been rescued.

"Were you in the war?" she asks Bill, who looks smug that she has noticed.

"You learn to be resourceful," he says. Towards evening they share out one of the bottles of ginger ale, and Bill allows them three peanuts each, telling them to scrape the salt off before eating them.

Annette goes to sleep thinking of a different story; it will have to be different now. She won't even have to write it, it will be her story As Told To, with a picture of herself, emaciated and sunburned but smiling bravely. Tomorrow she should take some pictures of the others.

During the night, which they spend under the sunshade, now a communal blanket, there is a scuffle. It's Greg the student and Bill, who has hit him and now claims he was making a try for the last bottle of ginger ale. They shout angrily at each other until Verna says it must have been a mistake, the boy was having a bad dream. All is quiet again but Annette is awake, she gazes up at the stars, you can't see stars like that in the city.

After a while there is heavy breathing, surely she's imagining it, but there's a distinct sound of furtive copulation. Who can it be? Julia and Mike, Julia and Greg? Not Verna, surely, in her corset which Annette is positive she has not taken off. Annette is a little disappointed that no one has made a pass at her, if that sort of thing is going around. But it was probably initiated by Julia, that suntanned solitary voyager, this must be what she goes on vacations for. Annette thinks of Jeff, wonders how he reacted to the fact that she is missing. She wishes he was here, he would be able to do something, though she doesn't know what. They could make love anyway.

In the morning she scans their faces for signs, revealing clues as to who did what, but finds nothing. They brush their teeth once more, then rub hand lotion onto their faces, which is refreshing. Bill passes round a package of Tums and more cough drops; he's saving the peanuts and the ginger ale for the evening meal. He devises a strainer out of his shirt and trails it over the side of the boat to catch plankton, he says. He brings in some messy green stuff, squeezes out the salt water and chews a handful thoughtfully. The others each take a mouthful, except Julia who says she can't swallow it. Verna tries, but spits hers out. Annette gets it down; it's salty and tastes of fish. Later, Bill does manage to catch a small fish and they eat chunks of that also; the hot fish smell mingles with the other smells, unwashed bodies and slept-in clothes, which are rubbing against Annette's nerves. She's irritable, she's stopped taking the pills, maybe that's why.

Bill has a knife, and with it he slices the plastic sandwich trays in two, then cuts slits in them to make sun goggles, "like the Eskimos," he says. He has definite leadership ability. He unravels part of Verna's sweater, then twists the pink wool to make the strings to tie them with. They have abandoned the coat sunshade, it was too hot and the paddles had to be held upright all the time, so they fasten the plastic trays over their faces. They smear their noses and lips and the exposed parts of their foreheads with lipstick from the purse collection; Bill says it will be protection against sunburn. Annette is disturbed by the effect, these masks and bloody markings. What bothers her is that she can't tell any more who these people are, it could be anyone behind the white plastic faces with slit eyes. But she must look like that too. It is exotic though, and she is still functioning well enough to think of taking a picture, though she doesn't take it. She ought to, for the same reason she's kept her watch conscientiously wound up, it would help morale by implying there is a future. But suddenly there's no point.

About two o'clock Greg the student starts thrashing around. He lunges for the side of the boat and tries to get his head over into the sea. Bill throws himself on top of him and after a minute Mike joins him. They hold Greg down on the bottom of the boat. "He was drinking sea water," Mike says, "I saw him, early this morning." The boy is gasping like a fish, and he looks like a fish too in his impersonal plastic face. Bill removes the mask, and the human features glare up into his. "He's delirious," Bill says. "If we let him up, he'll jump overboard." Bill's plastic mask turns, pointing itself toward the other members of the group. No one says anything, but they are thinking, Annette knows what they are thinking because she is thinking the same thing. They can't hold him down forever. If they let him up, he will die, and not only that, he will be lost to them, wasted. They themselves are dying slowly of thirst. Surely it would be better to . . . Verna is rummaging, slowly and painfully, like a crippled bumblebee, in the heap of clothing and debris; what is she looking for? Annette feels she is about to witness something mundane and horrible, doubly so because it will be bathed not in sinister blood-red lightning but in the ordinary sunlight she has walked in all her life; some tacky ritual put on for the tourists, tacky because it is put on for tourists, for those who are not responsible, for those who make the lives of others their transient spectacle and pleasure. She is a professional tourist, she works at being pleased and at not participating; at sitting still and watching. But they are going to slit his throat, like that pig on the beach at Mexico, and for once she does not find it quaint and unusual. "Stay out of it," the man in the light-green suit had said to his wife, who was sentimental about animals. Could you stay out by wishing to?

I can always say it wasn't me, I couldn't help it, she thinks, visualizing the newspaper interview. But there may not be one, and she is therefore stuck in the present, with four Martians and one madman waiting for her to say something. So this is what goes on behind her back, so this is what it means to be alive, she's sorry she wondered. But the sky is not flat any more, it's bluer than ever and recedes away from her, clear but unfocused. You are my sunshine, Annette thinks; when skies are grey. The quality of the light has not changed. Am I one of them or not?

The Resplendent Quetzal

Sarah was sitting near the edge of the sacrificial well. She had imagined something smaller, more like a wishing well, but this was huge, and the water at the bottom wasn't clear at all. It was mud-brown; a few clumps of reeds were growing over to one side, and the trees at the top dangled their roots, or were they vines, down the limestone walls into the water. Sarah thought there might be some point to being a sacrificial victim if the well were nicer, but you would never get her to jump into a muddy hole like that. They were probably pushed, or knocked on the head and thrown in. According to the guide-book the water was deep but it looked more like a swamp to her.

Beside her a group of tourists were being rounded up by the guide, who obviously wanted to get the whole thing over with so he could cram them back onto their pink-and-purple-striped *turismo* bus and relax. These were Mexican tourists, and Sarah found it reassuring that other people besides Canadians and Americans wore big hats and sunglasses and took pictures of everything. She wished she and Edward could make these excursions at a less crowded time of year, if they had to make them at all, but because of Edward's teaching job they were limited to school holidays. Christmas was the worst. It would be the same even if he had a different job and they had children, though; but they didn't have any.

The guide shooed his charges back along the gravel path as if they were chickens, which was what they sounded like. He himself lingered beside Sarah, finishing his cigarette, one foot on a stone block, like a conquistador. He was a small dark man with several gold teeth, which glinted when he smiled. He was smiling at Sarah now, sideways, and she smiled back serenely. She liked it when these men smiled at her or even when they made those juicy sucking noises with their mouths as they walked behind her on the street; so long as they didn't touch. Edward pretended not to hear them. Perhaps they did it so much because she was blonde: blondes were rare here. She didn't think of herself as beautiful, exactly; the word she had chosen for herself some time ago was "comely." Comely to look upon. You would never use that word for a thin woman.

The guide tossed his cigarette butt into the sacrificial well and turned to follow his flock. Sarah forgot about him immediately. She'd felt something crawling up her leg, but when she looked nothing was there. She tucked the full skirt of her cotton dress in under her thighs and clamped it between her knees. This was the kind of place you could get flea bites, places with dirt on the ground, where people sat. Parks and bus terminals. But she didn't care, her feet were tired and the sun was hot. She would rather sit in the shade and get bitten than rush around trying to see everything, which was what Edward wanted to do. Luckily the bites didn't swell up on her the way they did on Edward.

Edward was back along the path, out of sight among the bushes, peering around with his new Leitz binoculars. He didn't like sitting down, it made him restless. On these trips it was difficult for Sarah to sit by herself and just think. Her own binoculars, which were Edward's old ones, dangled around her neck; they weighed a ton. She took them off and put them into her purse.

His passion for birds had been one of the first things Edward had confided to her. Shyly, as if it had been some precious gift, he'd shown her the lined notebook he'd started keeping when he was nine, with its awkward, boyish printing—ROBIN, BLUE

JAY, KINGFISHER—and the day and the year recorded beside each name. She'd pretended to be touched and interested, and in fact she had been. She herself didn't have compulsions of this kind; whereas Edward plunged totally into things, as if they were oceans. For a while it was stamps; then he took up playing the flute and nearly drove her crazy with the practising. Now it was pre-Columbian ruins, and he was determined to climb up every heap of old stones he could get his hands on. A capacity for dedication, she guessed you would call it. At first Edward's obsessions had fascinated her, since she didn't understand them, but now they merely made her tired. Sooner or later he'd dropped them all anyway, just as he began to get really good or really knowledgeable; all but the birds. That had remained constant. She herself, she thought, had once been one of his obsessions.

It wouldn't be so bad if he didn't insist on dragging her into everything. Or rather, he had once insisted; he no longer did. And she had encouraged him, she'd let him think she shared or at least indulged his interests. She was becoming less indulgent as she grew older. The waste of energy bothered her, because it was a waste, he never stuck with anything, and what use was his encyclopædic knowledge of birds? It would be different if they had enough money, but they were always running short. If only he would take all that energy and do something productive with it, in his job, for instance. He could be a principal if he wanted to, she kept telling him that. But he wasn't interested, he was content to poke along doing the same thing year after year. His Grade Six children adored him, the boys especially. Perhaps it was because they sensed he was a lot like them.

He'd started asking her to go birding, as he called it, shortly after they'd met, and of course she had gone. It would have been an error to refuse. She hadn't complained, then, about her sore feet or standing in the rain under the dripping bushes trying to keep track of some nondescript sparrow, while Edward thumbed through his Peterson's Field Guide as if it were the Bible or the bird were the Holy Grail. She'd even become quite good at it. Edward was nearsighted, and she was quicker at spotting movement than he was. With his usual generosity he acknowledged this, and she'd fallen into the habit of using it when she wanted to get rid of him for a while. Just now, for instance.

"There's something over there." She'd pointed across the well to the tangle of greenery on the other side.

"Where?" Edward had squinted eagerly and raised his binoculars. He looked a little like a bird himself, she thought, with his long nose and stilt legs.

"That thing there, sitting in that thing, the one with the tufts. The sort of bean tree. It's got orange on it."

Edward focused. "An oriole?"

"I can't tell from here. Oh, it just flew." She pointed over their heads while Edward swept the sky in vain.

"I think it lit back there, behind us."

That was enough to send him off. She had to do this with enough real birds to keep him believing, however.

Edward sat down on the root of a tree and lit a cigarette. He had gone down the first side-path he'd come to; it smelled of piss, and he could see by the decomposing Kleenexes further along that this was one of the places people went when they couldn't make it back to the washroom behind the ticket counter.

He took off his glasses, then his hat, and wiped the sweat off his forehead. His face was red, he could feel it. Blushing, Sarah called it. She persisted in attributing it to shyness and boyish embarrassment; she hadn't yet deduced that it was simple rage. For someone so devious she was often incredibly stupid.

She didn't know, for instance, that he'd found out about her little trick with the birds at least three years ago. She'd pointed to a dead tree and said she saw a bird in it, but he himself had inspected that same tree only seconds earlier and there was nothing in it at all. And she was very careless: she described oriole-coloured birds behaving like kingbirds, woodpeckers where there would never be any woodpeckers, mute jays, neck-less herons. She must have decided he was a total idiot and any slipshod invention would do.

But why not, since he appeared to fall for it every time? And why did he do it, why did he chase off after her imaginary birds, pretending he believed her? It was partly that although he knew what she was doing to him, he had no idea why. It couldn't be simple malice, she had enough outlets for that. He didn't want to know the real reason, which loomed in his mind as something formless, threatening and final. Her lie about the birds was one of the many lies that propped things up. He was afraid to confront her, that would be the end, all the pretences would come crashing down and they would be left standing in the rubble, staring at each other. There would be nothing left to say and Edward wasn't ready for that.

She would deny everything anyway. "What do you mean? Of course I saw it. It flew right over there. Why would I make up such a thing?" With her level gaze, blonde and stolid and immoveable as a rock.

Edward had a sudden image of himself, crashing out of the undergrowth like King Kong, picking Sarah up and hurling her over the edge, down into the sacrificial well. Anything to shatter that imperturbable expression, bland and pale and plump and smug, like a Flemish Madonna's. Self-righteous, that's what it was. Nothing was ever her fault. She hadn't been like that when he'd met her. But it wouldn't work: as she fell she would glance at him, not with fear but with maternal irritation, as if he'd spilled chocolate milk on a white tablecloth. And she'd pull her skirt down. She was concerned for appearances, always.

Though there would be something inappropriate about throwing Sarah into the sacrificial well, just as she was, with all her clothes on. He remembered snatches from the several books he'd read before they came down. (And that was another thing: Sarah didn't believe in reading up on places beforehand. "Don't you want to understand what you're looking at?" he'd asked her. "I'll see the same thing in any case, won't I?" she said. "I mean, knowing all those facts doesn't change the actual statue or whatever." Edward found this attitude infuriating;

and now that they were here, she resisted his attempts to explain things to her by her usual passive method of pretending not to hear.

("That's a Chac-Mool, see that? That round thing on the stomach held the bowl where they put the hearts, and the butterfly on the head means the soul flying up to the sun.")

("Could you get out the suntan lotion, Edward? I think it's in the tote bag, in the left-hand pocket.")

And he would hand her the suntan lotion, defeated once again.)

No, she wouldn't be a fit sacrifice, with or without lotion. They only threw people in—or perhaps they jumped in, of their own free will—for the water god, to make it rain and ensure fertility. The drowned were messengers, sent to carry requests to the god. Sarah would have to be purified first, in the stone sweat-house beside the well. Then, naked, she would kneel before him, one arm across her breast in the attitude of submission. He added some ornaments: a gold necklace with a jade medallion, a gold circlet adorned with feathers. Her hair, which she usually wore in a braid coiled at the back of her head, would be hanging down. He thought of her body, which he made slimmer and more taut, with an abstract desire which was as unrelated as he could make it to Sarah herself. This was the only kind of desire he could feel for her any more: he had to dress her up before he could make love to her at all. He thought about their earlier days, before they'd married. It was almost as if he'd had an affair with another woman, she had been so different. He'd treated her body then as something holy, a white-and-gold chalice, to be touched with care and tenderness. And she had liked this; even though she was two years older than he was and much more experienced she hadn't minded his awkwardness and reverence, she hadn't laughed at him. Why had she changed?

Sometimes he thought it was the baby, which had died at birth. At the time he'd urged her to have another right away, and she'd said yes, but nothing had happened. It wasn't something they talked about. "Well, that's that," she said in the hospital afterwards. A perfect child, the doctor said; a freak accident, one of those things that happen. She'd never gone back to university either and she wouldn't get a job. She sat at home, tidying the apartment, looking over his shoulder, towards the door, out the window, as if she was waiting for something.

Sarah bowed her head before him. He, in the feathered costume and long-nosed, toothed mask of the high priest, sprinkled her with blood drawn with thorns from his own tongue and penis. Now he was supposed to give her the message to take to the god. But he couldn't think of anything he wanted to ask for.

And at the same time he thought: what a terrific idea for a Grade Six special project! He'd have them build scale models of the temples, he'd show the slides he'd taken, he'd bring in canned tortillas and tamales for a Mexican lunch, he'd have them make little Chac-Mools out of papier-mâché . . . and the ball game where the captain of the losing team had his head cut off, that would appeal to them, they were bloodthirsty at that age. He could see himself up there in front of them, pouring out his own enthusiasm, gesturing, posturing, acting it out for them, and their response. Yet afterwards he knew he would be depressed. What were his special projects anyway but a substitute for television, something to keep them entertained? They liked him because he danced for them, a funny puppet, inexhaustible and a little absurd. No wonder Sarah despised him.

Edward stepped on the remains of his cigarette. He put his hat back on, a wide-brimmed white hat Sarah had bought for him at the market. He had wanted one with a narrower brim, so he could look up through his binoculars without the hat getting in his way; but she'd told him he would look like an American golfer. It was always there, that gentle, patronizing mockery.

He would wait long enough to be plausible; then he would go back.

· ·

Sarah was speculating about how she would be doing this whole trip if Edward had conveniently died. It wasn't that she wished him dead, but she couldn't imagine any other way for him to disappear. He was omnipresent, he pervaded her life like a kind of smell; it was hard for her to think or act except in reference to him. So she found it harmless and pleasant to walk herself through the same itinerary they were following now, but with Edward removed, cut neatly out of the picture. Not that she would be here at all if it wasn't for him. She would prefer to lie in a deck chair in, say, Acapulco, and drink cooling drinks. She threw in a few dark young men in bathing suits, but took them out: that would be too complicated and not relaxing. She had often thought about cheating on Edward—somehow it would serve him right, though she wasn't sure what for—but she had never actually done it. She didn't know anyone suitable, any more.

Suppose she was here, then, with no Edward. She would stay at a better hotel, for one thing. One that had a plug in the sink; they had not yet stayed in a hotel with a plug. Of course that would cost more money, but she thought of herself as having more money if Edward were dead: she would have all of his salary instead of just part of it. She knew there wouldn't be any salary if he really were dead, but it spoiled the fantasy to remember this. And she would travel on planes, if possible, or first-class buses, instead of the noisy, crowded second-class ones he insisted on taking. He said you saw more of the local colour that way and there was no point going to another country if you spent all your time with other tourists. In theory she agreed with this, but the buses gave her headaches and she could do without the closeup tour of squalor, the miserable thatched or thin-roofed huts, the turkeys and tethered pigs.

He applied the same logic to restaurants. There was a perfectly nice one in the village where they were staying, she'd seen it from the bus and it didn't look that expensive; but no, they had to eat in a seedy linoleum-tiled hutch, with plastic-covered tablecloths. They were the only customers in the place Behind them four adolescent boys were playing dominoes and

151

drinking beer, with a lot of annoying laughter, and some smaller children watched television, a program that Sarah realized was a re-run of *The Cisco Kid*, with dubbed voices.

On the bar beside the television set there was a crèche, with three painted plaster Wise Men, one on an elephant, the others on camels. The first Wise Man was missing his head. Inside the stable a stunted Joseph and Mary adored an enormous Christ Child which was more than half as big as the elephant. Sarah wondered how the Mary could possibly have squeezed out this colossus; it made her uncomfortable to think about it. Beside the crèche was a Santa Claus haloed with flashing lights, and beside that a radio in the shape of Fred Flintstone, which was playing American popular songs, all of them ancient.

"Oh someone help me, help me, plee-ee-ee-eeze . . ."

"Isn't that Paul Anka?" Sarah asked.

But this wasn't the sort of thing Edward could be expected to know. He launched into a defence of the food, the best he'd had in Mexico, he said. Sarah refused to give him the consolation of her agreement. She found the restaurant even more depressing than it should have been, especially the crèche. It was painful, like a cripple trying to walk, one of the last spastic gestures of a religion no one, surely, could believe in much longer.

Another group of tourists was coming up the path behind her, Americans by the sound of them. The guide was Mexican, though. He scrambled up onto the altar, preparing to give his spiel.

"Don't go too near the edge, now."

"Who me, I'm afraid of heights. What d'you see down there?"

"Water, what am I supposed to see?"

The guide clapped his hands for attention. Sarah only half-listened: she didn't really want to know anything more about it.

"Before, people said they threw nothing but virgins in here," the guide began. "How they could tell that, I do not know. It is always hard to tell." He waited for the expected laughter, which came. "But this is not true. Soon, I will tell you how we have found this out. Here we have the altar to the rain god Tlaloc . . ."

Two women sat down near Sarah. They were both wearing cotton slacks, high-heeled sandals and wide-brimmed straw hats.

"You go up the big one?"

"Not on your life. I made Alf go up, I took a picture of him at the top."

"What beats me is why they built all those things in the first place."

"It was their religion, that's what he said."

"Well, at least it would keep people busy."

"Solve the unemployment problem." They both laughed.

"How many more of these ruins is he gonna make us walk around?"

"Beats me. I'm about ruined out. I'd rather go back and sit on the bus."

"I'd rather go shopping. Not that there's much to buy."

Sarah, listening, suddenly felt indignant. Did they have no respect? The sentiments weren't that far from her own of a moment ago, but to hear them from these women, one of whom had a handbag decorated with tasteless straw flowers, made her want to defend the well.

"Nature is very definitely calling," said the woman with the handbag. "I couldn't get in before, there was such a lineup."

"Take a Kleenex," the other woman said. "There's no paper. Not only that, you just about have to wade in. There's water all over the floor."

"Maybe I'll just duck into the bushes," the first woman said.

Edward stood up and massaged his left leg, which had gone to sleep. It was time to go back. If he stayed away too long, Sarah would be querulous, despite the fact that it was she herself who had sent him off on this fool's expedition.

He started to walk back along the path. But then there was a flash of orange, at the corner of his eye. Edward swivelled and raised his binoculars. They were there when you least expected it. It was an oriole, partly hidden behind the leaves; he could see the breast, bright orange, and the dark barred wing. He wanted it to be a hooded oriole, he had not yet seen one.

He talked to it silently, begging it to come out into the open. It was strange the way birds were completely magic for him the first time only, when he had never seen them before. But there were hundreds of kinds he would never see; no matter how many he saw there would always be one more. Perhaps this was why he kept looking. The bird was hopping further away from him, into the foliage. *Come back*, he called to it wordlessly, but it was gone.

Edward was suddenly happy. Maybe Sarah hadn't been lying to him after all, maybe she had really seen this bird. Even if she hadn't, it had come anyway, in answer to his need for it. Edward felt he was allowed to see birds only when they wanted him to, as if they had something to tell him, a secret, a message. The Aztecs thought hummingbirds were the souls of dead warriors, but why not all birds, why just warriors? Or perhaps they were the souls of the unborn, as some believed. "A jewel, a precious feather," they called an unborn baby, according to *The Daily Life of the Aztecs*. *Quetzal*, that was *feather*.

"This is the bird I want to see," Sarah said when they were looking through *The Birds of Mexico* before coming down.

"The Resplendent Quetzal," Edward said. It was a green-and-red bird with spectacular iridescent-blue tail plumes. He explained to her that Quetzal Bird meant Feather Bird. "I don't think we're likely to see it," he said. He looked up the habitat. "*Cloud forests*. I don't think we'll be in any cloud forests."

"Well, that's the one I want," Sarah said. "That's the only one I want."

Sarah was always very determined about what she wanted and what she didn't want. If there wasn't anything on a restaurant menu that appealed to her, she would refuse to order anything; or she would permit him to order for her and then pick around the edges, as she had last night. It was no use telling her that this was the best meal they'd had since coming. She never lost her temper or her self-possession, but she was stubborn. Who but Sarah, for instance, would have insisted on bringing a collapsible umbrella to Mexico in the dry season?

He'd argued and argued, pointing out its uselessness and the extra weight, but she'd brought it anyway. And then yesterday afternoon it had rained, a real cloudburst. Everyone else had run for shelter, huddling against walls and inside the temple doorways, but Sarah had put up her umbrella and stood under it, smugly. This had infuriated him. Even when she was wrong, she always managed, somehow, to be right. If only just once she would admit . . . what? That she could make mistakes. This was what really disturbed him: her assumption of infallibility.

And he knew that when the baby had died she had blamed it on him. He still didn't know why. Perhaps it was because he'd gone out for cigarettes, not expecting it to be born so soon. He wasn't there when she was told; she'd had to take the news alone.

"It was nobody's fault," he told her repeatedly. "Not the doctor's, not yours. The cord was twisted."

"I know," she said, and she had never accused him; nevertheless he could feel the reproach, hanging around her like a fog. As if there was anything he could have done.

"I wanted it as much as you did," he told her. And this was true. He hadn't thought of marrying Sarah at all, he'd never mentioned it because it had never occurred to him she would agree, until she told him she was pregnant. Up until that time, she had been the one in control; he was sure he was just an amusement for her. But the marriage hadn't been her suggestion, it had been his. He'd dropped out of Theology, he'd taken his public-school teaching certificate that summer in order to support them. Every evening he had massaged her belly, feeling the child move, touching it through her skin. To him it was a sacred thing, and he included her in his worship. In the sixth month, when she had taken to lying on her back, she had begun to snore, and he would lie awake at night listening to these gentle snores, white and silver they seemed to him, almost songs, mysterious talismans. Unfortunately Sarah had retained this habit, but he no longer felt the same way about it.

When the child had died, he was the one who had cried, not

Sarah. She had never cried. She got up and walked around almost immediately, she wanted to get out of the hospital as quickly as possible. The baby clothes she'd been buying disappeared from the apartment; he never found out what she'd done with them, he'd been afraid to ask.

Since that time he'd come to wonder why they were still married. It was illogical. If they'd married because of the child and there was no child, and there continued to be no child, why didn't they separate? But he wasn't sure he wanted this. Maybe he was still hoping something would happen, there would be another child. But there was no use demanding it. They came when they wanted to, not when you wanted them to. They came when you least expected it. A jewel, a precious feather.

"Now I will tell you," said the guide. "The archæologists have dived down into the well. They have dredged up more than fifty skeletons, and they have found that some of them were not virgins at all but men. Also, most of them were children. So as you can see, that is the end of the popular legend." He made an odd little movement from the top of the altar, almost like a bow, but there was no applause. "They do not do these things to be cruel," he continued. "They believe these people will take a message to the rain god, and live forever in his paradise at the bottom of the well."

The woman with the handbag got up. "Some paradise," she said to her friend. "I'm starting back. You coming?"

In fact the whole group was moving off now, in the scattered way they had. Sarah waited until they had gone. Then she opened her purse and took out the plaster Christ Child she had stolen from the crèche the night before. It was inconceivable to her that she had done such a thing, but there it was, she really had.

She hadn't planned it beforehand. She'd been standing beside the crèche while Edward was paying the bill, he'd had to go into the kitchen to do it as they were very slow about bringing it to the table. No one was watching her: the domino-playing boys were absorbed in their game and the children were riveted to the television. She'd just suddenly reached out her hand, past the Wise Men and through the door of the stable, picked the child up and put it into her purse.

She turned it over in her hands. Separated from the dwarfish Virgin and Joseph, it didn't look quite so absurd. Its diaper was cast as part of it, more like a tunic, it had glass eyes and a sort of pageboy haircut, quite long for a newborn. A perfect child, except for the chip out of the back, luckily where it would not be noticed. Someone must have dropped it on the floor.

You could never be too careful. All the time she was pregnant, she'd taken meticulous care of herself, counting out the vitamin pills prescribed by the doctor and eating only what the books recommended. She had drunk four glasses of milk a day, even though she hated milk. She had done the exercises and gone to the classes. No one would be able to say she had not done the right things. Yet she had been disturbed by the thought that the child would be born with something wrong, it would be a mongoloid or a cripple, or a hydrocephalic with a huge liquid head like the ones she'd seen taking the sun in their wheelchairs on the lawn of the hospital one day. But the child had been perfect.

She would never take that risk, go through all that work again. Let Edward strain his pelvis till he was blue in the face; "trying again," he called it. She took the pill every day, without telling him. She wasn't going to try again. It was too much for anyone to expect of her.

What had she done wrong? She hadn't done anything wrong, that was the trouble. There was nothing and no one to blame, except, obscurely, Edward; and he couldn't be blamed for the child's death, just for not being there. Increasingly since that time he had simply absented himself. When she no longer had the child inside her he had lost interest, he had deserted her. This, she realized, was what she resented most about him. He had left her alone with the corpse, a corpse for which there was no explanation.

"Lost," people called it. They spoke of her as having lost the child, as though it was wandering around looking for her, crying plaintively, as though she had neglected it or misplaced it somewhere. But where? What limbo had it gone to, what watery paradise? Sometimes she felt as if there had been some mistake, the child had not been born yet. She could still feel it moving, ever so slightly, holding on to her from the inside.

Sarah placed the baby on the rock beside her. She stood up, smoothing out the wrinkles in her skirt. She was sure there would be more flea bites when she got back to the hotel. She picked up the child and walked slowly towards the well, until she was standing at the very brink.

Edward, coming back up the path, saw Sarah at the well's edge, her arms raised above her head. My God, he thought, she's going to jump. He wanted to shout to her, tell her to stop, but he was afraid to startle her. He could run up behind her, grab her . . . but she would hear him. So he waited, paralyzed, while Sarah stood immobile. He expected her to hurtle downwards, and then what would he do? But she merely drew back her right arm and threw something into the well. Then she turned, half stumbling, towards the rock where he had left her and crouched down.

"Sarah," he said. She had her hands over her face; she didn't lift them. He kneeled so he was level with her. "What is it? Are you sick?"

She shook her head. She seemed to be crying, behind her hands, soundlessly and without moving. Edward was dismayed. The ordinary Sarah, with all her perversity, was something he could cope with, he'd invented ways of coping. But he was unprepared for this. She had always been the one in control.

"Come on," he said, trying to disguise his desperation, "you need some lunch, you'll feel better." He realized as he said this how fatuous it must sound, but for once there was no patronizing smile, no indulgent answer.

"This isn't like you," Edward said, pleading, as if that was a final argument which would snap her out of it, bring back the old calm Sarah.

Sarah took her hands away from her face, and as she did so Edward felt cold fear. Surely what he would see would be the face of someone else, someone entirely different, a woman he had never seen before in his life. Or there would be no face at all. But (and this was almost worse) it was only Sarah, looking much as she always did.

She took a Kleenex out of her purse and wiped her nose. It is like me, she thought. She stood up and smoothed her skirt once more, then collected her purse and her collapsible umbrella.

"I'd like an orange," she said. "They have them, across from the ticket office. I saw them when we came in. Did you find your bird?"

Training

It must have taken Rob several minutes to notice that the sun was in her eyes. When he did notice, because she was squinting, he moved her sideways a little so she could see better. He felt the padded arms of the chair, where her thin bare arms were kept at rest by the leather straps, to make sure they were not overheated. She should have a hat, they were always being warned about sunburn. So far it had always been sunny during the day, though there had been a thunderstorm the night before. But no hat had been wheeled out with her.

"They forgot your hat," he said to her. "That was stupid of them, wasn't it?" Then he offered her another piece of the wooden puzzle, giving her time to consider it and to look also at the half-finished puzzle on the tray.

"This way?" he said. He watched her left hand for the slight movement towards him that would say *yes*. It was one of the few controlled movements she could make.

He also watched her eyes and face. She could move her eyes, though her head jerked around like a hooked fish if she tried to swivel it too fast. But she had little control of the muscles of her face, so he could never tell if she was trying to smile or whether the contortion of her mouth was caused by the spontaneous knotting and unknotting of her jumpy flesh, the body that would not respond to the enormous will he saw, or thought he saw, sealed up in her eyes like some small fierce animal captured in a metal net. She couldn't get out! She was strapped into the wheelchair, prisoned in her cage of braces, trays, steel wheels, but only because she was strapped into her own body as into some bumpy, sickening carnival ride. Let out of her chair, she would thrash, topple, flail, hurtle through space. It was one of the worst cases they'd ever taken, Pam the physiotherapist had told him.

But everyone agreed she was bright, very bright; it was amazing really what she could do. She could say *yes* by moving her left hand, and therefore she could play games, answer questions, indicate what she wanted. It just needed more work than usual on the part of the counsellor, and you had to do a lot of guessing. It took time, but after she had beaten him twice in a row at chequers, with no collusion on his part, Rob was willing to spend the time. He wondered about teaching her to play chess. But there were too many pieces, too many moves, a game would take weeks. He thought of her, sitting impatiently inside her body, waiting for him to get to the piece she wanted to move and figure out where she wanted to move it.

She hadn't said anything. He turned the puzzle piece around. *Yes*, her hand said immediately, and he fitted it in. It was a giraffe, two giraffes, a funny-animal picture, a caricature. It struck him that she might not know what a giraffe was; she might never have seen a real one or even a picture of one.

"Is this puzzle boring?" he asked her. *Yes*, she said.

"How about a game of chequers?"

That was fine with her. "Okay, killer," he said, "but this time I'm going to beat you." Her blue eyes stared at him; her mouth wavered. He wished she could smile. He wheeled her off to get out the chequers and return the puzzle.

It was her brightness that fascinated him. It was amazing, but it was horrible too, that mind trapped and strangling. Maybe she was a genius; who could ever tell? Surely she knew things and could sense things that would escape other people. When she looked at him with her ice-blue eyes, clear and cold, hard like mint candies, it was as if she could see into him, past the desperately cheerful kind-uncle act he knew was only an act. He had to be careful what he thought about when he was with her. She would pick it up, and for some reason it mattered what she felt about him.

Sometimes he thought she would be better off if she were like some of the others. The hydrocephalics, for instance, with their watery pumpkin heads and infant's bodies; there were three of them at the camp right now, and they could all talk, but they weren't very bright. Or the muscular dystrophy cases, who looked so normal the first time you saw them, slumped in their wheelchairs, wan and limp as orphans. They would be dead soon; some of them would be dead even before the next summer. Rob found the camp song so painful he could not bring himself to sing it.

> Where do you find the girls and boys
> Who grow to be women and men?
> Eff ay eye ar
> EE—ee—dee-ee en!

The tune was the Mickey Mouse song, which made it worse for Rob by conjuring up an image of the Mouseketeers, those plump, pert children with functional arms and legs who had chosen to use their normal, beautiful bodies for *that*, for prancing and jiggling and acting on television. He would stand looking down, looking away, looking anywhere but at the rows of doomed children ranged in the auditorium, brought there so Bert the Assistant Director could finger his accordion and generate what he called "camp spirit." But the children sang the song with gusto. They liked to sing. Those who could clapped their hands.

Jordan could not clap. But on the other hand, she would live a long time. You didn't die from what she had. She was only nine years old.

GAMES was in the right-hand half of the cabin nearest the main house. The front window had been enlarged and fitted with an awning, a wooden shutter for when it rained and a counter. Jo-Anne Johnson, who had the shift this week, was sitting behind the counter on a high stool, reading a paperback. She was wearing a white terry T-shirt with an anchor on the left breast and red short-shorts, and she had her legs crossed. Rob looked at the line on her thigh where the tan ended, then switched to the shelves behind her where the volleyballs and baseball bats were stored. She had brown hair, in a pony-tail held with a gold clip, and tortoise-shell sunglasses. When she walked she limped a little. She was one of the former campers who had come back as a counsellor. Rob thought of her as a nice girl; at least she was always nice to him.

"We'd like to exchange this puzzle," he told her. "We'd like to get out some chequers."

"Chequers again, eh?" she said. "You must be sick of chequers. That's the fourth time this week."

Rob didn't like the way some people talked in front of Jordan as if she couldn't hear. "Oh no," he said. "I'm playing Jordan. She's beaten me twice."

Jo-Anne smiled at him as if they shared a secret. Then she smiled down at Jordan, who stared back at her, not moving much. "Yes, I've heard she's a real whiz," she said. She crossed out the puzzle in the lined notebook on the counter and wrote in the chequer set opposite his name. "See you later," she said. "Have a good game."

"Let's find some shade," Rob said to Jordan. He wheeled her along the cement pathway, beside the row of cabins. The cabins were white, neat, identical. Each one had a front ramp instead of a doorstep; inside them were the special beds, the special toilets, and the curious smell that was not like the smell of children but was sweeter, heavier and more humid, and reminded him of a greenhouse. A smell of warm earth and baby powder, of things mouldering slightly. Of course there was always a lot of laundry, sitting in bags, waiting to be taken away. Some of the children wore diapers, grotesque when you saw them on a twelve-year-old. In the mornings, before the beds had been changed, the smell was stronger. It took a long time to get everyone ready for the day. The girl counsellors were forbidden to lift the children out of the beds or out of the wheelchairs; only the boys could do that. Rob lifted his own cabin and two girls' cabins, Number Seven and Number Eight, Jordan's cabin. With her Dutch-boy haircut and tough wilful little face, she looked out of place in the frilled pink nightgowns they put on her. He wondered if she were ever allowed to help choose her own clothes.

They reached the corner of the walk and turned left. From the open windows of the auditorium, which doubled as a gym, came the sound of recorded music and a woman's voice: "No, back to your places and try again. You can do it, Susie." Now they had reached the end of the boys' side. The girls' side was across the central field, where there was a baseball game going on, as there had been the day he had arrived. The camp van had stopped in the circular driveway. From the front, the main house could have been a rich man's mansion, and in fact it once had been. Some figures that looked at first like grandmothers in rocking chairs were placed at intervals along the wide verandah. The Director had greeted them and had deputized Bert to give them the tour for new counsellors. Around the corner was the baseball game, and Rob had thought, Well, it's not going to be so bad, because from a distance, on the green field, in the full sunlight that seemed to have been shining ever since, the game had seemed almost normal.

The strange thing about it was the silence. Boys that age ought to be shouting, that was part of the game; but games here were played with quiet concentration. These were mostly children who could walk, with the aid of braces or crutches; some could even run. But a few of the players were double, one boy being pushed around the bases in a wheelchair by another. Rob knew from having played that the games were conducted with a politeness and consideration that he found eerie. During baseball games these children behaved as adults were always telling children to behave. The only noisy one at the moment was Bert, the umpire, who was waving his arms and yelling encouragement as Dave Snider, paralyzed by polio from the waist down, knocked the ball straight out past second base.

Two outfielders on crutches hobbled after it while Dave spun onto first.

Rob knew he should be volunteering for more sports and supervision, but he wanted to spend the time with Jordan. Besides, he hated baseball. It was his family's game, the one he was expected to excel at as a matter of course, just as he was expected to become a doctor. His father was the one who insisted on the games, with some echo in his mind perhaps of the golden Kennedys, as featured recently in *Life* magazine playing touch football. Joseph Kennedy and his three fine boys. His father wore a T-shirt with CHAMP on it, given to him by his mother. His two older brothers were good players, and so were the Miller boys. Dr. Miller was a surgeon, too, like his father; they had the place next door. His father did hearts, Dr. Miller did brains, and both of the Miller boys were going to be doctors, too.

They played on the beach, and for Rob the sense of hopelessness and failure that went with these games went also with blue skies, full sunlight and waves breaking on sand. These things, that for other people meant carefree vacations, meant for him an almost intolerable bondage. To refuse to play would have been unthinkable. If he'd been a better player, he would have been able to say he didn't feel like a game, but, as it was, the cries of spoilsport and poor loser would have been too truthful. No one held it against him that he was so wretched a player, that he could barely hit the ball, because of his bad eyesight perhaps, the sunlight glinting into his eyes from the frames of his glasses, that he would not see the ball when it came hurtling towards him out of the sizzling blue sky like an assassin's bomb, numbing his fingers when he raised his hands to fend it off, knocking him on the head or neck, or, even more humiliating, ignoring him so completely so that he had to run after it, chase it down the beach or into the lake. His family treated him as a joke, even, and especially, his mother. "What did you hurt today?" she would ask him, as she doled out the snacks afterwards on the patio deck above the boathouse, sandwiches and Cokes for the boys, beers for the men. In the city his father drank Scotch, but at the cottage, which he called his "summer place," he drank beer. The others would tell funny stories about Rob's blunderings, his losing duels with the demonic white ball, while he would grin. The grin was obligatory, to show he was a good sport and didn't mind. "You have to be able to take it," his father was fond of saying, without being too specific about what *it* was. He also said, after almost every game, that competitive sports were good for you because they taught you how to handle failure. Rob knew his father was only trying to make him feel better; nevertheless, he felt like answering that he'd had enough practice at that and he wouldn't mind being taught how to handle success.

But he had to be careful about saying things like that. "He's the sensitive one," his mother was in the habit of telling her friends, half proud, half rueful. Her favourite picture of him was the one in his choirboy surplice, taken the year before his voice cracked. His oldest brother was supposed to be the handsome one, his middle brother was the smart one, Rob was the sensitive one. For this reason it was necessary, he knew, to appear as insensitive as possible. Lately he had begun to succeed, and his mother was now complaining that he never talked to her any more. He found even her moments of solicitous interest painful.

She trusted the others to make their own way, but she didn't trust him, and secretly Rob agreed with her estimate. He knew he could never be a doctor, although he felt he wanted to. He wanted to be good at baseball too, but he wasn't, and all he could see ahead for himself at Medical School was catastrophe. How to confess that even the drawings in his father's medical books, those interiors of bodies abstract as plaster models, made him queasy, that he'd actually fainted—though no one knew, because he'd been lying down anyway—when he'd given blood this year at the clinic and had seen for the first time the hot purple worm of his own blood inching through the clear tube across his bare arm? His father thought it was a great treat for his boys to be allowed into the observation bubble at the hospital while he was doing open heart surgery, but Rob was unable to turn down the offer or admit his nausea. (*Red rubber, it's only red rubber,* he would repeat to himself over and over, closing his eyes when his brothers weren't watching.) He would come away from these ordeals with his knees jellied and his palms scored with the marks of his jagged, bitten nails. He couldn't do it, he could never do it.

James, the handsome one, was already interning, and the family made jokes at the Sunday dinner table about pretty nurses. Adrian was cleaning up the top marks in third year. Both of them fit so easily into the definitions that had been provided for them. And who was he supposed to be, what had been left over for him when they were dishing out the roles? The bumbling third son in a fairy tale, with no princess and no good luck. But friendly and generous, kind to old women and dwarves in the forest. He despised his own generosity, which he felt was mostly cowardice.

Rob was supposed to go into Pre-Meds in the fall, and dutifully he would do it. But sooner or later he would be forced to drop out, and what then? He saw himself on top of a boxcar like some waif from the thirties, penniless, fleeing his family's disappointment, heading for some form of oblivion so foreign to him he could not even picture it. But there was no one he could talk to about his knowledge of his own doom. A year ago his father had taken him aside for the pep-talk Rob was sure he'd had with both of the others. Medicine wasn't just a job, he told Rob. It was a calling, a vocation. One of the noblest things a man could do was to dedicate his life selflessly to the saving of others. His father's eyes gleamed piously: was Rob worthy? (Speedboat, Rob thought, summer place on the bay, two cars, Forest Hill house.) "Your grandfather was a doctor," his father said, as if this was the clincher. His grandfather had been a doctor, but he'd been a country doctor, driving a sleigh and team through blizzards to deliver babies. They had often heard these heroic stories. "He wasn't very good at collecting his bills," Rob's father would say, shaking his head with a mixture of admiration and indulgent contempt. This was not one of his own weaknesses. "During the Depression we lived on chickens; the farmers gave them to us instead of money. I had only one pair of shoes." Rob thought of the shoe rack that ran the length of his father's triple-doored closet, the twinkling shoes arranged on it like testimonials.

He would not be able to take the scene when they found out, he would just disappear. He thought of the final catastrophe as happening in a classroom. They would all be dissecting a cadaver, and he would suddenly begin to scream. He would run out of the room and down the corridor, reeking of formaldehyde, he would forget his coat and the galoshes that were a fetish of his mother's, it would be snowing. He would wake up the next morning in a greenish-grey hotel room, with no recollection of what he had done.

It was his family who had chosen this job, this camp. They felt it would be good practice for him to spend the summer with crippled children; it would be part of the *it* he had to learn to take. His father knew the Director, and it was all arranged before Rob was told about it. His father and mother had been so enthusiastic, so full of their sense of the wonderful opportunity they'd arranged for him, how could he refuse? "Use your powers of observation," his father had said to him at the train station. "I wish I'd had this chance when I was your age."

For the first week Rob had had nightmares. The dreams were of bodies, pieces of bodies, arms and legs and torsos, detached and floating in mid-air; or he would feel he couldn't move, couldn't breathe, and he would wake up with his skin wet from effort. He found the sight of the children, especially the younger ones, unbearably painful, and he didn't understand how the other staff members could go around all day with expressions of such bluff professional cheer. Except that he did it himself. Though apparently with less success than he'd thought, since Pam the physiotherapist had come over to sit beside him in the staff lounge after the second-day orientation meeting. She had dull blonde hair held back by a velvet band that matched the blue of her plaid Bermuda shorts. She was pretty, but Rob felt she had too many teeth. Too many and too solid. "It's rough working with kids like this," she said, "but it's so rewarding." Rob nodded dutifully: what did she mean, rewarding? He still felt sick to his stomach. He'd been on shift for dinner that evening, and he could barely stand the milk dribbling from the bent plastic feeding tubes, the chair trays splattered with food ("Let them do as much for themselves as they can"), the slurps and suction noises. Pam lit a cigarette and Rob watched the red fingernails on her strong, competent hands. "It doesn't do *them* any good for you to be depressed," she said. "They'll use it against you. A lot of them don't know the difference. They've never been any other way." She was going to do this for a living, she was going to do this for the rest of her life! "You'll get used to it," she said, and patted his arm in a way that Rob found insulting. She's trying to be nice, he corrected himself quickly.

"I know your brother James," she said, smiling again with her solid teeth. "I met him on a double-date. He's quite the boy."

Rob excused himself and got up. She was older than him anyway, she was probably twenty.

But she'd been right, he was getting used to it. The nightmares had gone away, though not before he'd aroused the interest of the boys in his cabin. They nicknamed him "The Groaner." They had nicknames for everyone in the camp.

"Hey, ya hear The Groaner last night?"

"Yeah. *Uh. Uh.* Getting his rocks off good."

"Ya have a good time, Groaner?"

Rob, blushing, would mumble, "I was having a nightmare," but they would hoot with laughter.

"Oh yeah. *We* heard ya. Wish I had nightmares like that." They were the oldest boys' cabin, fourteen- to sixteen-year-olds, and he'd had trouble with them from the first. They weren't like the younger children, polite, eager to enjoy themselves in whatever way they could, grateful for help. Instead they were cynical about the camp, about the Director, about Bert (whom they nicknamed "Bert the Nert") and about themselves and their lives. They drank beer, when they could get hold of it; they smoked furtive cigarettes. They kept girlie magazines hidden under their mattresses, and they told some of the foulest jokes Rob had ever heard. They divided the world into two camps, the "crips" and the "norms," and for the most part they accepted only the crips. The norms were seen as their oppressors, the dimwits who would never understand, who would never get it right, and whom it was their duty to war against and exploit. It gave them a bitter pleasure to outrage norm and sensibility whenever possible, and they'd found Rob an easy target.

"Hey, Pete," Dave Snider would start. He'd be sitting in his chair, wearing one of the T-shirts with the cut-off arms that displayed his overdeveloped biceps to advantage. He had a Charles Atlas set at home, Rob knew, and subscribed to body-building magazines.

"Yeah, Dave?" Pete would answer. They both had classic ducktails, which they wore covered with grease. They found Rob's private-school English-style haircut ludicrous. Pete was paralyzed from the neck down, but he'd somehow gained second place in the cabin's pecking order. Dave combed his duck's ass for him.

"What's black and crawls and catches flies?"

"Roy Campanella!"

Raucous laughter, in which the rest of the cabin joined while Rob blushed. "I don't think that's very nice," he'd said the first time.

"He doesn't think it's very *nice*," Dave mimicked. "What weighs two thousand pounds and twitches?"

"Moby Spaz!"

They called these jokes "spaz jokes." What bothered Rob most about them was that they reminded him of the kinds of jokes his brothers and their medical-student friends would tell, having a game of pool in their father's rec room, to relax after classes ("Bring your friends over anytime, boys. You too, Rob.") Except that theirs were supposed to be true stories. They played endless practical jokes on each other, most of them involving parts of cadavers they would cut off during dissection: eyeballs in the teacup, hands in the coat pocket.

"Hey, we were doing this old guy, and I thought, What the hell, and I cut off his tool, it's all brown and shrivelled up, like they get, and I slipped it into my briefcase. So I go down to the Babloor, and I have a few beers, and I go into the can and I open my fly, but I stick this old boy's dork out instead of my own. So I stand there like I'm pissing, and I wait till another guy comes in, and I shake it and it comes off in my hand. So I throw it down and I say, 'Damn thing never worked anyway.' You should've seen the look on his face!"

They related rumours from Emergency at the hospital, most of which seemed to involve women with broken Coke bottles stuck in them or men who had been masturbating with the hot-water tap. "Had to get a plumber to saw him out. Came in with the tap still on and two feet of pipe." "I heard of one with a crayon. Got stuck in the bladder. He came in because he was pissing blue and he couldn't figure out why."

"I heard about one with a snake."

"Why do you tell those stories?" Rob asked them one night when he felt courageous.

"Why do you listen to them?" James grinned.

"You'll do it, too," Adrian told him. "Wait and see." Then, after the others had gone home, he said, more seriously, "You have to tell them. I know you think it's pretty gross, but you don't know what it's like. It's real life out there. You have to laugh or go crazy." Rob tried to reject this, but it haunted him. Real life would be too much for him, he would not be able to take it. He would not be able to laugh. He would go crazy. He would run out into the snow with no galoshes, he would vanish, he would be lost forever.

"What weighs two thousand pounds and has an exploding head?"

"Moby Hydrocephalic!"

"That's enough!" Rob said, trying to assert his authority.

"Look, Groaner," Dave said, "you're here to see we have a good time, right? Well, we're having a good time."

"Yeah," Pete said. "You don't like it, you can beat me up."

"Sure, go on," Dave said. "Do your Boy Scout good deed for the week. Kill a cripple." Bullying him with his own guilt.

It didn't help that the other counsellor, Gordon Holmes, encouraged them. He smuggled beer and cigarettes into the cabin for them, ogled their girlie magazines, and told them which of the girl counsellors were "easy outs."

"Hey, make out last night?" Dave would ask him in the morning.

"Not bad, not bad."

"She go down for ya?"

Gordon's secretive smile. Patting Old Spice on the back of his neck.

"Who was it, Pammer the Slammer?"

"Every time she pounds my back I get a bone on."

"Hey, was it Jo-Anne?"

"Naw, she's a crip. Gord wouldn't take out a crip, would ya, Gord?"

"You got to go along with them," Gordon told Rob. "Kid them a little. They're frustrated, they got normal emotions just like you and me." He punched Rob on the shoulder. "Take it easy, man, you think too much."

Gordon went to a public high school in East York. His mother and father were divorced and he lived with his mother, whom he called "the old lady." He'd got the job with the camp through the Big Brothers. He wasn't a juvenile delinquent, and Rob could think of many good points about him, but he couldn't bear to be around him for long. It did no good for Rob to tell himself that Gord would probably end up as a garage mechanic, that the kind of girls he talked about so freely were what his own mother would call "cheap," that he would get one of them pregnant and have to get married and end up in a dingy, overcrowded apartment, drinking beer in front of the TV while his wife nagged him about the laundry. He was envious anyway, listening despite himself to the sagas of back seats and forbidden mickeys at the drive-in, of heavy petting, forays into undergarments by Gord's daring fingers, triumphs over hostile elastic straps, conquests of breasts. He resented this sleazy freedom even though he knew he wouldn't enjoy it himself, wouldn't know what to say, or where to put his hands.

He himself had never taken out anyone but his mother's friends' daughters, pallid little girls who needed to be escorted to their own private-school dances and didn't know anyone else to ask. He bought them wrist corsages and steered them swiftly, correctly, around the floor in their dresses like layers of pastel toilet paper, their small wired bosoms pressing lightly into his chest, his hand against their backs feeling the rows of hooks that might conceivably be undone; but no, that would be too embarrassing. Though he'd sometimes felt his crotch tighten during the joyless fox-trots (he stood out the few chaste rock numbers the hired band would attempt), he hadn't liked any of these girls, though he tried to make sure they had a good time. He had even kissed one of them good night, because he felt she was expecting it. It was three years ago, when he was still wearing bands on his teeth. So was the girl, and when he'd kissed her harder than he'd intended, their teeth had locked painfully together, at her front door, in full view of the entire street. Anyone watching would have thought it was a passionate embrace, but he could still remember the panic in her eyes, though he'd repressed her name.

Rob turned Jordan right, onto the Nature Walk that ran in a meandering oval through the small woods behind the boys' cabins. It was paved, like all the other walks. The trees were labelled, and there was a little glass case at the far end of the oval where Bert the Nert, who was a nature buff, put a new exhibit every day. He'd taken Jordan on the Nature Walk several times before, stopping to read the labels on the trees, pointing out chipmunks and once a stray cat. Hardly anyone else seemed to go on it. He liked to wheel her along through the trees, whistling or singing songs to her. He wasn't shy about his voice when there was no one else but her, he even sang songs from Bert's repertoire that stuck in his throat when the assembled children sang them, led by red-faced Bert, his master-of-ceremonies smile, and his energetic accordion.

> Jordan River is chilly and cold,
> Hallelujah,
> Chills the body but not the soul,
> Hallelujah.

"Your name is the name of a famous river," he told her. He hoped she would be pleased by that. He wondered if her parents had known about her, about what she was going to be like, when they named her, and whether they'd felt later that the expensive-sounding name was wasted because she would never match it, never sip cocktails on a terrace or smile like Grace Kelly in cool lipstick. But they must have known; it said in her file that it was a birth defect. She had one brother and one sister, both normal, and her father was something in a bank.

Sometimes, thinking of the catastrophe ahead of him, his failure and his flight, he thought about taking her with him. That was her clinging to his neck as he scrambled up the boxcar (but she couldn't cling!), she was with him in the hotel room when he woke up, sitting in her chair (how had he got her there?), looking into his eyes with her icy blue ones, her face miraculously still. Then she would open her mouth and words would come out, she would stand up, he would somehow have cured her. Sometimes, very quickly (and he would repress it immediately), he would see both of them hurtling from the top of a building. An accident, an accident, he would tell himself. I don't mean that.

> "Jordan River is chilly and wide,
> Hallelujah,"

Rob crooned. He was heading for a bench, there was one up ahead, where he could sit and they could have their game of chequers.

"Hey, look at this." It was Bert's glass case. "*Shelf fungus*," he read from the typed card. "*There are several species of shelf fungus. The shelf fungus is a saprophyte which feeds on decaying vegetable matter and can often be found growing on dead trees.* You can write your name on the bottom with a stick," he said. He used to do that at the cottage, without removing the fungus from the tree, and it gave him pleasure to think of his name growing in secret, getting a little bigger every year. It was hard to tell whether or not she was interested.

He found the bench, turned Jordan to face it and unfolded the board. "I was red last time," he said, "so you get it this time, okay?" There was one chequer missing, on her side. "We'll use something else," he said. He looked around for a flat stone, but there wasn't one. Finally he pulled a button off his shirt-sleeve. "That okay?" he said.

Jordan's hand moved *yes*. He began the laborious trial-and-error process of determining how she wanted to move. He would point at each chequer in turn until she signalled. Then he would point to each possible square. They could get through a game a lot faster now that he was used to playing this way. Her face would fold and unfold, screw itself up, twitch, movements he found distressing in the other CP children still, but not in her. Concentrating made her worse.

They had hardly gone through the opening moves when the bell sounded from the main building. That meant the Play Period was over and it was time for the afternoon group activities. Jordan, he knew, had swimming with the rest of her cabin. She couldn't swim, but someone held her in the water, where her movements, they said, were more controlled than on land. He himself was supposed to help with Occupational Therapy. "Mud pies," the boys in his cabin called it. They liked making obscene statues out of clay in order to shock Wilda, the OT instructor, who wanted so much to be able to tell them they were being creative.

Rob put his shirt button into his pocket. He took out the notebook they used and marked down their respective positions. "We'll finish it tomorrow," he told Jordan. He wheeled her along the path in the same direction they'd been going, which would get them back sooner, since they were three-quarters of the way around the oval already.

To the north side of the cement path there was a clearing, a stretch of grass and across it the silver of water: the stream that was always there, usually a sluggish trickle but swollen now by last night's rain. Rob thought, She's probably never felt grass before, she's probably never had her hand in a real stream. He suddenly wanted to give her something that no one else ever had, that no one else would ever think of.

"I'm going to take you out," he told her. "I'm going to put you down on the grass, so you can feel it. Okay?"

There was a hesitation before she signalled *yes*. She was looking into his face; perhaps she didn't understand. "It's fun," he told her, "it feels nice," thinking of the many times he had sprawled on the lawn of the back garden eight or ten years ago, chewing on the white soft ends of grass blades and reading the almost-forbidden Captain Marvel comic books.

He unbuckled the straps that held her in and lifted her thin body. She was so light, lighter even than she looked, a creature of balsa wood and paper. But tough, he told himself. She could take it, you could see it in her eyes. He put her down on the grass, on her side, where she could see the flowing stream.

"There," he said. He knelt beside her, took her left hand and put it into the cold stream. "That's real water, not like a swimming pool." He smiled, feeling magnanimous, a giver, a healer; but she had closed her eyes, and from somewhere a curious sound, a whine, a growl . . . Her body was limp, her arm jerking; suddenly her leg shot out and her foot in its steel-crusted boot kicked him in the shin.

"Jordan," he said, "are you all right?" More growling: was it joy or terror? He couldn't tell, and he was frightened. Maybe this was too much for her, too exciting. He wrapped his arms around her, pulling her up to put her back into the chair. The grass had been damper than he'd thought, and the right side of her face was streaked with mud.

"What the hell are you doing with that child?" Pam's voice behind him. Rob turned, still holding Jordan, who was thrashing her arms like a propeller gone crazy. Pam was standing on the cement walk, hands on her hips, the posture of an accusing mother coming upon the children playing Doctor in the bushes. Her face was red, her hair mussed, as if she'd been running. There was a twig dangling above her ear.

"Nothing," Rob said, "I was just . . ." *She thinks I'm some kind of a pervert,* he saw, and felt himself blushing. "I thought she would like to see what the grass felt like," he said.

"You know that's dangerous," Pam said. "You know she isn't

supposed to be taken out. She could hit her head, injure herself."

"I was watching her the whole time," Rob said. Who was she to be bossing him around like this?

"I think you spend far too much time with that child," Pam said, less angry now but definitely not convinced by his explanation. "You should spend more time with some of the others. It's not good for *them*, you know, forming . . . attachments . . . that can't possibly be kept up after camp." Jordan's eyes were open now; she was looking at Rob.

"What the hell are you talking about?" Rob said, almost shouting. "How do *you* know, you don't know . . ." She was accusing him, in advance, of betraying Jordan, abandoning her.

"Don't get your girdle in a knot about it," Pam said. "But I think you should have a word with Bert, after Staff Lounge tonight. I've discussed this problem with him already."

She turned away from him and walked quickly off towards the main house. On the back of her Bermuda shorts there was a small patch of wet mud.

Rob buckled Jordan back into the chair. *This problem.* Why was it a problem? There wasn't much time, he would be assigned to other children, discouraged from seeing her, and she would think . . . What could he say to her, how convince her? He knelt in front of her, resting his arms on the chair tray, and took hold of her left hand.

"I'm sorry if it frightened you, being on the ground," he said. "Did it?" Her left hand did not move. "Don't pay any attention to what Pam just said. I'm going to write you letters after camp, lots of letters." Would he? "And someone at your house can read them to you." But of course they might forget, or lose the letters. In Pre-Meds, dissecting corpses, would he have time to remember her? Her eyes watched his face. She could see through him.

"I'm going to give you something special," he told her, casting around desperately for something to give. He searched his pocket with his free hand. "This is my button, and it's magic. I wore it on my shirt cuff like that just to keep it disguised." He placed it in her hand, folded the fingers around it. "I'm giving it to you, and whenever you see it . . . ." No, that wouldn't do; someone was bound to find it in her pocket and throw it out, and she would have no way of explaining. "You don't even have to see it, because it's invisible sometimes. All you have to do is think about it. And every time you think about it, you'll know I'm thinking specially about you. Okay?" He'd tried to make it as convincing as possible, but she was probably too old and too bright, she probably knew he was just trying to reassure her. In any case, she moved her hand *yes*. Whether it was real belief or embarrassed kindness he could never know.

After OT, Rob went back to his own cabin, to help with the pre-dinner change into clean clothes that Bert felt was good for morale. The boys were unusually boisterous, but it was probably only his own anxiety and need for peace that made them seem that way. Or it might have been the show that was being put on that evening, by a number of the seniors. All of these boys were in it, even Pete, who was going to be the MC, with a mike strapped to his shoulder near his mouth. None of the ordinary counsellors were involved; they and the younger children were to be the audience, while Scott and Martina, Drama and Dance respectively, ran the show. Rob knew the boys had been practising for two weeks at least, but he had not been interested enough to ask them what the show was about.

"Lemme borrow your zit cream."

"Wouldn't do you any good, pusface."

"Yeah, he's got pimples on his pimples."

"You spaz!" A scuffle.

"Cut that out, prickhead!"

Rob wondered if he could be transferred to another cabin. He was helping Dave Snider into his clean shirt, a pink one with charcoal stripes ("Cheap," his mother's voice said), when Gordon strolled into the cabin, late. Rob suspected him of thumbing into town for a quick drink in the beer-parlour, which wasn't choosy about your age. He had been late a number of times recently, leaving Rob to attempt control of the cabin single-handed. He looked very smug; he didn't reply to the admiring mock cheers that always accompanied his entrances, but dug into his pocket and, very casual, very cool, draped something over his bedpost. A pair of black panties, with red lace edges.

"Hey! Wow! Hey, Gord, whose are they?"

Out with the comb, patting the blond pompadour into place. "That's for me to know and you to find out."

"Hey, come on, Gord, eh, Gord?"

"Hey, no fair, Gord! Bet you stole 'em from the laundry!"

"Take a look, smart boy. They're not from any laundry."

Dave wheeled over and grabbed the panties. He stuck them on his head and circled the cabin floor. "Mickey Mouse, Mickey Mouse," he sang. "Forever let us hold our whammers high. Hey, Groaner, you wanna try them on? Bet they'd fit, you got a big head."

Other hands snatched at the panties. Rob left the room, went down the hall into the washroom. They must have been in the woods, near him, near Jordan. Her outrage, lecturing him like that with the twigs still in her hair, what gave her the right? Mud on her rump.

His face, his nice face, bland and freckled, framed in neatly trimmed sandy hair, watched him from the mirror. He would have preferred a scar, a patch over one eye, sunburned wrinkles, a fang. How untouched he looked, like the fat on uncooked bacon: nobody's fingerprints on him, no dirt, and he despised this purity. At the same time he could never be like the others, gloat over some woman's musky underpants. Maybe I'm not normal, he thought with gloomy pride.

After the chaos and mess of dinner had been endured, Rob went to the auditorium with the others. The stage, which was like a school stage except for the ramps at either side, had its red curtains closed. There were no chairs. Those in wheelchairs didn't need them, and the others sat on the floor, wherever they liked. Rob sought out Jordan and moved closer to her. He prepared to applaud, dutifully, whatever was set before him.

The lights in the room dimmed, there was some fumbling

behind the curtains, and Pete in his chair was pushed out by several pairs of hands. The audience clapped, some cheered. Pete was quite popular.

"Don't push me off the edge, you spaz," he said into the mike, which got a laugh from some of the older boys. He was wearing a vaudeville straw hat with a red crepe-paper band, and someone had glued a false moustache unevenly to his upper lip.

"Ladies and gents," he said. He made his moustache wiggle at one side, then at the other, and the younger children giggled. At that moment Rob almost liked him. "This here is the Fair-Eden Follies, and you better believe it, anyways, we all did a lot of falling down practising it." His voice went serious. "We've all worked hard to make this a good show, and I want you to give a big hand to the first number, which is—a square dance, by the Fair-Eden Wheeler Dealers. Thank you."

Pete was jerked backwards, became briefly entangled, and disappeared. After a pause the curtains parted haltingly. In front of a brown-paper backdrop with a poster-painted apple tree and a cow, four boys and four girls faced each other in standard square dance formation. They were all in wheelchairs, without the trays.

The girls were two polio cases and two paraplegic CPs. They were wearing lipstick and had red paper bows at the necks of their white blouses; their emaciated legs and braces were hidden by long printed cotton skirts, and one of them, the one without the glasses, was astonishingly pretty. Dave Snider was the front corner boy. Like the others, he had on a Western string tie and a cardboard cowboy hat. The dancers looked self-conscious, but proud. None of them was smiling.

Martina was off to the side, with the primitive record player. "Now," she prompted, and the scratchy fiddle music started up. She clapped her hands in time. "Honour your partners," she called, and the two lines bowed to each other from the waist. "Honour your corners!" Then the two opposite corners shot forward, met each other in the centre of the square, passed, and by quick hand-turnings of their wheels executed a perfect do-si-do.

Jesus, Rob thought. They must have practised for hours. He saw the concentration in Dave Snider's face and thought for a brief second, He cares about it, and, triumphantly, Now I've got something on him. Immediately he was ashamed of himself. The dancers whizzed out again, locked wheels and arms, and swung, careening dangerously. They seemed to have forgotten about the audience: their attention was held entirely by the rhythm and by the intricate manipulations of the wheels needed at such close quarters.

Rob looked over at Jordan. She was sitting almost still, her arms moving slightly, aimlessly, under the leather straps. He wanted her to turn her eyes so he could smile at her, but she was gazing straight at the dancers, her eyes shining with what he saw, with a quick jolt of his heart, were tears. She had never cried before: he hadn't known she could, he'd thought of her as a little changeling, from another planet perhaps, but not quite human. What was wrong? He tried to see as she was seeing, and, of course, it wasn't anything he could give her that she wanted. She wanted something she could imagine, something almost possible for her, she wanted to do this! A square dance in a wheelchair. She longed to be able to do just this much, this particular dance, that would be wonderful. And it was wonderful. He had wasted himself, his body, why couldn't he have moved with such abandon, such joy in precision, during those interminable formal dances when his legs went stiff as wood, his feet compressed themselves to clumsy blocks inside his polished shoes. . . .

But it was grotesque, he saw also, he couldn't help seeing. It was a mockery, of themselves and of the dance; who had ever allowed them to do it? All their effort, their perfection even, amounted to this: they were ludicrous in their cumbersome machines. They danced like comic robots. They danced like him.

Rob felt something inside him, coming up, bursting out. He doubled over, his hands clenched to his mouth. He was laughing! He tried to hold the laughter back, stifle it, turn it to coughing, but it was no use. He was red with shame and shaking all over; he couldn't stop. He crouched towards the door, hands across his face, stumbled through it, and collapsed onto the grass of the baseball field. He hoped they would think he was being sick to his stomach. That's what he would tell them afterwards. How could he, how could he have been so incredibly callous and rude? But he was still laughing so hard his stomach hurt. And she had seen him, she had turned her wet eyes and seen him just as it happened, she would think he had betrayed her.

Rob took off his glasses and wiped his eyes. Then he pressed his forehead into the grass, which was damp and cool with dew. From the open windows of the auditorium the tinny music ground on, to the rumble of wheels. *I'll have to leave, I can't explain, I'll never be able to face them.* But then he realized that *nobody had really seen but her, and she couldn't tell.* He was safe. And who was that, in the bright room at the back of his head, that man in the green gown and the mask, under the glass bubble, raising the knife?

Lives of the Poets

Lying on the bathroom floor of this anonymous hotel room, my feet upon the edge of the bathtub and a cold wet washcloth balled at the back of my neck. Bloody nosebleed. A good adjective, it works, as the students say in those creative writing classes that are sometimes part of the package. So colourful. Never had a nosebleed before, what are you supposed to do? An ice cube would be nice. Image of the Coke-and-ice machine at the end of the hall, me streaking toward it, a white towel over my head, the bloodstain spreading through it. A hotel guest opens his room door. Horrors, an accident. Stabbed in the nose. Doesn't want to get involved, the room door shuts, my quarter jams the machine. I'll stick with the washcloth.

The air's too dry, that must be it, nothing to do with me or the protests of the soggy body. Osmosis. Blood to the outside because there's not enough water vapour; they keep the radiators going full blast and no switch to shut them off. Cheapskates, why couldn't I stay at the Holiday Inn? Instead it's this one, pseudo-Elizabethan motifs tacked to a mouse-eaten frame, somebody's last-ditch attempt to make something out of this corner of the woods. The outskirts of Sudbury, nickel-smelting capital of the world. Can we show you around? they said. I'd like to see the slag heaps, and the places where the vegetation has all been scorched off. Oh, ha-ha, they said. It's growing back, they raised the stacks. It's turning into quite a, you know, civilized place. I used to like it, I said, it looked like the moon. There's something to be said for a place where absolutely nothing grows. Bald. Dead. Clean as a bone. Know what I mean? Furtive glances at one another, young beardy faces, one pipesmokes, they write footnotes, on their way up, why do we always get stuck with the visiting poet? Last one threw up on the car rug. Just wait till we get tenure.

Julia moved her head. The blood trickled gently down the back of her throat, thick and purple-tasting. She had been sitting there in front of the phone, trying to figure out the instructions for calling long-distance through the hotel operator, when she'd sneezed and the page in front of her had suddenly been spattered with blood. Totally unprovoked. And Bernie would be hanging around at home, waiting for her to call. In two hours she had to give the reading. A gracious introduction, she would rise and move to the microphone, smiling, she would open her mouth and blood would start to drip from her nose. Would they clap? Would they pretend not to notice? Would they think it was part of the poem? She would have to start rooting around in her purse for a Kleenex, or, better still, she'd faint, and someone else would have to cope. (But everyone would think she was drunk.) How upsetting for the committee. Would they pay her anyway? She could imagine them discussing it.

She raised her head a little, to see if it had stopped. Something that felt like a warm slug crawled down towards her upper lip. She licked, tasting salt. How was she going to get to the phone? On her back, crawling supine across the floor, using her elbows and pushing with her feet, a swimming motion, like a giant aquatic insect. She shouldn't be calling Bernie, she should be calling a doctor. But it wasn't serious enough. Something like this always happened when she had to give a reading, something painful but too minor for a doctor. Besides, it was always out of town, she never knew any doctors. Once it was a bad cold; her voice had sounded as if it was coming through a layer of mud. Once her hands and ankles had swelled up. Headaches were standard: she never got headaches at home. It was as if something was against these readings and was trying to keep her from giving them. She was waiting for it to take a more drastic form, paralysis of the jaw muscles, temporary blindness, fits. This was what she thought about during the introductions, always: herself on a stretcher, the waiting ambulance, then waking up, safe and cured, with Bernie sitting beside the bed. He would smile at her, he would kiss her forehead, he would tell her—what? Some magical thing. They had won the Wintario Lottery. He'd been left a lot of money. The gallery was solvent. Something that would mean she didn't have to do this any more.

That was the problem: they needed the money. They had always needed the money, for the whole four years they had lived together, and they still needed it. At first it hadn't seemed so important. Bernie was on a grant then, painting, and after that he got a renewal. She had a part-time job, cataloguing in a library. Then she had a book published, by one of the medium-sized houses, and got a grant herself. Of course she quit her job, to make the best use of the time. But Bernie ran out of money, and he had trouble selling paintings. Even when he did sell one, the dealer got most of it. The dealer system was wrong, he told her, and he and two other painters opened a co-operative artists' gallery which, after a lot of talk, they decided to call The Notes from Underground. One of the other painters had money, but they didn't want to take advantage of him; they would go strict thirds. Bernie explained all this to her, and he was so enthusiastic it had seemed natural to lend him half of her grant money, just to get things going. As soon as they began to show a profit, he said, he would pay her back. He even gave her two shares in the gallery. They hadn't started to show a profit yet, though, and, as Bernie pointed out, she didn't really need the money back right at the moment. She could get some more. She now had a reputation; a small one, but still, she could earn money easier and faster than he could, travelling around and giving readings on college campuses. She was "promising," which meant that she was cheaper than those who were more than promising. She got enough invitations to keep them going, and though she debated the merits of each one with Bernie, hoping he would veto, he had never yet advised her to turn one down. But to be fair, she had never told him quite how much she hated it, the stares of the eyes, her own voice detached and floating, the one destructive question that was sure to lurk there among all the blank ones. *I mean, do you really think you have anything to say?*

Deep in February, deep in the snow, bleeding on the tiles of this bathroom floor. By turning her head she could see them, white hexagons linked like a honeycomb, with a single black tile at regular intervals.

For a measly hundred and twenty-five dollars—but it's half the rent, don't forget that—and twenty-five a day for expenses. Had to take the morning plane, no seats in the afternoon, who the hell goes to Sudbury in February? A bunch of engineers. Practical citizens, digging out the ore, making a bundle, two cars and a swimming pool. They don't stay at this place, anyway. Dining room at lunchtime almost empty. Just me and a very old man who talked to himself out loud. What's wrong with him? I said to the waitress. Is he crazy? In a whisper I said it. It's okay, he's deaf, she said. No, he's just lonely, he's been real lonely ever since his wife died. He lives here. I guess it's better than an old-age home, you know? There are more people here in the summertime. And we get a lot of men who're separating from their wives. You can always tell them, by what they order.

Didn't pursue that. Should have though, now I'll never know. What they order. Was looking as usual for the cheapest thing on the menu. Need that whole hundred and twenty-five, why waste it on food? This food. The menu a skewed effort to be Elizabethan, everything spelled with an *e* at the end. Got the Anne Boleyn Special, a hamburger with no bun, garnished with a square of red Jell-O and followed by "a glass of skime milke." Do they know that Anne Boleyn's head was cut off? Is that why the hamburger has no bun? What goes on in people's minds? Everyone thinks writers must know more about the inside of the human head, but that is wrong. They know less, that's why they write. Trying to find out what everyone else takes for granted. The symbolism of the menu, for god's sake, why am I even thinking about it? The menu has no symbolism, it's just some dimwit's ill-informed attempt to be cute. Isn't it?

You're too complicated, Bernie used to tell her, when they were still stroking and picking at each other's psyches. You should take it easy. Lie back. Eat an orange. Paint your toenails.

All very well for him.

Maybe he wasn't even up yet. He used to take naps in the afternoons, he'd be lying there under the heaped-up blankets of their Queen Street West apartment (over the store that had once sold hardware but was now a weaving boutique, and the rent was climbing), face down, arms flung out to either side, his socks on the floor where he'd discarded them, one after the other, like deflated feet or stiffened blue footprints leading to the bed. Even in the mornings he would wake up slowly and fumble his way to the kitchen for some coffee, which she would already have made. That was one of their few luxuries, real coffee. She'd have been up for hours, crouching at the kitchen table, worrying away at a piece of paper, gnawing words, shredding the language. He would place his mouth, still full of sleep, on hers, and perhaps pull her back into the bedroom and down into the bed with him, into that liquid pool of flesh, his mouth sliding over her, furry pleasure, the covers closing over them as they sank into weightlessness. But he hadn't done that for some time. He had been waking earlier and earlier; she, on the other hand, had been having trouble getting out of bed. She was losing that compulsion, that joy, whatever had nagged her out into the cold morning air, driven her to fill all those notebooks, all those printed pages. Instead she would roll herself up in the blankets after Bernie got up, tucking in all the corners, muffling herself in wool. She had begun to have the feeling that nothing was waiting for her outside the bed's edge. Not emptiness but nothing, the zero with legs in the arithmetic book.

"I'm off," he'd say to her groggy bundled back. She'd be awake enough to hear this; then she would lapse back into a humid sleep. His absence was one more reason for not getting up. He would be going to The Notes from Underground, which was where he seemed to spend most of his time now. He was pleased with the way it had been going, they'd had several interviews in the papers, and it was easy for her to understand how something could be thought of as a qualified success and still not make money, since the same thing had happened to her book. But she worried a little because he wasn't doing very much painting any more. His last picture had been a try at Magic Realism. It was her, sitting at the kitchen table, wrapped in the plaid rug off the foot of the bed, with her hair in a sleazy bun at the back of her neck, looking like some kind of famine victim. Too bad the kitchen was yellow; it made her skin green. He hadn't finished it though. Paper work, he would say. That was what he spent his morning at the gallery doing, that and answering the phone. The three of them were supposed to take turns and he should have been off at twelve, but he usually ended up there in the afternoons, too. The gallery had attracted a few younger painters, who sat around drinking plastic cups of Nescafé and cans of beer and arguing about whether or not anyone who bought a share in the gallery should be able to have a show there and whether the gallery should take commissions, and if not how it was going to survive. They had various schemes, and they'd recently hired a girl to do public relations, posters and mailings and bothering the media. She was free-lance and did it for two other small galleries and one commercial photographer. She was just starting out, Bernie said. She talked about building them up. Her name was Marika; Julia had met her at the gallery, back in the days when she'd been in the habit of dropping around in the afternoons. That seemed a long time ago.

Marika was a peach-cheeked blonde, about twenty-two or

three, anyway no more than five or six years younger than Julia. Although her name suggested the exotic, a Hungarian perhaps, her accent was flat Ontario and her last name was Hunt. Either a fanciful mother or a name-changing father, or perhaps Marika had adopted the name herself. She had been very friendly to Julia. "I've read your book," she said. "I don't find time to read too many books, but I got yours out of the library because of Bernie. I didn't think I was going to like it, but actually it's quite good." Julia was grateful, Bernie said too grateful, to people who said they liked her work or who had even read it. Nevertheless, she heard a voice inside her head saying, *Piss right off*. It was the way Marika offered her compliment: like a biscuit to a dog, part reward, part bribe, and condescending.

Since then they'd had coffee together several times. It was always Marika who dropped over, on some errand or other from Bernie. They sat in the kitchen and talked, but no real connections were made. They were like two mothers at a birthday party, sitting on the sidelines while their children whooped and gobbled: they were polite to each other, but the real focus of their attention was elsewhere. Once Marika had said, "I've always thought I might like to write myself," and Julia had felt a small red explosion at the back of her neck and had almost thrown her cup of coffee at her, until she realized Marika didn't mean it that way, she was just trying to appear interested. "Aren't you afraid you'll run out of material?"

"Not material, energy," she'd said, making it sound like a joke; but it had been true, that was her fear. Weren't they the same thing? "According to Einstein," she said, and Marika, having missed the connection, gave her a funny look and changed the subject to films.

The last time Marika came over, Julia wasn't even out of bed. She had no excuse, no explanation. She almost told her to go away, but Bernie needed his black notebook, the one with the phone numbers, so she had to let her in. Marika leaned in the bedroom doorway, trim in her little layered look, dangling her handwoven bag, while Julia, with unwashed hair straggling over the shoulders of her nightgown, moss-mouthed and blurry-minded, knelt on the floor and scrabbled through Bernie's discarded pockets. For the first time in their life she wished he would bloody well pick up his clothes. She felt exposed by them, though she shouldn't, they weren't her clothes, she hadn't dropped them. Marika exuded surprise, embarrassment and a certain glee, as if Bernie's dirty socks and trampled jeans were Julia's soft underbelly, which she'd always wanted to get a look at.

"I don't know where he's put it," Julia said, irritated. "He's supposed to pick them up himself," and added, far too defensively she knew, "We share everything."

"Of course, with your work and all," Marika said. She was scanning the room, the greyish bed, Julia's sweater slumped in the corner chair, the avocado with brown-edged leaves on the windowsill, their only plant. She'd grown it from the pit of a celebration avocado—she could no longer remember the reason for the rejoicing—but there was something wrong with it. Tea-leaves, you were supposed to put tea-leaves on them, or was it charcoal?

The notebook was finally under the bed. Julia pulled it out; a dustball clung to it. She saw in her mind a small plaque, like the ones on historical houses: DUSTBALL. *Once the property of Julia Morse, Poetess.* With a few bored schoolchildren looking at it through the glass of a case. That was the future, if there was a future, if she kept on writing, if she became at least marginally significant, an obligatory footnote in someone's thesis. Fragments left over after the general decay, classified, gathering dust, like the vertebrae of dinosaurs. Bloodless.

She handed the notebook over. "Would you like some coffee?" she asked, in a voice meant to discourage.

"I don't want to put you out," Marika said, but she had some anyway, chatting brightly about their plans for a collective show, to be called "Up from Under." Her eyes shifted around the kitchen, taking in the dripping tap, the smelly cloth draped over it, the ancient toaster with the crumbs around its base like the debris from a tiny landslide. "I'm really glad we can be friends," she said just before leaving. "Bernie says we have nothing in common, but I think we get on real well. They're mostly men down there." This could have been some ersatz variety of women's lib, Julia thought, but it wasn't: Marika's voice stank of bridge club. "Real well." How incongruous, with those three-inch platforms, that trendy bum. Marika's visits made her feel like a welfare case. She wondered how she could get her to stop coming, without being too rude. She begrudged the time, too, she could be using it for work. Though increasingly there was no work.

Bernie didn't seem to notice that she was doing next to nothing. He no longer asked to read what she might have written during the day. When he came home for dinner he would talk obsessively about the gallery, eating plate after plate of spaghetti and, it seemed to her, whole loaves of bread. His appetite had increased, and they had recently begun to argue about the food bills and who was supposed to do the cooking and shopping. In the beginning they had shared everything, that was the agreement. Julia wanted to point out that since he was now eating twice as much as she was, he really ought to do more of the shopping and pay more than half, but she felt it would be mingy of her to say this. Especially since, whenever they talked about money, he would say, "Don't worry, you'll get paid off," as if she begrudged him the gallery loan. Which she supposed she did.

What time is it? Life the wrist: six-thirty. The blood seems to have slowed down, but it's still there, a thickening like sludge at the back of the throat. A teacher, once, in public school, who came into the classroom with her teeth outlined in blood. She must have been to the dentist and then not checked in the mirror, but we were all so afraid of her none of us said anything and we spent the afternoon drawing three tulips in a vase, presided over by that bloodthirsty smile. Have to remember to brush my teeth and clean my face carefully, a drop of blood on the chin might be disturbing to the audience. Blood, the elemental fluid, the juice of life, by-product of birth, prelude to death. The red badge of courage. The people's flag. Maybe I could get a job writing political speeches, if all else fails. But when it comes out of your nose, not magic or even symbolic, just ridiculous. Pinned by the nose to the geometric net of this bathroom floor. Don't be completely stupid, get started. Stand up carefully: if the blood keeps flowing, call off the reading and get on the plane. (Leaving a trail of clots?) I could be home tonight. Bernie's there now, waiting for me to call, it's past the time.

She pulled herself up, slowly, holding on to the sink, and walked into the bedroom with her head tilted back precariously. She groped for the phone and picked it up. She dialled 0 and got the operator to place the call for her. She listened to the outer-space noises the phone made, anticipating Bernie's voice, feeling his tongue already on the inside of her mouth. They would go to bed and after that they would have a late supper, the two of them in the kitchen with the gas oven lit and open to keep them warm, the way they used to. (Her mind skipped the details of what they would eat. She knew there had been nothing in the refrigerator when she left but a couple of aging wieners. Not even any buns.) Things would get better, time would reverse itself, they would talk, she would tell him how much she had missed him (for surely she had been away much longer than a day), silence would open, language would flow again.

The line was busy.

She did not want to think about her disappointment. She would phone later. There was no more blood, though she could feel it crusted inside her head. So she would stay, she would do the reading, she would collect the fee and use it to pay the rent. What else was possible?

It was dinnertime and she was hungry, but she couldn't afford another meal. Sometimes they took the poet out for dinner, sometimes they gave a party afterwards where she could fill up on crackers and cheese. Here there was nothing. They picked her up at the airport, that was it. She could tell there had been no posters, no advance publicity. A small audience, nervous because they were there and nobody else was, caught out attending the wrong reading. And she didn't even look like a poet, she was wearing a neat navy-blue pantsuit, easy for stairs and cars. Maybe a robe would help, something flowing and ethereal. Bangles, a scarf?

She sat on the edge of the straight-backed chair, facing a picture of two dead ducks and an Irish setter. There was time to be filled. No television set. Read the Gideon Bible? No, nothing too strenuous, she didn't want to start bleeding again. In half an hour they would come to pick her up. Then the eyes, the polite hands, the fixed smiles. Afterwards everyone would murmur. "Don't you feel exposed up there?" a young girl had asked her once. "No," she'd said, and she didn't, it wasn't her, she read only her most soothing poems, she didn't want to disturb anyone. But they distrusted her anyway. At least she never got drunk beforehand the way a lot of the others did. She wanted to be nice, and everyone approved of that.

Except the few hungry ones, the ones who wanted to know the secret, who believed there was a secret. They would straggle up afterwards, she knew, hanging around the edges, behind the murmuring committee members, clutching little packets of poems, extending them to her gingerly, as if the pages were raw flesh they could not bear to have touched. She could remember when she had felt like that. Most of the poems would be dismal, but now and then there would be one that had something, the energy, the thing that could not be defined. *Don't do it*, she wanted to tell them, *don't make the mistake I made*. But what was her mistake? Thinking she could save her soul, no doubt. By the word alone.

Did I really believe that? Did I really believe that language could seize me by the hair and draw me straight up, out into the free air? But if you stop believing, you can't do it any longer, you can't fly. So I'm stuck here on this chair. A *sixty-year-old smiling public man*. Crisis of faith? Faith in what? Resurrection, that's what is needed. Up from under. Get rid of these haunts, these fictions, *he said, she said,* counting up points and grievances; the dialogues of shadows. Otherwise there will be nothing left but the rest of my life. Something is frozen.

Bernie, save me.

He was so nice this morning, before she left. The phone again, the voice flies through the darkness of space. Hollow ringing, a click.

"Hi." A woman's voice, Marika, she knew who it would be.

"Could I please speak to Bernie?" Stupid to act as though she didn't recognize the voice.

"Hi, Julia," Marika said. "Bernie's not here right now. He had to go away for a couple of days, but he knew you'd be calling tonight so he asked me to come over. So you wouldn't worry or anything. He said to have a good reading, and don't forget to water the plant when you get back."

"Oh, thanks, Marika," she said. As if she was his secretary, leaving her with messages for the idiot wife while he . . . She couldn't ask where he had gone. She herself went away, why couldn't he? If he wanted her to know where, he'd tell her. She said goodbye. As she put down the phone, she thought she heard something. A voice, a laugh?

He hasn't gone anywhere. He's there, in the apartment, I can see it, it must have been going on for weeks, months, down at the gallery, *I've read your book,* checking out the competition. I must be feeble-minded, everyone knew but me. Trotting over to have coffee with me, casing the joint. Hope they have the grace to change the sheets. Didn't have the guts to talk to me himself, water the plant my ass, it's dead anyway. Melodrama in a parking lot, long stretches of asphalt with here and there a splotch of crushed animal, is that what my life has become?

Rock bottom in this room among the slag heaps, outer space, on the dead moon, with two slaughtered ducks and a stuffed dog, why did you have to do it that way, when I'm out here, you know it cripples me, these ordeals, walking through the

194

eyes, couldn't you have waited? You set it up so well, I'll come back and yell and scream, and you'll deny it all, you'll look at me, very cool, and say, *What are you talking about?* And what will I be talking about, maybe I'm wrong, I'll never know. Beautiful.

It's almost time.

They will arrive, the two young men who are polite and who do not yet have tenure. She will get into the front seat of their Volvo, and all the way to the reading, as they drive between the snowdrifts piled halfway up the telephone poles, the two young men will discuss the virtues of this car and the relative virtues of the car belonging to the one who is not driving but who is sitting in the back seat with his legs doubled like a grasshopper's.

She will not be able to say anything at all. She will watch the snow coming at the windshield and being wiped away by the windshield wipers, and it will be red, it will be like a solid red wall. A violation, that is what she hates, they had promised never to lie.

Stomach full of blood, head full of blood, burning red, she can feel it at last, this rage that has been going on for a long time, energy, words swarming behind her eyes like spring bees. Something is hungry, something is coiling itself. A long song coils and uncoils itself just in front of the windshield, where the red snow is falling, bringing everything to life. They park the virtuous car and she is led by the two young men into the auditorium, grey cinder-block, where a gathering of polite faces waits to hear the word. Hands will clap, things will be said about her, nothing astonishing, she is supposed to be good for them, they must open their mouths and take her in, like vitamins, like bland medicine. No. No sweet identity, she will clench herself against it. She will step across the stage, words coiled, she will open her mouth and the room will explode in blood.

Dancing Girls

The first sign of the new man was the knock on the door. It was the landlady, knocking not at Ann's door, as she'd thought, but on the other door, the one east of the bathroom. Knock, knock, knock; then a pause, soft footsteps, the sound of unlocking. Ann, who had been reading a book on canals, put it down and lit herself a cigarette. It wasn't that she tried to overhear: in this house you couldn't help it.

"Hi!" Mrs. Nolan's voice loud, overly friendly. "I was wondering, my kids would love to see your native costume. You think you could put it on, like, and come down?"

A soft voice, unintelligible.

"Gee, that's great! We'd sure appreciate it!"

Closing and locking, Mrs. Nolan slip-slopping along the hall in, Ann knew, her mauve terry-cloth scuffies and flowered housecoat, down the stairs, hollering at her two boys. "You get into this room right now!" Her voice came up through Ann's hot-air register as if the grate were a PA system. It isn't those kids who want to see him, she thought. It's her. She put out the cigarette, reserving the other half for later, and opened her book again. What costume? Which land, this time?

Unlocking, opening, soft feet down the hall. They sounded bare. Ann closed the book and opened her own door. A white robe, the back of a brown head, moving with a certain stealth or caution towards the stairs. Ann went into the bathroom and turned on the light. They would share it; the person in that room always shared her bathroom. She hoped he would be better than the man before, who always seemed to forget his razor and would knock on the door while Ann was having a bath. You wouldn't have to worry about getting raped or anything in this house though, that was one good thing. Mrs. Nolan was better than any burglar alarm, and she was always there.

That one had been from France, studying Cinema. Before him there had been a girl, from Turkey, studying Comparative Literature. Lelah, or that was how it was pronounced. Ann used to find her beautiful long auburn hairs in the washbasin fairly regularly; she'd run her thumb and index finger along them, enviously, before discarding them. She had to keep her own hair chopped off at ear level, as it was brittle and broke easily. Lelah also had a gold tooth, right at the front on the outside where it showed when she smiled. Curiously, Ann was envious of this tooth as well. It and the hair and the turquoise-studded earrings Lelah wore gave her a gypsy look, a wise look that Ann, with her beige eyebrows and delicate mouth, knew she would never be able to develop, no matter how wise she got. She herself went in for "classics," tailored skirts and Shetland sweaters; it was the only look she could carry off. But she and Lelah had been friends, smoking cigarettes in each other's rooms commiserating with each other about the difficulties of their courses and the loudness of Mrs. Nolan's voice. So Ann was familiar with that room; she knew what it looked like inside and how much it cost. It was no luxury suite, certainly, and she wasn't surprised at the high rate of turnover. It had an even more direct pipeline to the sounds of the Nolan family than hers had. Lelah had left because she couldn't stand the noise.

The room was smaller and cheaper than her room, though painted the same depressing shade of green. Unlike hers, it did not have its own tiny refrigerator, sink and stove; you had to use the kitchen at the front of the house, which had been staked out much earlier by a small enclave of mathematicians, two men and one woman, from Hong Kong. Whoever took that room either had to eat out all the time or run the gamut of their conversation, which even when not in Chinese was so rarefied as to be unintelligible. And you could never find any space in the refrigerator, it was always full of mushrooms. This from Lelah; Ann herself never had to deal with them since she could cook in her own room. She could see them, though, as she went in and out. At mealtimes they usually sat quietly at their kitchen table, discussing surds, she assumed. Ann suspected that what Lelah had really resented about them was not the mushrooms: they simply made her feel stupid.

Every morning, before she left for classes, Ann checked the bathroom for signs of the new man—hairs, cosmetics—but there was nothing. She hardly ever heard him; sometimes there was that soft, barefooted pacing, the click of his lock, but there were no radio noises, no coughs, no conversations. For the first couple of weeks, apart from the one glimpse of a tall, billowing figure, she didn't even see him. He didn't appear to use the kitchen, where the mathematicians continued their mysteries undisturbed; or if he did, he cooked while no one else was there. Ann would have forgotten about him completely if it hadn't been for Mrs. Nolan.

"He's real nice, not like some you get," she said to Ann in her piercing whisper. Although she shouted at her husband, when he was home, and especially at her children, she always whispered when she was talking to Ann, a hoarse, avid whisper, as if they shared disreputable secrets. Ann was standing in front of her door with the room key in her hand, her usual location during these confidences. Mrs. Nolan knew Ann's routine. It wasn't difficult for her to pretend to be cleaning the bathroom, to pop out and waylay Ann, Ajax and rag in hand, whenever she felt she had something to tell her. She was a short, barrel-shaped woman: the top of her head came only to Ann's nose, so she had to look up at Ann, which at these moments made her seem oddly childlike.

"He's from one of them Arabian countries. Though I thought

tney wore turbans, or not turbans, those white things, like. He just has this funny hat, sort of like the Shriners. He don't look much like an Arab to me. He's got these tattoo marks on his face. But he's real nice."

Ann stood, her umbrella dripping onto the floor, waiting for Mrs. Nolan to finish. She never had to say anything much; it wasn't expected. "You think you could get me the rent on Wednesday?" Mrs. Nolan asked. Three days early; the real point of the conversation, probably. Still, as Mrs. Nolan had said back in September, she didn't have much of anyone to talk to. Her husband was away much of the time and her children escaped outdoors whenever they could. She never went out herself except to shop, and for Mass on Sundays.

"I'm glad it was you took the room," she'd said to Ann. "I can talk to you. You're not, like, foreign. Not like most of them. It was his idea, getting this big house to rent out. Not that he has to do the work or put up with them. You never know what they'll do."

Ann wanted to point out to her that she was indeed foreign, that she was just as foreign as any of the others, but she knew Mrs. Nolan would not understand. It would be like that fiasco in October. *Wear your native costumes.* She had responded to the invitation out of a sense of duty, as well as one of irony. Wait till they get a load of my native costume, she'd thought, contemplating snowshoes and a parka but actually putting on her good blue wool suit. There was only one thing *native costume* reminded her of: the cover picture on the Missionary Sunday School paper they'd once handed out, which showed children from all the countries of the world dancing in a circle around a smiling white-faced Jesus in a bedsheet. That, and the poem in the *Golden Windows Reader:*

> Little Indian, Sioux or Cree,
> Oh, don't you wish that you were me?

The awful thing, as she told Lelah later, was that she was the only one who'd gone. "She had all this food ready, and not a single other person was there. She was really upset, and I was so embarrassed for her. It was some Friends of Foreign Students thing, just for women: students and the wives of students. She obviously didn't think I was foreign enough, and she couldn't figure out why no one else came." Neither could Ann, who had stayed far too long and had eaten platefuls of crackers and cheese she didn't want in order to soothe her hostess's thwarted sense of hospitality. The woman, who had tastefully streaked ash-blonde hair and a living room filled with polished and satiny traditional surfaces, had alternately urged her to eat and stared at the door, as if expecting a parade of foreigners in their native costumes to come trooping gratefully through it.

Lelah smiled, showing her wise tooth. "Don't they know any better than to throw those things at night?" she said. "Those men aren't going to let their wives go out by themselves at night. And the single ones are afraid to walk on the streets alone, I know I am."

"I'm not," Ann said, "as long as you stay on the main ones, where it's lighted."

"Then you're a fool," Lelah said. "Don't you know there was a girl murdered three blocks from here? Left her bathroom window unlocked. Some man climbed through the window and cut her throat."

"I always carry my umbrella," Ann said. Of course there were certain places where you just didn't go. Scollay Square, for instance, where the prostitutes hung out and you might get followed, or worse. She tried to explain to Lelah that she wasn't used to this, to any of this, that in Toronto you could walk all over the city, well, almost anywhere, and never have any trouble. She went on to say that no one here seemed to understand that she wasn't like them, she came from a different country, it wasn't the same; but Lelah was quickly bored by this. She had to get back to Tolstoy, she said, putting out her cigarette in her unfinished cup of instant coffee. (Not strong enough for her, I suppose, Ann thought.)

"You shouldn't worry," she said. "You're well off. At least

your family doesn't almost disown you for doing what you want to do." Lelah's father kept writing her letters, urging her to return to Turkey, where the family had decided on the perfect husband for her. Lelah had stalled them for one year, and maybe she could stall them for one more, but that would be her limit. She couldn't possibly finish her thesis in that time.

Ann hadn't seen much of her since she'd moved out. You lost sight of people quickly here, in the ever-shifting population of hopeful and despairing transients.

No one wrote her letters urging her to come home, no one had picked out the perfect husband for her. On the contrary. She could imagine her mother's defeated look, the greying and sinking of her face, if she were suddenly to announce that she was going to quit school, trade in her ambitions for fate, and get married. Even her father wouldn't like it. *Finish what you start*, he'd say, *I didn't and look what happened to me*. The bungalow at the top of Avenue Road, beside a gas station, with the roar of the expressway always there, like the sea, and fumes blighting the Chinese elm hedge her mother had planted to conceal the pumps. Both her brothers had dropped out of high school; they weren't the good students Ann had been. One worked in a print shop now and had a wife; the other had drifted to Vancouver, and no one knew what he did. She remembered her first real boyfriend, beefy, easygoing Bill Decker, with his two-tone car that kept losing the muffler. They'd spent a lot of time parked on side streets, rubbing against each other through all those layers of clothes. But even in that sensual mist, the cocoon of breath and skin they'd spun around each other, those phone conversations that existed as a form of touch, she'd known this was not something she could get too involved in. He was probably flabby by now, settled. She'd had relationships with men since then, but she had treated them the same way. *Circumspect*.

Not that Mrs. Nolan's back room was any step up. Out one window there was a view of the funeral home next door; out the other was the yard, which the Nolan kids had scraped clean of grass and which was now a bog of half-frozen mud.

Their dog, a mongrelized German shepherd, was kept tied there, where the kids alternately hugged and tormented it. ("Jimmy! Donny! Now you leave that dog alone!" "Don't do that, he's filthy! Look at you!" Ann covering her ears, reading about underground malls.) She'd tried to fix the room up, she'd hung a madras spread as a curtain in front of the cooking area, she'd put up several prints, Braque still-lifes of guitars and soothing Cubist fruit, and she was growing herbs on her windowsill; she needed surroundings that at least tried not to be ugly. But none of these things helped much. At night she wore earplugs. She hadn't known about the scarcity of good rooms, hadn't realized that the whole area was a student slum, that the rents would be so high, the available places so dismal. Next year would be different; she'd get here early and have the pick of the crop. Mrs. Nolan's was definitely a leftover. You could do much better for the money; you could even have a whole apartment, if you were willing to live in the real slum that spread in narrow streets of three-storey frame houses, fading mustard yellow and soot grey, nearer the river. Though Ann didn't think she was quite up to that. Something in one of the good old houses, on a quiet back street, with a little stained glass, would be more like it. Her friend Jetske had a place like that.

But she was doing what she wanted, no doubt of that. In high school she had planned to be an architect, but while finishing the preliminary courses at university she had realized that the buildings she wanted to design were either impossible—who could afford them?—or futile. They would be lost, smothered, ruined by all the other buildings jammed inharmoniously around them. This was why she had decided to go into Urban Design, and she had come here because this school was the best. Or rumoured to be the best. By the time she finished, she intended to be so well-qualified, so armoured with qualifications, that no one back home would dare turn her down for the job she coveted. She wanted to rearrange Toronto. Toronto would do for a start.

She wasn't yet too certain of the specific details. What she saw were spaces, beautiful green spaces, with water flowing through them, and trees. Not big golf-course lawns, though; something more winding, something with sudden turns, private niches, surprising vistas. And no formal flower beds. The houses, or whatever they were, set unobtrusively among the trees, the cars kept where? And where would people shop, and who would live in these places? This was the problem: she could see the vistas, the trees and the streams or canals, quite clearly, but she could never visualize the people. Her green spaces were always empty.

She didn't see her next-door neighbour again until February. She was coming back from the small local supermarket where she bought the food for her cheap, carefully balanced meals. He was leaning in the doorway of what, at home, she would have called a vestibule, smoking a cigarette and staring out at the rain, through the glass panes at the side of the front door. He should have moved a little to give Ann room to put down her umbrella, but he didn't. He didn't even look at her. She squeezed in, shook her deflated umbrella and checked her mailbox, which didn't have a key. There weren't usually any letters in it, and today was no exception. He was wearing a white shirt that was too big for him and some greenish trousers. His feet were not bare, in fact he was wearing a pair of prosaic brown shoes. He did have tattoo marks, though, or rather scars, a set of them running across each cheek. It was the first time she had seen him from the front. He seemed a little shorter than he had when she'd glimpsed him heading towards the stairs, but perhaps it was because he had no hat on. He was curved so listlessly against the doorframe, it was almost as if he had no bones.

There was nothing to see through the front of Mrs. Nolan's door except the traffic, sizzling by the way it did every day. He was depressed, it must be that. This weather would depress anyone. Ann sympathized with his loneliness, but she did not wish to become involved in it, implicated by it. She had enough trouble dealing with her own. She smiled at him, though since he wasn't looking at her this smile was lost. She went past him and up the stairs.

As she fumbled in her purse for her key, Mrs. Nolan stumped out of the bathroom. "You see him?" she whispered.

"Who?" Ann said.

"*Him.*" Mrs. Nolan jerked her thumb. "Standing down there, by the door. He does that a lot. He's bothering me, like. I don't have such good nerves."

"He's not doing anything," Ann said.

"That's what I mean," Mrs. Nolan whispered ominously. "He never does nothing. Far as I can tell, he never goes out much. All he does is borrow my vacuum cleaner."

"Your vacuum cleaner?" Ann said, startled into responding.

"That's what I said." Mrs. Nolan had a rubber plunger which she was fingering. "And there's more of them. They come in the other night, up to his room. Two more, with the same marks and everything, on their faces. It's like some kind of, like, a religion or something. And he never gave the vacuum cleaner back till the next day."

"Does he pay the rent?" Ann said, trying to switch the conversation to practical matters. Mrs. Nolan was letting her imagination get out of control.

"Regular," Mrs. Nolan said. "Except I don't like the way he comes down, so quiet like, right into my house. With Fred away so much."

"I wouldn't worry," Ann said in what she hoped was a soothing voice. "He seems perfectly nice."

"It's always that kind," Mrs. Nolan said.

Ann cooked her dinner, a chicken breast, some peas, a digestive biscuit. Then she washed her hair in the bathroom and put it up in rollers. She had to do that, to give it body. With her head encased in the plastic hood of her portable dryer she sat at her table, drinking instant coffee, smoking her usual half cigarette, and attempting to read a book about Roman aqueducts, from which she hoped to get some novel ideas for her current project. (An aqueduct, going right through the middle of the obligatory shopping centre? Would anyone care?) Her mind kept flicking, though, to the problem of the man next door. Ann did not often try to think about what it would be like to be a man. But this particular man . . . Who was he, and what was happening to him? He must be a student, everyone here was a student. And he would be intelligent, that went without saying. Probably on scholarship. Everyone here in the graduate school was on scholarship, except the real Americans, who sometimes weren't. Or rather, the women were, but some of the men were still avoiding the draft, though President Johnson had announced he was going to do away with all that. She herself would never have made it this far without scholarships; her parents could not have afforded it.

So he was here on scholarship, studying something practical, no doubt, nuclear physics or the construction of dams, and, like herself and the other foreigners, he was expected to go away again as soon as he'd learned what he'd come for. But he never went out of the house; he stood at the front door and watched the brutish flow of cars, the winter rain, while those back in his own country, the ones who had sent him, were confidently expecting him to return someday, crammed with knowledge, ready to solve their lives. He's lost his nerve, Ann thought. He'll fail. It was too late in the year for him ever to catch up. Such failures, such paralysis, were fairly common here, especially among the foreigners. He was far from home, from the language he shared, the wearers of his native costume; he was in exile, he was drowning. What did he do, alone by himself in his room at night?

Ann switched her hair dryer to COOL and wrenched her mind back to aqueducts. She could see he was drowning but there was nothing she could do. Unless you were good at it you shouldn't even try, she was wise enough to know that. All you could do for the drowning was to make sure you were not one of them.

The aqueduct, now. It would be made of natural brick, an earthy red; it would have low arches, in the shade of which there would be ferns and, perhaps, some delphiniums, in varying tones of blue. She must learn more about plants. Before entering the shopping complex (trust him to assign a shopping complex; before that he had demanded a public housing project), it would flow through her green space, in which, she could now see, there were people walking. Children? *But not children like Mrs. Nolan's.* They would turn her grass to mud, they'd nail things to her trees, their mangy dogs would shit on her ferns, they'd throw bottles and pop cans into her aqueduct. And Mrs. Nolan herself, and her Noah's Ark of seedy, brilliant foreigners, where would she put them? For the houses of the Mrs. Nolans of this world would have to go; that was one of the axioms of Urban Design. She could convert them to small offices, or single-floor apartments; some shrubs and hanging plants and a new coat of paint would do wonders. But she knew this was temporizing. Around her green space, she could see, there was now a high wire fence. Inside it were trees, flowers and grass, outside the dirty snow, the endless rain, the grunting cars and the half-frozen mud of Mrs. Nolan's drab backyard. That was what *exclusive* meant, it meant that some people were excluded. Her parents stood in the rain outside the fence, watching with dreary pride while she strolled about in the eternal sunlight. Their one success.

Stop it, she commanded herself. *They want me to be doing this.* She unwound her hair and brushed it out. Three hours from now, she knew, it would be limp as ever because of the damp.

The next day, she tried to raise her new theoretical problem with her friend Jetske. Jetske was in Urban Design, too. She was from Holland, and could remember running through the devastated streets as a child, begging small change, first from the Germans, later from the American soldiers, who were always good for a chocolate bar or two.

"You learn how to take care of yourself," she'd said. "It didn't seem hard at the time, but when you are a child, nothing is that hard. We were all the same, nobody had anything." Because of this background, which was more exotic and cruel than anything Ann herself had experienced (what was growing up next to a gas pump compared with the Nazis?), Ann respected her opinions. She liked her also because she was the only person she'd met here who seemed to know where Canada was. There were a lot of Canadian soldiers buried in Holland. This provided Ann with at least a shadowy identity, which she felt she needed. She didn't have a native costume, but at least she had some heroic dead bodies with which she was connected, however remotely.

"The trouble with what we're doing . . ." she said to Jetske, as they walked towards the library under Ann's umbrella. "I mean, you can rebuild one part, but what do you do about the rest?"

"Of the city?" Jetske said.

"No," Ann said slowly, "I guess I mean of the world."

Jetske laughed. She had what Ann now thought of as Dutch teeth, even and white, with quite a lot of gum showing above them and below the lip. "I didn't know you were a socialist," she said. Her cheeks were pink and healthy, like a cheese ad.

"I'm not," Ann said. "But I thought we were supposed to be thinking in total patterns."

Jetske laughed again. "Did you know," she said, "that in some countries you have to get official permission to move from one town to another?"

Ann didn't like this idea at all. "It controls the population flow," Jetske said. "You can't really have Urban Design without that, you know."

"I think that's awful," Ann said.

"Of course you do," Jetske said, as close to bitterness as she ever got. "You've never had to do it. Over here you are soft in the belly, you think you can always have everything. You think there is freedom of choice. The whole world will come to it. You will see." She began teasing Ann again about her plastic headscarf. Jetske never wore anything on her head.

Ann designed her shopping complex, putting in a skylight and banks of indoor plants, leaving out the aqueduct. She got an A.

In the third week of March, Ann went with Jetske and some of the others to a Buckminster Fuller lecture. Afterwards they all went to the pub on the corner of the Square for a couple of beers. Ann left with Jetske about eleven o'clock and walked a couple of blocks with her before Jetske turned off towards her lovely old house with the stained glass. Ann continued by herself, warily, keeping to the lighted streets. She carried her purse under her elbow and held her furled umbrella at the ready. For once it wasn't raining.

When she got back to the house and started to climb the stairs, it struck her that something was different. Upstairs, she knew. Absolutely, something was out of line. There was curious music coming from the room next door, a high flute rising over drums, thumping noises, the sound of voices. The man next door was throwing a party, it seemed. Good for him, Ann thought. He might as well do something. She settled down for an hour's reading.

But the noises were getting louder. From the bathroom came the sound of retching. There was going to be trouble. Ann checked her door to make sure it was locked, got out the bottle of sherry she kept in the cupboard next to the oven and poured herself a drink. Then she turned out the light and sat with her back against the door, drinking her sherry in the faint blue light from the funeral home next door. There was no point in going to bed: even with her earplugs in, she could never sleep.

The music and thumpings got louder. After a while there was a banging on the floor, then some shouting, which came quite clearly through Ann's hot-air register. "I'm calling the police! You hear? I'm calling the police! You get them out of here and get out yourself!" The music switched off, the door opened and there was a clattering down the stairs. Then more footsteps—Ann couldn't tell whether they were going up or down—and more shouting. The front door banged and the shouts continued on down the street. Ann undressed and put on her nightgown, still without turning on the light, and crept into the bathroom. The bathtub was full of vomit.

This time Mrs. Nolan didn't even wait for Ann to get back from classes. She waylaid her in the morning as she was comıng out of her room. Mrs. Nolan was holding a can of Drano and had dark circles under her eyes. Somehow this made her look younger. She's probably not much older than I am, Ann thought. Until now she had considered her middle-aged.

"I guess you saw the mess in there," she whispered.

"Yes, I did," Ann said.

"I guess you heard all that last night." She paused.

"What happened?" Ann asked. In fact she really wanted to know.

"He had some dancing girls in there! Three dancing girls, and two other men, in that little room! I thought the ceiling was gonna come right down on our heads!"

"I did hear something like dancing," Ann said.

"Dancing! They was jumping, it sounded like they jumped right off the bed onto the floor. The plaster was coming off. Fred wasn't home, he's not home yet. I was afraid for the kids. Like, with those tattoos, who knows what they was working themselves up to?" Her sibilant voice hinted of ritual murders, young Jimmy and runny-nosed Donny sacrificed to some obscure god.

"What did you do?" Ann asked.

"I called the police. Well, the dancing girls, as soon as they heard I was calling the police, they got out of here, I can tell you. Put on their coats and was down the stairs and out the door like nothing. You can bet they didn't want no trouble with the police. But not the others, they don't seem to know what police means."

She paused again, and Ann asked, "Did they come?"

"Who?"

"The police.'

"Well, you know around here it always takes the police a while to get there, unless there's some right outside. I know that, it's not the first time I've had to call them So who knows what they would've done in the meantime? I could hear them coming downstairs, like, so I just grabs the broom and I chased them out. I chased them all the way down the street."

Ann saw that she thought she had done something very brave, which meant that in fact she had. She really believed that the man next door and his friends were dangerous, that they were a threat to her children. She had chased them single-handedly, yelling with fear and defiance. But he had only been throwing a party.

"Heavens," she said weakly.

"You can say that again," said Mrs. Nolan. "I went in there this morning, to get his things and put them out front where he could get them without me having to see him. I don't have such good nerves, I didn't sleep at all, even after they was gone. Fred is just gonna have to stop driving nights, I can't take it. But you know? He didn't have no things in there. Not one. Just an old empty suitcase?"

"What about his native costume?" Ann said.

"He had it on," Mrs. Nolan said. "He just went running down the street in it, like some kind of a loony. And you know what else I found in there? In one corner, there was this pile of empty bottles. Liquor. He must've been drinking like a fish for months, and never threw out the bottles. And in another corner, there was this pile of burnt matches. He could've burnt the house down, throwing them on the floor like that. But the worst thing was, you know all the times he borrowed my vacuum cleaner?"

"Yes," Ann said.

"Well, he never threw away the dirt. There it all was, in the other corner of the room. He must've just emptied it out and left it there. I don't get it." Mrs. Nolan, by now, was puzzled rather than angry.

"Well," Ann said, "that certainly is strange."

"Strange?" Mrs. Nolan said. "I'll tell you it's strange. He always paid the rent though, right on time. Never a day late. Why would he put the dirt in a corner like that, when he could've put it out in a bag like everyone else? It's not like he didn't know. I told him real clear which were the garbage days, when he moved in."

Ann said she was going to be late for class if she didn't hurry. At the front door she tucked her hair under her plastic scarf. Today it was just a drizzle, not heavy enough for the umbrella.

She started off, walking quickly along beside the double line of traffic.

She wondered where he had gone, chased down the street by Mrs. Nolan in her scuffies and flowered housecoat, shouting and flailing at him with a broom. She must have been at least as terrifying a spectacle to him as he was to her, and just as inexplicable. Why would this woman, this fat crazy woman, wish to burst in upon a scene of harmless hospitality, banging and raving? He and his friends could easily have overpowered her, but they would not even have thought about doing that. They would have been too frightened. What unspoken taboo had they violated? What would these cold, mad people do next?

Anyway, he did have some friends. They would take care of him, at least for the time being. Which was a relief, she guessed. But what she really felt was a childish regret that she had not seen the dancing girls. If she had known they were there, she might even have risked opening her door. She knew they were not real dancing girls, they were probably just some whores from Scollay Square. Mrs. Nolan had called them that as a euphemism, or perhaps because of an unconscious association with the word *Arabian*, the vaguely Arabian country. She never had found out what it was. Nevertheless, she wished she had seen them. Jetske would find all of this quite amusing, especially the image of her backed against the door, drinking sherry in the dark. It would have been better if she'd had the courage to look.

She began to think about her green space, as she often did during this walk. The green, perfect space of the future. She knew by now that it was cancelled in advance, that it would never come into being, that it was already too late. Once she was qualified, she would return to plan tasteful mixes of residential units and shopping complexes, with a lot of underground malls and arcades to protect people from the snow. But she could allow herself to see it one last time.

The fence was gone now, and the green stretched out endlessly, fields and trees and flowing water, as far as she could see. In the distance, beneath the arches of the aqueduct, a herd of animals, deer or something, was grazing. (She must learn more about animals.) Groups of people were walking happily among the trees, holding hands, not just in twos but in threes, fours, fives. The man from next door was there, in his native costume, and the mathematicians, they were all in their native costumes. Beside the stream a man was playing the flute; and around him, in long flowered robes and mauve scuffies, their auburn hair floating around their healthy pink faces, smiling their Dutch smiles, the dancing girls were sedately dancing.

The Sin Eater

This is Joseph, in maroon leather bedroom slippers, flattened at the heels, scuffed at the toes, wearing also a seedy cardigan of muddy off-yellow that reeks of bargain basements, sucking at his pipe, his hair greying and stringy, his articulation as beautiful and precise and English as ever:

"In Wales," he says, "mostly in the rural areas, there was a personage known as the Sin Eater. When someone was dying the Sin Eater would be sent for. The people of the house would prepare a meal and place it on the coffin. They would have the coffin all ready, of course: once they'd decided you were going off, you had scarcely any choice in the matter. According to other versions, the meal would be placed on the dead person's body, which must have made for some sloppy eating one would have thought. In any case the Sin Eater would devour this meal and would also be given a sum of money. It was believed that all the sins the dying person had accumulated during his lifetime would be removed from him and transmitted to the Sin Eater. The Sin Eater thus became absolutely bloated with other people's sins. She'd accumulate such a heavy load of them that nobody wanted to have anything to do with her; a kind of syphilitic of the soul, you might say. They'd even avoid speaking to her, except of course when it was time to summon her to another meal."

"Her?" I say.

Joseph smiles, that lopsided grin that shows the teeth in one side of his mouth, the side not engaged with the stem of his pipe. An ironic grin, wolvish, picking up on what? What have I given away this time?

"I think of them as old women," he says, "though there's no reason why they shouldn't have been men, I suppose. They could be anything as long as they were willing to eat the sins. Destitute old creatures who had no other way of keeping body and soul together, wouldn't you think? A sort of geriatric spiritual whoring."

He gazes at me, grinning away, and I remember certain stories I've heard about him, him and women. He's had three wives, to begin with. Nothing with me though, ever, though he does try to help me on with my coat a bit too lingeringly. Why should I worry? It's not as though I'm susceptible. Besides which he's at least sixty, and the cardigan is truly gross, as my sons would say.

"It was bad luck to kill one of them, though," he says, "and there must have been other perks. In point of fact I think Sin Eating has a lot to be said for it."

Joseph's not one of the kind who'll wait in sensitive, indulgent silence when you've frozen on him or run out of things to say. If you won't talk to him, he'll bloody well talk to you, about the most boring things he can think of, usually. I've heard all about his flower beds and his three wives and how to raise calla lilies in your cellar; I've heard all about the cellar too, I could give guided tours. He says he thinks it's healthy for his patients—he won't call them "clients," no pussyfooting around, with Joseph—to know he's a human being too, and God do we know it. He'll drone on and on until you figure out that you aren't paying him so you can listen to him talk about his house plants, you're paying him so he can listen to you talk about yours.

Sometimes, though, he's really telling you something. I pick up my coffee cup, wondering whether this is one of those occasions.

"Okay," I say, "I'll bite. Why?"

"It's obvious," he says, lighting his pipe again, spewing out fumes. "First, the patients have to wait until they're dying. A

214

true life crisis, no fakery and invention. They aren't permitted to bother you until then, until they can demonstrate that they're serious, you might say. Second, somebody gets a good square meal out of it." He laughs ruefully. We both know that half his patients don't bother to pay him, not even the money the government pays them. Joseph has a habit of taking on people nobody else will touch with a barge pole, not because they're too sick but because they're too poor. Mothers on welfare and so on; bad credit risks, like Joseph himself. He once got fired from a loony bin for trying to institute worker control.

"And think of the time saving," he goes on. "A couple of hours per patient, sum total, as opposed to twice a week for years and years, with the same result in the end."

"That's pretty cynical," I say disapprovingly. I'm supposed to be the cynical one, but maybe he's outflanking me, to force me to give up this corner. Cynicism is a defence, according to Joseph.

"You wouldn't even have to listen to them," he says. "Not a blessed word. The sins are transmitted in the food."

Suddenly he looks sad and tired. "You're telling me I'm wasting your time?" I say.

"Not mine, my dear," he says. "I've got all the time in the world."

I interpret this as condescension, the one thing above all that I can't stand. I don't throw my coffee cup at him, however. I'm not as angry as I would have been once.

We've spent a lot of time on it, this anger of mine. It was only because I found reality so unsatisfactory; that was my story. So unfinished, so sloppy, so pointless, so endless. I wanted things to make sense.

I thought Joseph would try to convince me that reality was actually fine and dandy and then try to adjust me to it, but he didn't do that. Instead he agreed with me, cheerfully and at once. Life in most ways was a big pile of shit, he said. That was axiomatic. "Think of it as a desert island," he said. "You're stuck on it, now you have to decide how best to cope."

"Until rescued?" I said.

"Forget about the rescue," he said.

"I can't," I said.

This conversation is taking place in Joseph's office, which is just as tatty as he is and smells of unemptied ashtrays, feet, misery and twice-breathed air. But it's also taking place in my bedroom, on the day of the funeral. Joseph's, who didn't have all the time in the world.

"He fell out of a tree," said Karen, notifying me. She'd come to do this in person, rather than using the phone. Joseph didn't trust phones. Most of the message in any act of communication, he said, was non-verbal.

Karen stood in my doorway, oozing tears. She was one of his too, one of us; it was through her I'd got him. By now there's a network of us, it's like recommending a hairdresser, we've passed him from hand to hand like the proverbial eye or tooth. Smart women with detachable husbands or genius-afflicted children with nervous tics, smart women with deranged lives, overjoyed to find someone who wouldn't tell us we were too smart for our own good and should all have frontal lobotomies. Smartness was an asset, Joseph maintained. We should only see what happened to the dumb ones.

"Out of a *tree*?" I said, almost screaming.

"Sixty feet, onto his head," said Karen. She began weeping again. I wanted to shake her.

"What the bloody hell was he doing up at the top of a sixty-foot *tree*?" I said.

"Pruning it," said Karen. "It was in his garden. It was cutting off the light to his flower beds."

"The old fart," I said. I was furious with him. It was an act of desertion. What made him think he had the right to go climbing up to the top of a sixty-foot tree, risking all our lives? Did his flower beds mean more to him than we did?

"What are we going to do?" said Karen.

What am I going to do? is one question. It can always be replaced by *What am I going to wear?* For some people it's the same thing. I go through the cupboard, looking for the blackest things I can find. What I wear will be the non-verbal part of the communication. Joseph will notice. I have a horrible feeling I'll turn up at the funeral home and find they've laid him out in his awful yellow cardigan and those tacky maroon leather bedroom slippers.

I needn't have bothered with the black. It's no longer demanded. The three wives are in pastels, the first in blue, the second in mauve, the third, the current one, in beige. I know a lot about the three wives, from those off-days of mine when I didn't feel like talking.

Karen is here too, in an Indian-print dress, snivelling softly to herself. I envy her. I want to feel grief, but I can't quite believe Joseph is dead. It seems like some joke he's playing, some anecdote that's supposed to make us learn something. Fakery and invention. *All right, Joseph,* I want to call, *we have the answer, you can come out now.* But nothing happens, the closed coffin remains closed, no wisps of smoke issue from it to show there's life.

The closed coffin is the third wife's idea. She thinks it's more dignified, says the grapevine, and it probably is. The coffin is of dark wood, in good taste, no showy trim. No one has made a meal and placed it on this coffin, no one has eaten from it. No destitute old creature, gobbling down the turnips and mash and the heavy secrecies of Joseph's life along with them. I have no idea what Joseph might have had on his conscience. Nevertheless I feel this as an omission: what then have become of Joseph's sins? They hover around us, in the air, over the bowed heads, while a male relative of Joseph's, unknown to me, tells us all what a fine man he was.

After the funeral we go back to Joseph's house, to the third wife's house, for what used to be called the wake. Not any more: now it's coffee and refreshments.

The flower beds are tidy, gladioli at this time of year, already fading and a little ragged. The tree branch, the one that broke, is still on the lawn.

"I kept having the feeling he wasn't really there," says Karen as we go up the walk.

"Really where?" I say.

"There," says Karen. "In the coffin."

"For Christ's sake," I say, "don't start that." I can tolerate that kind of sentimental fiction in myself, just barely, as long as I don't do it out loud. "Dead is dead, that's what he'd say. Deal with here and now, remember?"

Karen, who'd once tried suicide, nodded and started to cry again. Joseph is an expert on people who try suicide. He's never lost one yet.

"How does he do it?" I asked Karen once. Suicide wasn't one of my addictions, so I didn't know.

"He makes it sound so *boring*," she said.

"That can't be all," I said.

"He makes you imagine," she said, "what it's like to be dead."

There are people moving around quietly, in the living room and in the dining room, where the table stands, arranged by the third wife with a silver tea urn and a vase of chrysanthemums, pink and yellow. Nothing too funereal, you can hear her thinking. On the white tablecloth there are cups, plates, cookies, coffee, cakes. I don't know why funerals are supposed to make people hungry, but they do. If you can still chew you know you're alive.

Karen is beside me, stuffing down a piece of chocolate cake. On the other side is the first wife.

"I hope you aren't one of the loonies," she says to me abruptly. I've never really met her before, she's just been pointed out to me, by Karen, at the funeral. She's wiping her fingers on a paper napkin. On her powder-blue lapel is a gold brooch in the shape of a bird's nest, complete with the eggs. It reminds me of high school: felt skirts with appliqués of cats and telephones, a world of replicas.

I ponder my reply. Does she mean *client*, or is she asking whether I am by chance genuinely out of my mind?

"No," I say.

"Didn't think so," says the first wife. "You don't look like it. A lot of them were, the place was crawling with them. I was afraid there might be an *incident*. When I lived with Joseph there were always these *incidents*, phone calls at two in the morning, always killing themselves, throwing themselves all over him, you couldn't believe what went on. Some of them were *devoted* to him. If he'd told them to shoot the Pope or something, they'd have done it just like that."

"He was very highly thought of," I say carefully.

"You're telling *me*," says the first wife. "Had the idea he was God himself, some of them. Not that he minded all that much."

The paper napkin isn't adequate, she's licking her fingers. "Too rich," she says. "*Hers*." She jerks her head in the direction of the second wife, who is wispier than the first wife and is walking past us, somewhat aimlessly, in the direction of the living room. "You can have it, I told him finally. I just want some peace and quiet before I have to start pushing up the daisies." Despite the richness, she helps herself to another piece of chocolate cake. "*She* had this nutty idea that we should have some of them stand up and give little testimonies about him, right at the ceremony. Are you totally out of your tree? I told her. It's your funeral, but if I was you I'd try to keep it in mind that some of the people there are going to be a whole lot saner than others. Luckily she listened to me."

"Yes," I say. There's chocolate icing on her cheek: I wonder if I should tell her.

"I did what I could," she says, "which wasn't that much, but still. I was fond of him in a way. You can't just wipe out ten years of your life. I brought the cookies," she adds, rather smugly. "Least I could do."

I look down at the cookies. They're white, cut into the shapes of stars and moons and decorated with coloured sugar and little silver balls. They remind me of Christmas, of festivals and celebrations. They're the kind of cookies you make to please someone; to please a child.

I've been here long enough. I look around for the third wife, the one in charge, to say goodbye. I finally locate her, standing in an open doorway. She's crying, something she didn't do at the funeral. The first wife is beside her, holding her hand.

"I'm keeping it just like this," says the first wife, to no one in particular. Past her shoulder I can see into the room, Joseph's study evidently. It would take a lot of strength to leave that rummage sale untouched, untidied. Not to mention the begonias withering on the sill. But for her it will take no strength at all, because Joseph is in this room, unfinished, a huge boxful of loose ends. He refuses to be packed up and put away.

"Who do you hate the most?" says Joseph. This, in the middle of a lecture he's been giving me about the proper kind of birdbath for one's garden. He knows of course that I don't have a garden.

"I have absolutely no idea," I say.

"Then you should find out," says Joseph. "I myself cherish an abiding hatred for the boy who lived next door to me when I was eight."

"Why is that?" I ask, pleased to be let off the hook.

"He picked my sunflower," he says. "I grew up in a slum, you know. We had an area of sorts at the front, but it was solid cinders. However I did manage to grow this one stunted little sunflower, God knows how. I used to get up early every morning just to look at it. And the little bugger picked it. Pure bloody malice. I've forgiven a lot of later transgressions but if I ran into the little sod tomorrow I'd stick a knife into him."

I'm shocked, as Joseph intends me to be. "He was only a child," I say.

"So was I," he says. "The early ones are the hardest to forgive. Children have no charity; it has to be learned."

Is this Joseph proving yet once more that he's a human being, or am I intended to understand something about myself? Maybe, maybe not. Sometimes Joseph's stories are parables, but sometimes they're just running off at the mouth.

In the front hall the second wife, she of the mauve wisps, ambushes me. "He didn't fall," she whispers.

"Pardon?" I say.

The three wives have a family resemblance—they're all blondish and vague around the edges—but there's something else about this one, a glittering of the eyes. Maybe it's grief; or maybe Joseph didn't always draw a totally firm line between his personal and his professional lives. The second wife has a faint aroma of client.

"He wasn't happy," she says. "I could tell. We were still very close, you know."

What she wants me to infer is that he jumped. "He seemed all right to me," I say.

"He was good at keeping up a front," she says. She takes a breath, she's about to confide in me, but whatever these revelations are I don't want to hear them. I want Joseph to remain as he appeared: solid, capable, wise and sane. I do not need his darkness.

I go back to the apartment. My sons are away for the weekend. I wonder whether I should bother making dinner just for myself. It's hardly worth it. I wander around the too-small living room, picking things up. No longer my husband's: as befits the half-divorced, he lives elsewhere.

One of my sons has just reached the shower-and-shave phase, the other hasn't, but both of them leave a deposit every time they pass through a room. A sort of bathtub ring of objects— socks, paperback books left face-down and open in the middle, sandwiches with bites taken out of them, and, lately, cigarette butts.

Under a dirty T-shirt I discover the Hare Krishna magazine my younger son brought home a week ago. I was worried that it was a spate of adolescent religious mania, but no, he'd given them a quarter because he felt sorry for them. He was a dead-robin-burier as a child. I take the magazine into the kitchen to put it in the trash. On the front there's a picture of Krishna playing the flute, surrounded by adoring maidens. His face is bright blue, which makes me think of corpses: some things are not cross-cultural. If I read on I could find out why meat and sex are bad for you. Not such a poor idea when you think about it: no more terrified cows, no more divorces. A life of abstinence and prayer. I think of myself, standing on a street corner, ringing a bell, swathed in flowing garments. Selfless and removed, free from sin. Sin is this world, says Krishna. This world is all we have, says Joseph. It's all you have to work with. It is not too much for you. You will not be rescued.

I could walk to the corner for a hamburger or I could phone out for pizza. I decide on the pizza.

"Do you like me?" Joseph says from his armchair.

"What do you mean, do I *like* you?" I say. It's early on; I haven't given any thought to whether or not I like Joseph.

"Well, do you?" he says.

"Look," I say. I'm speaking calmly but in fact I'm outraged. This is a demand, and Joseph is not supposed to make demands of me. There are too many demands being made of me already. That's why I'm here, isn't it? Because the demands exceed the supply. "You're like my dentist," I say. "I don't think about whether or not I like my dentist. I don't *have* to like him. I'm paying him to fix my teeth. You and my dentist are the only people in the whole world that I don't *have* to *like*."

"But if you met me under other circumstances," Joseph persists, "would you like me?"

"I have no idea," I say. "I can't imagine any other circumstances."

This is a room at night, a night empty except for me. I'm looking at the ceiling, across which the light from a car passing outside is slowly moving. My apartment is on the first floor: I don't like heights. Before this I always lived in a house.

I've been having a dream about Joseph. Joseph was never much interested in dreams. At the beginning I used to save them up for him and tell them to him, the ones I thought were of interest, but he would always refuse to say what they meant. He'd make me tell him, instead. Being awake, according to Joseph, was more important than being asleep. He wanted me to prefer it.

Nevertheless, there was Joseph in my dream. It's the first time he's made an appearance. I think that it will please him to have made it, finally, after all those other dreams about preparations for dinner parties, always one plate short. But then I remember that he's no longer around to be told. Here it is, finally, the shape of my bereavement: Joseph is no longer around to be told. There is no one left in my life who is there only to be told.

I'm in an airport terminal. The plane's been delayed, all the planes have been delayed, perhaps there's a strike, and people are crammed in and milling around. Some of them are upset, there are children crying, some of the women are crying too, they've lost people, they push through the crowd calling out names, but elsewhere there are clumps of men and women laughing and singing, they've had the foresight to bring cases of beer with them to the airport and they're passing the bottles around. I try to get some information but there's no one at any of the ticket counters. Then I realize I've forgotten my passport. I decide to take a taxi home to get it, and by the time I make it back maybe they'll have everything straightened out.

I push towards the exit doors, but someone is waving to me across the heads of the crowd. It's Joseph. I'm not at all surprised to see him, though I do wonder about the winter overcoat he's wearing, since it's still summer. He also has a yellow muffler wound around his neck, and a hat. I've never seen him in any of these clothes before. Of course, I think, he's cold, but now he's pushed through the people, he's beside me. He's wearing a pair of heavy leather gloves and he takes the right one off to shake my hand. His own hand is bright blue, a flat tempera-paint blue, a picture-book blue. I hesitate, then I shake the hand, but he doesn't let go, he holds my hand, confidingly, like a child, smiling at me as if we haven't met for a long time.

"I'm glad you got the invitation," he says.

Now he's leading me towards a doorway. There are fewer people now. To one side there's a stand selling orange juice. Joseph's three wives are behind the counter, all in identical costumes, white hats and frilly aprons, like waitresses of the forties. We go through the doorway; inside, people are sitting at small round tables, though there's nothing on the tables in front of them, they appear to be waiting.

I sit down at one of the tables and Joseph sits opposite me. He doesn't take off his hat or his coat, but his hands are on the table, no gloves, they're the normal colour again. There's a man standing beside us, trying to attract our attention. He's holding out a small white card covered with symbols, hands and fingers. A deaf-mute, I decide, and sure enough when I look his mouth is sewn shut. Now he's tugging at Joseph's arm, he's holding out something else, it's a large yellow flower. Joseph doesn't see him.

"Look," I say to Joseph, but the man is already gone and one of the waitresses has come instead. I resent the interruption, I have so much to tell Joseph and there's so little time, the plane will go in a minute, in the other room I can already hear the crackle of announcements, but the woman pushes in between us, smiling officiously. It's the first wife; behind her, the other two wives stand in attendance. She sets a large plate in front of us on the table.

"Will that be all?" she says, before she retreats.

The plate is filled with cookies, children's-party cookies, white ones, cut into the shapes of moons and stars, decorated with silver balls and coloured sugar. They look too rich.

"My sins," Joseph says. His voice sounds wistful but when I glance up he's smiling at me. Is he making a joke?

I look down at the plate again. I have a moment of panic: this is not what I ordered, it's too much for me, I might get sick. Maybe I could send it back; but I know this isn't possible.

I remember now that Joseph is dead. The plate floats up towards me, there is no table, around us is dark space. There are thousands of stars, thousands of moons, and as I reach out for one they begin to shine.

Giving Birth

But who gives it? And to whom is it given? Certainly it doesn't feel like giving, which implies a flow, a gentle handing over, no coercion. But there is scant gentleness here; it's too strenuous, the belly like a knotted fist, squeezing, the heavy trudge of the heart, every muscle in the body tight and moving, as in a slow-motion shot of a high-jump, the faceless body sailing up, turning, hanging for a moment in the air, and then—back to real time again—the plunge, the rush down, the result. Maybe the phrase was made by someone viewing the result only: in this case, the rows of babies to whom birth has occurred, lying like neat packages in their expertly wrapped blankets, pink or blue, with their labels Scotch Taped to their clear plastic cots, behind the plate-glass window.

No one ever says *giving death*, although they are in some ways the same, events, not things. And *delivering*, that act the doctor is generally believed to perform: who delivers what? Is it the mother who is delivered, like a prisoner being released? Surely not; nor is the child delivered to the mother like a letter through a slot. How can you be both the sender and the receiver at once? Was someone in bondage, is someone made free? Thus language, muttering in its archaic tongues of something, yet one more thing, that needs to be re-named.

It won't be by me, though. These are the only words I have,

I'm stuck with them, stuck in them. (That image of the tar sands, old tableau in the Royal Ontario Museum, second floor north, how persistent it is. Will I break free, or will I be sucked down, fossilized, a sabre-toothed tiger or lumbering brontosaurus who ventured out too far? Words ripple at my feet, black, sluggish, lethal. Let me try once more, before the sun gets me, before I starve or drown, while I can. It's only a tableau after all, it's only a metaphor. See, I can speak, I am not trapped, and you on your part can understand. So we will go ahead as if there were no problem about language.)

This story about giving birth is not about me. In order to convince you of that I should tell you what I did this morning, before I sat down at this desk—a door on top of two filing cabinets, radio to the left, calendar to the right, these devices by which I place myself in time. I got up at twenty-to-seven, and, halfway down the stairs, met my daughter, who was ascending, autonomously she thought, actually in the arms of her father. We greeted each other with hugs and smiles; we then played with the alarm clock and the hot water bottle, a ritual we go through only on the days her father has to leave the house early to drive into the city. This ritual exists to give me the illusion that I am sleeping in. When she finally decided it was time for me to get up, she began pulling my hair. I got dressed while she explored the bathroom scales and the mysterious white altar of the toilet. I took her downstairs and we had the usual struggle over her clothes. Already she is wearing miniature jeans, miniature T-shirts. After this she fed herself: orange, banana, muffin, porridge.

We then went out to the sun porch, where we recognized anew, and by their names, the dog, the cats and the birds, blue jays and goldfinches at this time of year, which is winter. She puts her fingers on my lips as I pronounce these words; she hasn't yet learned the secret of making them. I am waiting for her first word: surely it will be miraculous, something that has never yet been said. But if so, perhaps she's already said it and I, in my entrapment, my addiction to the usual, have not heard it.

In her playpen I discovered the first alarming thing of the day. It was a small naked woman, made of that soft plastic from which jiggly spiders and lizards and the other things people hang in their car windows are also made. She was given to my daughter by a friend, a woman who does props for movies, she was supposed to have been a prop but she wasn't used. The baby loved her and would crawl around the floor holding her in her mouth like a dog carrying a bone, with the head sticking out one side and the feet out the other. She seemed chewy and harmless, but the other day I noticed that the baby had managed to make a tear in the body with her new teeth. I put the woman into the cardboard box I use for toy storage.

But this morning she was back in the playpen and the feet were gone. The baby must have eaten them, and I worried about whether or not the plastic would dissolve in her stomach, whether it was toxic. Sooner or later, in the contents of her diaper, which I examine with the usual amount of maternal brooding, I knew I would find two small pink plastic feet. I removed the doll and later, while she was still singing to the dog outside the window, dropped it into the garbage. I am not up to finding tiny female arms, breasts, a head, in my daughter's disposable diapers, partially covered by undigested carrots and the husks of raisins, like the relics of some gruesome and demented murder.

Now she's having her nap and I am writing this story. From what I have said, you can see that my life (despite these occasional surprises, reminders of another world) is calm and orderly, suffused with that warm, reddish light, those well-placed blue highlights and reflecting surfaces (mirrors, plates, oblong window-panes) you think of as belonging to Dutch genre paintings; and like them it is realistic in detail and slightly sentimental. Or at least it has an aura of sentiment. (Already I'm having moments of muted grief over those of my daughter's baby clothes which are too small for her to wear any more. I will be a keeper of hair, I will store things in trunks, I will weep over photos.) But above all it's solid, everything here has solidity. No more of those washes of light, those shifts, nebulous effects of cloud, Turner sunsets, vague fears, the impalpables Jeanie used to concern herself with.

I call this woman Jeanie after the song. I can't remember any more of the song, only the title. The point (for in language there are always these "points," these reflections; this is what makes it so rich and sticky, this is why so many have disappeared beneath its dark and shining surface, why you should never try to see your own reflection in it; you will lean over too far, a strand of your hair will fall in and come out gold, and, thinking it is gold all the way down, you yourself will follow, sliding into those outstretched arms, towards the mouth you think is opening to pronounce your name but instead, just before your ears fill with pure sound, will form a word you have never heard before. . . .)

The point, for me, is in the hair. My own hair is not light brown, but Jeanie's was. This is one difference between us. The other point is the dreaming; for Jeanie isn't real in the same way that I am real. But by now, and I mean your time, both of us will have the same degree of reality, we will be equal: wraiths, echoes, reverberations in your own brain. At the moment though Jeanie is to me as I will someday be to you. So she is real enough.

Jeanie is on her way to the hospital, to give birth, to be delivered. She is not quibbling over these terms. She's sitting in the back seat of the car, with her eyes closed and her coat spread over her like a blanket. She is doing her breathing exercises and timing her contractions with a stopwatch. She has been up since two-thirty in the morning, when she took a bath and ate some lime Jell-O, and it's now almost ten. She has learned to count, during the slow breathing, in numbers (from one to ten while breathing in, from ten to one while breathing out) which she can actually see while she is silently pronouncing them. Each number is a different colour and, if she's concentrating very hard, a different typeface. They range from plain roman to ornamented circus numbers, red with gold filigree and dots. This is a refinement not mentioned in any of the numerous books she's read on the subject. Jeanie is a devotee of handbooks. She has at least two shelves of books that cover everything from building kitchen cabinets to auto repairs to smoking your own hams. She doesn't do many of these things, but she does some of them, and in her suitcase, along with a washcloth, a package of lemon Life Savers, a pair of glasses, a hot water bottle, some talcum powder and a paper bag, is the book that suggested she take along all of these things.

(By this time you may be thinking that I've invented Jeanie in order to distance myself from these experiences. Nothing could be further from the truth. I am, in fact, trying to bring myself closer to something that time has already made distant. As for Jeanie, my intention is simple: I am bringing her back to life.)

There are two other people in the car with Jeanie. One is a man, whom I will call A., for convenience. A. is driving. When Jeanie opens her eyes, at the end of every contraction, she can see the back of his slightly balding head and his reassuring shoulders. A. drives well and not too quickly. From time to time he asks her how she is, and she tells him how long the contractions are lasting and how long there is between them. When they stop for gas he buys them each a Styrofoam container of coffee. For months he has helped her with the breathing exercises, pressing on her knee as recommended by the book, and he will be present at the delivery. (Perhaps it's to him that the birth will be given, in the same sense that one gives a performance.) Together they have toured the hospital maternity ward, in company with a small group of other pairs like them: one thin solicitous person, one slow bulbous person. They have been shown the rooms, shared and private, the sitz-baths, the delivery room itself, which gave the impression of being white. The nurse was light-brown, with limber hips and elbows; she laughed a lot as she answered questions.

"First they'll give you an enema. You know what it is? They take a tube of water and put it up your behind. Now, the gentlemen must put on this—and these, over your shoes. And these hats, this one for those with long hair, this for those with short hair."

"What about those with no hair?" says A.

The nurse looks up at his head and laughs. "Oh, you still have some," she says. "If you have a question, do not be afraid to ask."

They have also seen the film made by the hospital, a full-colour film of a woman giving birth to, can it be a baby? "Not all babies will be this large at birth," the Australian nurse who introduces the movie says. Still, the audience, half of which is pregnant, doesn't look very relaxed when the lights go on. ("If you don't like the visuals," a friend of Jeanie's has told her, "you can always close your eyes.") It isn't the blood so much as the brownish-red disinfectant that bothers her. "I've decided to call this whole thing off," she says to A., smiling to show it's a joke. He gives her a hug and says, "Everything's going to be fine."

And she knows it is. Everything will be fine. But there is another woman in the car. She's sitting in the front seat, and she hasn't turned or acknowledged Jeanie in any way. She, like Jeanie, is going to the hospital. She too is pregnant. She is not going to the hospital to give birth, however, because the words, the words, are too alien to her experience, the experience she is about to have, to be used about it at all. She's wearing a cloth coat with checks in maroon and brown, and she has a kerchief tied over her hair. Jeanie has seen her before, but she knows little about her except that she is a woman who did not wish to become pregnant, who did not choose to divide herself like this, who did not choose any of these ordeals, these initiations. It would be no use telling her that everything is going to be fine. The word in English for unwanted intercourse is rape. But there is no word in the language for what is about to happen to this woman.

Jeanie has seen this woman from time to time throughout her pregnancy, always in the same coat, always with the same kerchief. Naturally, being pregnant herself has made her more aware of other pregnant women, and she has watched them, examined them covertly, every time she has seen one. But not every other pregnant woman is this woman. She did not, for instance, attend Jeanie's pre-natal classes at the hospital, where the women were all young, younger than Jeanie.

"How many will be breast-feeding?" asks the Australian nurse with the hefty shoulders.

All hands but one shoot up. A modern group, the new generation, and the one lone bottle-feeder, who might have (who knows?) something wrong with her breasts, is ashamed of herself. The others look politely away from her. What they want most to discuss, it seems, are the differences between one kind of disposable diaper and another. Sometimes they lie on mats and squeeze each other's hands, simulating contractions and counting breaths. It's all very hopeful. The Australian nurse tells them not to get in and out of the bathtub by themselves. At the end of an hour they are each given a glass of apple juice.

There is only one woman in the class who has already given birth. She's there, she says, to make sure they give her a shot this time. They delayed it last time and she went through hell. The others look at her with mild disapproval. *They* are not clamouring for shots, they do not intend to go through hell. Hell comes from the wrong attitude, they feel. The books talk about *discomfort*.

"It's not discomfort, it's pain, baby," the woman says.

The others smile uneasily and the conversation slides back to disposable diapers.

Vitaminized, conscientious, well-read Jeanie, who has managed to avoid morning sickness, varicose veins, stretch marks, toxemia and depression, who has had no aberrations of appetite, no blurrings of vision—why is she followed, then, by this other? At first it was only a glimpse now and then, at the infants' clothing section in Simpson's Basement, in the supermarket lineup, on street corners as she herself slid by in A.'s car: the haggard face, the bloated torso, the kerchief holding back the too-sparse hair. In any case, it was Jeanie who saw her, not the other way around. If she knew she was following Jeanie she gave no sign.

As Jeanie has come closer and closer to this day, the unknown day on which she will give birth, as time has thickened around her so that it has become something she must propel herself through, a kind of slush, wet earth underfoot, she has seen this woman more and more often, though always from distance. Depending on the light, she has appeared by turns as a young girl of perhaps twenty to an older woman of forty or forty-five, but there was never any doubt in Jeanie's mind that it was the same woman. In fact it did not occur to her that the woman was not real in the usual sense (and perhaps she was, originally, on the first or second sighting, as the voice that causes an echo is real), until A. stopped for a red light during this drive to the hospital and the woman, who had been standing on the corner with a brown paper bag in her arms, simply opened the front door of the car and got in. A. didn't react, and Jeanie knows better than to say anything to him. She is aware that the woman is not really there: Jeanie is not crazy. She could even make the woman disappear by opening her eyes wider, by staring, but it is only the shape that would go away, not the feeling. Jeanie isn't exactly afraid of this woman. She is afraid for her.

When they reach the hospital, the woman gets out of the car and is through the door by the time A. has come around to help Jeanie out of the back seat. In the lobby she is nowhere to be seen. Jeanie goes through Admission in the usual way, unshadowed.

There has been an epidemic of babies during the night and the maternity ward is overcrowded. Jeanie waits for her room behind a dividing screen. Nearby someone is screaming, screaming and mumbling between screams in what sounds like a foreign language. Portuguese, Jeanie thinks. She tells herself that for them it is different, you're supposed to scream, you're regarded as queer if you don't scream, it's a required part of giving birth. Nevertheless she knows that the woman screaming is the other woman and she is screaming from pain. Jeanie listens to the other voice, also a woman's, comforting, reassuring: her mother? A nurse?

A. arrives and they sit uneasily, listening to the screams. Finally Jeanie is sent for and she goes for her prep. Prep school, she thinks. She takes off her clothes—when will she see them again?—and puts on the hospital gown. She is examined, labelled around the wrist and given an enema. She tells the nurse she can't take Demerol because she's allergic to it, and the nurse writes this down. Jeanie doesn't know whether this is true or not but she doesn't want Demerol, she has read the books. She intends to put up a struggle over her pubic hair— surely she will lose her strength if it is all shaved off—but it turns out the nurse doesn't have very strong feelings about it. She is told her contractions are not far enough along to be taken seriously, she can even have lunch. She puts on her dressing gown and rejoins A., in the freshly vacated room, eats some tomato soup and a veal cutlet, and decides to take a nap while A. goes out for supplies.

Jeanie wakes up when A. comes back. He has brought a paper, some detective novels for Jeanie and a bottle of Scotch for himself. A. reads the paper and drinks Scotch, and Jeanie reads *Poirot's Early Cases*. There is no connection between Poirot and her labour, which is now intensifying, unless it is the egg-shape of Poirot's head and the vegetable marrows he is known to cultivate with strands of wet wool (placentae? umbilical cords?). She is glad the stories are short; she is walking around the room now, between contractions. Lunch was definitely a mistake.

"I think I have back labour," she says to A. They get out the handbook and look up the instructions for this. It's useful that everything has a name. Jeanie kneels on the bed and rests her forehead on her arms while A. rubs her back. A. pours himself another Scotch, in the hospital glass. The nurse, in pink, comes, looks, asks about the timing, and goes away again. Jeanie is beginning to sweat. She can only manage half a page or so of Poirot before she has to clamber back up on the bed again and begin breathing and running through the coloured numbers.

When the nurse comes back, she has a wheelchair. It's time to go down to the labour room, she says. Jeanie feels stupid sitting in the wheelchair. She tells herself about peasant women having babies in the fields, Indian women having them on portages with hardly a second thought. She feels effete. But the hospital wants her to ride, and considering the fact that the nurse is tiny, perhaps it's just as well. What if Jeanie were to collapse, after all? After all her courageous talk. An image of the tiny pink nurse, antlike, trundling large Jeanie through the corridors, rolling her along like a heavy beach ball.

As they go by the check-in desk a woman is wheeled past on a table, covered by a sheet. Her eyes are closed and there's a bottle feeding into her arm through a tube. Something is wrong. Jeanie looks back—she thinks it was the other woman—but the sheeted table is hidden now behind the counter.

In the dim labour room Jeanie takes off her dressing gown and is helped up onto the bed by the nurse. A. brings her suit-case, which is not a suitcase actually but a small flight bag, the significance of this has not been lost on Jeanie, and in fact she now has some of the apprehensive feelings she associates with planes, including the fear of a crash. She takes out her Life Savers, her glasses, her washcloth and the other things she thinks she will need. She removes her contact lenses and places them in their case, reminding A. that they must not be lost. Now she is purblind.

There is something else in her bag that she doesn't remove. It's a talisman, given to her several years ago as a souvenir by a travelling friend of hers. It's a rounded oblong of opaque blue glass, with four yellow-and-white eye shapes on it. In Turkey, her friend has told her, they hang them on mules to protect against the Evil Eye. Jeanie knows this talisman probably won't work for her, she is not Turkish and she isn't a mule, but it makes her feel safer to have it in the room with her. She had planned to hold it in her hand during the most difficult part of labour but somehow there is no longer any time for carrying out plans like this.

An old woman, a fat old woman dressed all in green, comes into the room and sits beside Jeanie. She says to A., who is sitting on the other side of Jeanie, "That is a good watch. They don't make watches like that any more." She is referring to his gold pocket watch, one of his few extravagances, which is on the night table. Then she places her hand on Jeanie's belly to feel the contraction. "This is good," she says, her accent is Swedish or German. "This, I call a contraction. Before, it was nothing." Jeanie can no longer remember having seen her before. "Good. Good."

"When will I have it?" Jeanie asks, when she can talk, when she is no longer counting.

The old woman laughs. Surely that laugh, those tribal hands, have presided over a thousand beds, a thousand kitchen tables . . . "A long time yet," she says. "Eight, ten hours."

"But I've been *doing* this for twelve hours already," Jeanie says.

"Not hard labour," the woman says. "Not good, like this."

Jeanie settles into herself for the long wait. At the moment she can't remember why she wanted to have a baby in the first place. That decision was made by someone else, whose motives are now unclear. She remembers the way women who had babies used to smile at one another, mysteriously, as if there was something they knew that she didn't, the way they would casually exclude her from their frame of reference. What was the knowledge, the mystery, or was having a baby really no more inexplicable than having a car accident or an orgasm? (But these too were indescribable, events of the body, all of them; why should the mind distress itself trying to find a language for them?) She has sworn she will never do that to any woman without children, engage in those passwords and exclusions. She's old enough, she's been put through enough years of it to find it tiresome and cruel.

But—and this is the part of Jeanie that goes with the talisman hidden in her bag, not with the part that longs to build kitchen cabinets and smoke hams—she is, secretly, hoping for a mystery. Something more than this, something else, a vision. After all she is risking her life, though it's not too likely she will die. Still, some women do. Internal bleeding, shock, heart failure, a mistake on the part of someone, a nurse, a doctor. She deserves a vision, she deserves to be allowed to bring something back with her from this dark place into which she is now rapidly descending.

She thinks momentarily about the other woman. Her motives, too, are unclear. Why doesn't she want to have a baby? Has she been raped, does she have ten other children, is she starving? Why hasn't she had an abortion? Jeanie doesn't know, and in fact it no longer matters why. *Uncross your fingers*, Jeanie thinks to her. Her face, distorted with pain and terror, floats briefly behind Jeanie's eyes before it too drifts away.

Jeanie tries to reach down to the baby, as she has many times before, sending waves of love, colour, music, down through her arteries to it, but she finds she can no longer do this. She can no longer feel the baby as a baby, its arms and legs poking, kicking, turning. It has collected itself together, it's a hard sphere, it does not have time right now to listen to her. She's grateful for this because she isn't sure anyway how good the message would be. She no longer has control of the numbers either, she can no longer see them, although she continues mechanically to count. She realizes she has practised for the wrong thing, A. squeezing her knee was nothing, she should have practised for this, whatever it is.

"Slow down," A. says. She's on her side now, he's holding her hand. "Slow it right down."

"I can't, I can't do it, I can't do this."

"Yes, you can."

"Will I sound like that?"

"Like what?" A. says. Perhaps he can't hear it: it's the other woman, in the room next door or the room next door to that. She's screaming and crying, screaming and crying. While she cries she is saying, over and over, "It hurts. It hurts."

"No, you won't," he says. So there is someone, after all.

A doctor comes in, not her own doctor. They want her to turn over on her back.

"I can't," she says. "I don't like it that way." Sounds have receded, she has trouble hearing them. She turns over and the doctor gropes with her rubber-gloved hand. Something wet and hot flows over her thighs.

"It was just ready to break," the doctor says. "All I had to do was touch it. Four centimetres," she says to A.

"Only *four?*" Jeanie says. She feels cheated; they must be wrong. The doctor says her own doctor will be called in time. Jeanie is outraged at them. They have not understood, but it's too late to say this and she slips back into the dark place, which is not hell, which is more like being inside, trying to get out. *Out*, she says or thinks. Then she is floating, the numbers are gone, if anyone told her to get up, go out of the room, stand on her head, she would do it. From minute to minute she comes up again, grabs for air.

"You're hyperventilating," A. says. "Slow it down." He is rubbing her back now, hard, and she takes his hand and shoves it viciously further down, to the right place, which is not the right place as soon as his hand is there. She remembers a story she read once, about the Nazis tying the legs of Jewish women together during labour. She never really understood before how that could kill you.

A nurse appears with a needle. "I don't want it," Jeanie says.

"Don't be hard on yourself," the nurse says. "You don't have to go through pain like that." What pain? Jeanie thinks. When there is no pain she feels nothing, when there is pain, she feels nothing because there is no *she*. This, finally, is the disappearance of language. *You don't remember afterwards*, she has been told by almost everyone.

Jeanie comes out of a contraction, gropes for control. "Will it hurt the baby?" she says.

"It's a mild analgesic," the doctor says. "We wouldn't allow anything that would hurt the baby." Jeanie doesn't believe this. Nevertheless she is jabbed, and the doctor is right, it is very mild, because it doesn't seem to do a thing for Jeanie, though A. later tells her she has slept briefly between contractions.

Suddenly she sits bolt upright. She is wide awake and lucid. "You have to ring that bell right now," she says. "This baby is being born."

A. clearly doesn't believe her. "I can feel it, I can feel the head," she says. A. pushes the button for the call bell. A nurse appears and checks, and now everything is happening too soon, nobody is ready. They set off down the hall, the nurse wheeling Jeanie feels fine. She watches the corridors, the edges of everything shadowy because she doesn't have her glasses on. She hopes A. will remember to bring them. They pass another doctor.

"Need me?" she asks.

"Oh no," the nurse answers breezily. "Natural childbirth."

Jeanie realizes that this woman must have been the anaesthetist. "What?" she says, but it's too late now, they are in the room itself, all those glossy surfaces, tubular strange apparatus like a science-fiction movie, and the nurse is telling her to get onto the delivery table. No one else is in the room.

"You must be crazy," Jeanie says.

"Don't push," the nurse says.

"What do you mean?" Jeanie says. This is absurd. Why should she wait, why should the baby wait for them because they're late?

"Breathe through your mouth," the nurse says. "Pant," and Jeanie finally remembers how. When the contraction is over she uses the nurse's arm as a lever and hauls herself across onto the table.

From somewhere her own doctor materializes, in her doctor suit already, looking even more like Mary Poppins than usual, and Jeanie says, "Bet you weren't expecting to see me so soon!" The baby is being born when Jeanie said it would, though just three days ago the doctor said it would be at least another week, and this makes Jeanie feel jubilant and smug. Not that she knew, she'd believed the doctor.

She's being covered with a green tablecloth, they are taking far too long, she feels like pushing the baby out now, before they are ready. A. is there by her head, swathed in robes, hats, masks. He has forgotten her glasses. "Push now," the doctor says. Jeanie grips with her hands, grits her teeth, face, her whole body together, a snarl, a fierce smile, the baby is enormous, a stone, a boulder, her bones unlock, and, once, twice, the third time, she opens like a birdcage turning slowly inside out.

A pause; a wet kitten slithers between her legs. "Why don't you look?" says the doctor, but Jeanie still has her eyes closed. No glasses, she couldn't have seen a thing anyway. "Why don't you look?" the doctor says again.

Jeanie opens her eyes. She can see the baby, who has been wheeled up beside her and is fading already from the alarming birth purple. A good baby, she thinks, meaning it as the old woman did: *a good watch*, well-made, substantial. The baby isn't crying; she squints in the new light. Birth isn't something that has been given to her, nor has she taken it. It was just something that has happened so they could greet each other like this. The nurse is stringing beads for her name. When the baby is bundled and tucked beside Jeanie, she goes to sleep.

As for the vision, there wasn't one. Jeanie is conscious of no special knowledge; already she's forgetting what it was like. She's tired and very cold; she is shaking, and asks for another blanket. A. comes back to the room with her; her clothes are still there. Everything is quiet, the other woman is no longer screaming. Something has happened to her, Jeanie knows. Is she dead? Is the baby dead? Perhaps she is one of those casualties (and how can Jeanie herself be sure, yet, that she will not be among them) who will go into postpartum depression and never come out. "You see, there was nothing to be afraid of," A. says before he leaves, but he was wrong.

The next morning Jeanie wakes up when it's light. She's been warned about getting out of bed the first time without the help of a nurse, but she decides to do it anyway (peasant in the field! Indian on the portage!). She's still running adrenaline, she's also weaker than she thought, but she wants very much to look out the window. She feels she's been inside too long, she wants to see the sun come up. Being awake this early always makes her feel a little unreal, a little insubstantial, as if she's partly transparent, partly dead.

(It was to me, after all, that the birth was given, Jeanie gave it, I am the result. What would she make of me? Would she be pleased?)

The window is two panes with a venetian blind sandwiched

between them; it turns by a knob at the side. Jeanie has never seen a window like this before. She closes and opens the blind several times. Then she leaves it open and looks out.

All she can see from the window is a building. It's an old stone building, heavy and Victorian, with a copper roof oxidized to green. It's solid, hard, darkened by soot, dour, leaden. But as she looks at this building, so old and seemingly immutable, she sees that it's made of water. Water, and some tenuous jelly-like substance. Light flows through it from behind (the sun is coming up), the building is so thin, so fragile, that it quivers in the slight dawn wind. Jeanie sees that if the building is this way (a touch could destroy it, a ripple of the earth, why has no one noticed, guarded it against accidents?) then the rest of the world must be like this too, the entire earth, the rocks, people, trees, everything needs to be protected, cared for, tended. The enormity of this task defeats her; she will never be up to it, and what will happen then?

Jeanie hears footsteps in the hall outside her door. She thinks it must be the other woman, in her brown-and-maroon-checked coat, carrying her paper bag, leaving the hospital now that her job is done. She has seen Jeanie safely through, she must go now to hunt through the streets of the city for her next case. But the door opens, it's a nurse, who is just in time to catch Jeanie as she sinks to the floor, holding on to the edge of the air-conditioning unit. The nurse scolds her for getting up too soon.

After that the baby is carried in, solid, substantial, packed together like an apple, Jeanie examines her, she is complete, and in the days that follow Jeanie herself becomes drifted over with new words, her hair slowly darkens, she ceases to be what she was and is replaced, gradually, by someone else.